AGAINST THE
WIND

**Center Point
Large Print**

Also by Bodie & Brock Thoene
and available from Center Point Large Print:

The Zion Diaries
The Gathering Storm

**This Large Print Book carries the
Seal of Approval of N.A.V.H.**

ZION DIARIES

AGAINST THE WIND

BODIE & BROCK THOENE

CENTER POINT PUBLISHING
THORNDIKE, MAINE

This Center Point Large Print edition is published in the year 2011 by arrangement with Riggins International Rights Services, Inc., agent for Summerside Press.

Scripture references marked KJV are taken from The Holy Bible, King James Version.
Scripture quotations marked ESV are from *The Holy Bible, English Standard Version®*, copyright © 2001 by Crossway Bibles, a publishing ministry of Good News Publishers. Used by permission. All rights reserved.
This novel is a work of fiction. Names, characters, places, and incidents either are the product of the authors' imaginations or are used fictitiously. Any resemblance to actual events, locales, organizations, or persons living or dead is entirely coincidental and beyond the intent of either the authors or publisher.

The text of this Large Print edition is unabridged. In other aspects, this book may vary from the original edition. Printed in the United States of America on permanent paper. Set in 16-point Times New Roman type.

ISBN: 978-1-61173-045-6

Library of Congress Cataloging-in-Publication Data

Thoene, Bodie, 1951–
Against the wind / Bodie & Brock Thoene. — Center Point large print ed.
p. cm.
ISBN 978-1-61173-045-6 (library binding : alk. paper)
1. World War, 1939-1945—Fiction.
  2. Refugees—Europe, Western—History—20th century—Fiction. 3. Large type books.
  I. Thoene, Brock, 1952– II. Title.
PS3570.H46A73 2011
813′.54—dc22
2010053697

DEDICATION

This story is written with love for
Robin Hanley, my true sister from the
beginning of everything. Your faith gives
us courage and light. You are one with those
who sail against the wind. Cast upon the sea,
you spread your wings and are lifted by
the gale to rise above the waves.

AGAINST THE
WIND

1

LIFEBOAT NUMBER 7
TENTH DAY—NORTH ATLANTIC
NOVEMBER 3, 1940

LAST WILL AND TESTAMENT of Elisa Lindheim Murphy.
Age: 27 yrs.
Born: February 3, 1913, Berlin, Germany.
Father: Theo Lindheim—Hebrew Christian. Patriot and hero of Germany in the Great War of 1918. Jewish refugee escaped Nazi Germany in 1937.
Mother: Anna Ibsen Lindheim—German Christian. Concert pianist.

I am the beloved wife of John Murphy, American journalist in London. I am foster mother of twin adopted sons, Charles and Louis Kronenberger, age 8. I am mother of a baby girl, Katie, 17 months, who is safe in America now with my husband's parents.

I have few material goods left to me after so many years as a refugee from the Nazis. All that I have I leave to my husband, John Murphy. More than material goods, I leave all my love.

・ ・ ・

To My Dear Ones:

It is ten days since the German U-boat attacked the SS *Newcastle* as we journeyed toward America. I am in Lifeboat Number 7, in the midst of the North Atlantic, among survivors—brave men, women, and children. As each day passes, we lose more of our company to death upon this cruel sea. Some among us have given up hope we will be found alive and rescued. I pray we will be spotted before it is too late. Our hope grows dim.

Perhaps God will grant us a second chance to live life with our families. But I do not know if I will survive. Others, stronger than I, have already perished. I feel I must write this love letter to my dearest Murphy and to our children. At the urging of my companions, who look at the empty horizon and no longer see hope, I will put down my final thoughts for my loved ones.

First, I think of my baby girl, who will never know me except perhaps from this letter and by what those closest to me will tell her. I pray the promises of Psalm 91 upon her sweet life. Beloved Murphy will tell our daughter who I was and why I sent her from England to America. My every thought and deed was motivated by love for my children.

I am a concert violinist, not a writer. Music is my first language, the language of my heart. Some among us in Number 7 will recount facts and details about our last days on the vast ocean.

"What was it like to be on the SS *Newcastle* when the German U-boat attacked?" some might ask.

If I could but lift my violin and play the music of Kol Nidre, I would feel the blast as the torpedo tears through the hull. I would feel the great ship shudder as the water rises. I could hear again the cries of children cast adrift in the seas. . . .

Voices! Voices! My heart hears them still as the wind lifts their souls from the waves into the arms of angels hovering just above us.

It is strange to think that I will no longer inhabit the earth. I fought bravely and traveled far in the hope that I would live on beyond the war, as others perished. I was distracted by the expectation of what tomorrow would bring. I thought the stars would not shine unless I was beneath them, looking up. As a music student, I played my violin beside the open window of our house on Wilhelmstrasse, believing my music would bring heaven down to those who passed by.

The stars will shine without me. Some other musician will inherit the music of Bach and Mozart. My violin will sing for new generations long after I am gone.

The breeze is in my face. My soul is like a seabird rising against the wind. Soon I will hover with joy above the earth. I am finished wishing wishes, and I leave only one great regret behind.

With plain words, how can I portray a tale of life and death—my struggle and my failure to save all the little ones entrusted to my care? I string together the letters of the alphabet as if they are musical notes on a treble clef. I long for ink to become black fire upon white fire, tympany and trumpet, kindling a requiem of courage and hope and self-sacrifice for those who survived and for those who did not.

As a child of mixed Jewish and Gentile parentage, I have spent all my youth, it seems, trying to escape the Nazis. I have left behind with Mama my personal diary, beginning the Christmas of 1936 when our family first fled Nazi Germany. I leave the diary to my husband now to translate into English for our children one day. Those terrible days, as our nation was lost to tyranny because good men failed to stand firm against evil, must never be forgotten.

Perhaps my diary is enough for my little ones to remember who their mother was and why I perished in the North Atlantic.

But there are those who cannot write down their thoughts. What can I say about those on the *Newcastle* who died so very young? Their parents, waiting for word in England, will want to know.

I see their faces, those beautiful children, so many lost in one night. They smile at me in my restless dreams upon the sea.

Who will write about them? If we do not survive, who will remember?

I raise my eyes now and squint against the sun. I see one child who is a hero in this story. He lies beside me in the bow of the lifeboat as our little vessel bobs in the waves. He is too weak now to write and, through parched lips, has asked me to recount what I could about his life. When I first met him, he was a choirboy at Westminster Abbey, a child from Primrose Hill Village. Sandy hair, fair, sun-freckled skin, wide, green-blue eyes that narrow when he laughs or thrusts his chin upward to consider a clever reply.

The name of this small hero is Connor Turner. If he does not survive, he will be remembered as one woman's darling son. He played the penny whistle, and everyone remarked that he sang like an angel. She was proud her son was selected to sing with the Abbey choir. She showed his school photograph to the girls round the telephone exchange where she worked. The language of a mother's love is the same everywhere. Her heartbreak is a melody everyone recognizes.

After the Westminster Boys' School closed because of the Blitz, Connor was sent home.

Brave and terrified at the same time, Connor's mother stood over his bed and wondered if he would survive the rain of bombs falling each night on London.

In a queue outside the bakery, she studied

casualty lists and noted the tender ages of the English dead.

While she uprooted roses and planted cabbages in her Victory Garden, her neighbor leaned across the fence and told her about the children's ships.

Ironing Connor's shirts, she dreamed that America might be the haven where her son could live safely until the war was over.

As the BBC announced grim news about the conflict, she listened at the kitchen table and filled out endless applications and forms.

She remembered that miracles are possible. Kneeling by the radio, she prayed her boy would be given a place on one of the evacuee ships sailing to America.

Celebration and sorrow arrived in the post with the letter accepting him and a handful of choirboys into the evacuee program. They would sing and bear witness to the Americans that England stood alone against the Nazis.

Connor would sail a few days before his eighth birthday.

Was she doing the right thing to let him go?

Connor assured his mother that a sea voyage to America would be a great adventure. He would celebrate his birthday somewhere on the sea.

On the day of parting, he raised his chin and kissed her good-bye. She wiped her tears with a white kerchief and tucked it into his pocket. "Don't cry, Mum. I'll see you soon. Mum, I'll be

14

back! You'll see. Don't cry!" As the ship slipped from the dock, courageous Connor plucked out the hankie, and with fierce and desperate cheerfulness, waved it like a banner.

Listen and walk beside me through those terrible hours.

The dissonant music of parting plays for all those who sent their children away from England during the Blitz. It was the same for us as we tried to escape from Nazi Germany in 1936.

How many will turn their backs on all they hold dear and set out, never to return?

Connor's face is the one I see when the wind whistles across the canvas shelter in the bow, and I dream again the desperate voices of children crying from the water.

We were three days out to sea, Connor's eighth birthday, when the torpedo struck our ship. But I began my journey toward this moment of life and death long before I ever boarded the SS *Newcastle*.

He shall give His angels charge over thee,
to keep thee in all thy ways.
PSALM 91:11 KJV

BERLIN, NAZI GERMANY
DECEMBER 10, 1936

Angels have charge over all my ways? As all I have known and loved changes before my eyes, I hope this is true.

Opened gifts early with family tonight. Uncles, aunts, and cousins gather here at the Wilhelmstrasse house for our annual family holiday party. Our gathering is always early, since both my uncles are pastors, and their calendars fill up. And I have holiday concerts to play back in Vienna.

Mama's present—this leather-bound diary—and one each of different colors to me and cousins Lori Ibsen and Loralei Bittick. Mine is red and stamped with roses. I thumb through blank pages. Scripture verses inscribed on each page.

I wonder what earth-changing events will fill the blank lines of our lives this year.

I pray there is an angel watching over every member of our family. I fear this will be our last family gathering in Berlin.

Cousins Lori and Loralei spend the night.

They are like little sisters to me. We look like sisters, though each of us has different parents. Both girls named for great-grandmother Koenig. They both look so much like Grandmother's old photos. Lori and Loralei are slender, pretty girls. Hair the color of ripe wheat. Bright blue eyes. Straight teeth. We laugh a lot and talk about the king of England giving up his throne today so he can marry the woman he loves. King Edward and the American Wallis Simpson will ride off into the sunset. So romantic. We prefer to think about falling in love in Buckingham Palace even though Berlin is cloaked with gloom and the whole world is crumbling around us. Do we still imagine everything will return to normal somehow?

We feel sad when our fathers discuss the future of the German church as Hitler enacts new racial laws.

The conversation becomes ominous. Other dissenters arrive at our holiday party. Dietrich B. comes with Eben G.

Eben G. is the man whom Loralei loves as much as her own life. I see Loralei blush when she hears Eben in the foyer. I smile at her in sympathy because I understand the heartache of an impossible love. Her eyes shine with tears when Eben speaks. He sees her but looks away quickly as if he does not have time for falling in love.

Loralei whispers, "He hates me. I told him I love him, and now he hates me."

Mama sees Loralei is about to crumble and suggests we three girls go upstairs to listen to the radio. We say good night but turn off the radio. We sit on the stair landing to hear the men discuss what must be done as the Nazis grow more vicious, anti-Christian, and anti-Semitic. We girls sit with our arms around one another and our heads close. I am not so afraid when we are together.

Eben warns that any with Jewish heritage should get out of the Reich while it is still possible. That means my father's family.

"The children," Eben says. "You are already helping, Theo. We must continue our work." Eben tells my father that the danger is very great and that our family is on a list with the Gestapo. What is coming against all Jews in Europe is worse than the Spanish Inquisition. It no longer matters if a Jew has converted to Christianity. The Nazis have declared war on all descendants of Abraham, Isaac, and Jacob. Since my father is Jewish, and I am half-Jewish, I feel his words very deeply. Papa says how thankful he is that I am playing in the orchestra in Vienna. He does not believe the Nazis will take over Austria.

Eben thinks Christians and Jews are all in danger in Hitler's Reich. "Make preparations to leave."

Lori murmurs, "If it's as bad as all that, I hope I never bring a child into this world. It would be too much to bear—living with fear that something might happen. I would rather never have a baby."

I say, "What's Christmas without children? I want a houseful. Just not here in Hitler's Reich."

Loralei, who is American, whispers, "If we can't be here for Christmas next year, then maybe in Jerusalem. Or maybe next year in New York? Or London. I fancy a Christmas with all of us together in London. Christmas tea at the Savoy. Oxford Street is even prettier than Berlin at Christmas. No Nazi flags. No danger of the Nazis ever landing in Piccadilly."

Lori is not as optimistic as Loralei. Lori confides that she believes her father (Uncle Karl) will remain in Berlin as pastor of New Church as long as possible. She says he has warned many friends with Jewish heritage that they must leave. Some think the crisis will blow over, but now I am sure it will only get worse.

Dietrich B. tells my father that there must be funds to organize home churches throughout Germany in case war breaks out.

Eben says it is already too late to change the course of events. There will be war against the church and against Jews and against democracy. The German church should have spoken up when Hitler was first elected. He says that the true shepherds who remain in the Reich will be arrested.

Papa agrees with Eben. I shall never forget Papa's words: "If the Church is silent in the face of Evil, in the end Evil will silence the Church."

I promise Lori and Loralei that I will be careful when I return to Austria. There are Nazis there too. We pray angels will go with us as we part. Lori remains in Berlin for the sake of Uncle Karl's church. Loralei will return to Belgium where her father (Uncle Robert) is headmaster of a seminary. I do not know when Papa and Mama will leave Berlin, but I think they will go until things blow over. Mama says Papa is turning over the management of the store to Aryan friends. That must mean something. I return to Vienna and the orchestra after our family ski trip to Kitzbühel.

I am already making plans for all of us to be together again. The Vienna Philharmonic Orchestra is scheduled to perform in England at the Albert Hall in the spring. Perhaps then Lori, Loralei, and our mothers can all meet for tea at the Savoy in London!

2

LONDON, ENGLAND
SUMMER 1940

How could I learn to say good-bye, knowing our parting could be forever? How could I embrace my children one last time and then let them go? How was it possible to say farewell at the quay and turn away as the mooring lines were cast off? How could I place my precious little ones in the care of others for the perilous journey, knowing they might end up adrift in a lifeboat in the North Atlantic, fighting to survive, in the middle of a war?

The question for all Londoners that summer of 1940 was this: "Would you rather your baby be bombed in London or risk being torpedoed on the North Atlantic?"

The decisive answer was delivered to us around afternoon teatime on September 7, 1940, in the opening salvo of the London Blitz.

Murphy was at the TENS news office on Fleet Street and I was at the BBC, preparing for the evening concert. A roar louder than thunder filled the air as 348 German bombers, escorted by 617 fighters, crossed the English Channel in a matter of minutes.

My mother, Anna Lindheim, was in London

that day, caring for our three children—Katie, a year old, and Charles and Louis, our eight-year-old adopted twins, while I rehearsed with the BBC Symphony Orchestra.

Murphy and I had shared our small flat in a Georgian town house near Regent's Park with my cousin Lori Kalner, her eighteen-month-old son, Alfie, and Lori's mother, Helen Ibsen. Our happy little home was very crowded.

When the air raid sounded that afternoon, my mother was pushing Katie's pram through Regent's Park. Charles and Louis skipped stones across the boating lake. While I sheltered in the basement of the BBC, Mama hurried with the children into the deep underground of the Baker Street tube station.

Even in the depths of the BBC bomb shelter, we heard the distant concussions. In that terrible moment we realized every horror England had hoped to prevent had finally come to pass. We raised our eyes to the concrete ceiling and prayed for the safety of our loved ones. My heart raced through every minute as I wondered about Murphy, my mother, and our children. In my fear, I remembered the painting in St. Paul's Cathedral of the angel guiding two small children across a bridge. Could the Lord keep my little ones safe beneath a sky raining fire and brimstone?

O God, protect them! Put Your angels around the ones I love!

Before one hour passed, the Luftwaffe emptied its deadly cargo, shattering forever the lives of citizens in the great city I had come to call my home.

A phone call after the all-clear alerted me that Mama and my little ones were alive and well and headed back home. We musicians picked ourselves up and resumed preparation for the evening concert as news of the devastation to the surrounding city trickled in. Fires raged in the East End. The rumors were horrific, but reality was worse.

Should tonight's concert broadcast go on the air in the face of such widespread tragedy?

The head of the BBC consulted with the British War Office. It was concluded for the sake of British morale, in spite of devastation and danger, the night's BBC performance must be aired without fail.

Churchill proclaimed, "It will send a message back to the Nazis that their bombs cannot and will not interrupt our lives or break the will of our island home."

I was in the practice room of the BBC when Mama rang me a second time. My mother's voice, almost always full of good cheer, was barely recognizable.

"Oh, Elisa!" she cried. "The house! The house is gone! Lori's little boy has been killed in the bombing! And her dear mother. Your aunt Helen. Yes, Helen dead too!"

I held the receiver for a long moment without speaking. Only the night before we had laughed and joked at the dining table. Could it really be true that their joy was silenced forever?

Other members of the BBC Orchestra surged around me, aware by my expression that personal tragedy had struck my family in the Luftwaffe's first great assault on London.

"Mama! Can this be?"

"Lori's darling baby boy. And Helen too. Gone! I can't bear it. I cannot bear it!"

My knees grew weak. My first thought was how lucky we were that Mama had been out for a stroll with my three children. The next thought slammed into my senses like a hammer blow. "Mama! Where is Lori?"

"St. John's Church is gone too. A stick of five bombs meant to strike the canal across the road. Instead, the bombs fell on the houses along Prince Albert Road . . . one after another. Starting with our house and ending with the church."

"Mama! Where is Lori? Where?" My panic drew a circle of friends close around me.

"Lori came back home and . . . she would not leave. Refused to leave the house until they found the bodies. She fought to get inside, in spite of the flames. They had to hold her back. And then they found them—Helen and Alfie. Oh Elisa! The poor girl. Poor dear girl! Her mother and baby boy . . . how will she ever forget such a sight?

Lori was up the hill in the village, shopping for a few dinner things. She came home and . . . everything gone. She asked to be taken to the shelter where Loralei works. St. Mark's, North Audley. I'm going there now."

Loralei Bittick, our Texas-born cousin, worked in a refugee center near the American Embassy.

I asked my mother, "Call Murphy for me, Mama. Ask him please to come to the church straight-away. I'll meet you there with the children."

I hung up. My hands were trembling. I knew I could not play the violin.

Fearing I might pass out, I handed my instrument to Henri Golden, the Jewish concertmaster, who had escaped from a half-dozen countries one step ahead of the Nazi army. Henri took stock. Still and wide-eyed, he pieced together what had just happened.

"Your children, Elisa?"

"Unharmed."

"Thanks be to God. Your home?"

I quietly replied, "Gone."

"Brick and mortar can be replaced."

"Henri, I won't be performing tonight. Our home . . . gone! A house is nothing. But my cousin Lori Kalner's little boy and my aunt—they were in the house."

His dark Sephardic eyes flashed. "Bombed." Not a question but a fact. "So very sorry. So very, very . . ."

I nodded and leaned back against the wall. Hands over my face, I tried to draw breath. I felt the room spin around me. *Little Alfie dead. Aunt Helen too. What if Mama had been there with Katie and Charles and Louis? What if Mama hadn't taken them for a walk in the park at the moment she did? She and Katie and Charles and Louis would be dead. The loss would be unbearable, as it must be now for my sweet cousin.*

On that first day when the skies were darkened with enemy aircraft, 1,364 civilians died; 1,666 Londoners were seriously injured.

Those hours were a foretaste of what lay ahead for us. Staggering numbers of dead and wounded are mere statistics. It is only when the numbers of dead are reduced to an ordinary person like you or me that the mind can comprehend the meaning of loss. How could we believe on that first evening that in the months following over 48,000 Londoners would die in the havoc raining down upon us? The reality is even more incomprehensible when I write the names of other target cities in Britain: Coventry, Newcastle, Manchester, Edinburgh, Glasgow, Plymouth, Liverpool, Blackpool . . .

Too many to record each heartache and loss. Yet as I close my eyes, I see the smiles and hear the laughter of two precious souls who were part of my own family. When I consider the meaning of the Blitz, I remember the smoke-blackened face of Lori Kalner, who had to be prevented from running into the flames in a futile attempt to save her little boy and her mother.

In the evening I met my mother at St. Mark's. She was praying in a side chapel. My children slept on a pew behind her.

Mama rose slowly and embraced me. "Loralei is in her office with Lori. You three girls. Always so close. I am praying you will find some word of comfort for poor Lori. After so much heartache, losing her father in Germany. Now this. Now this. I have no comfort to offer. I am broken. Broken."

I found Lori in Loralei's office. Both petite and nearly the same age, they had often pretended to be sisters when they were young. Years of persecution in Nazi Germany had strengthened our family ties.

Lori's shoulders hunched forward. With her fair hair, clothing, and skin covered with soot, she seemed very small and fragile, like a once-loved doll left in the rain. A cup of tea and toast were untouched at Lori's right hand. Loralei sat with her arm around her. Lori glanced up when I entered. Bright blue eyes were wide with bewilderment. Lips parted as if to ask, *How could this happen?*

"Lori," I whispered.

Lori shook her head. Her voice cracked as she tried to speak. "They're gone, Elisa. I only went to the market and . . . they're gone. I wish—I wish they would have come with me. The baby was napping. Oh, Elisa! I wish I would have stayed with him!"

Loralei, eyes brimming, pursed her lips and looked away.

"I know, Lori. I know, darling. I am so sorry." I sank down beside my cousins, and we three shed tears together.

What had happened in Spain, Poland, Holland, Belgium, and France had followed the flood of refugees here to the island fortress of Great Britain. Where was our hope? What hope for us now?

Lori wiped her eyes. "Oh, Elisa. You must get your babies to America if you can. Get them to America!"

We had no place to sleep, so Loralei gave us her house key and sent us to her flat. She offered to share her clothes with us. We just had time enough to bathe before the air raid siren sounded again. We hurried away to the Camden Town tube station as a fresh storm of incendiary bombs began to fall on London. I do believe Lori would have welcomed her own death that night. And, for all of us, this was only the beginning of sorrows.

Perhaps this is enough to help you understand why those of us who lived in England that year looked at our children and were able to answer the question, *"Would you rather your babies be bombed in London or risk being torpedoed on the North Atlantic?"*

"Six days to cross the Atlantic! Naval escorts will surround the evacuee ships. Only six days of danger before our kids'll be safe on a far shore!"

After that first day of the Blitz, the sight of a baby's tiny coffin made my reply certain. "Perhaps in a ship bound for America our children will have a chance. A crossing of only six days and then . . . LIFE!"

The morning of the funeral service for Helen Ibsen and little Alfie, Murphy sent a wire to his parents in Pennsylvania, asking Sean and Rosie Murphy for their help.

The LORD is my light and my salvation;
whom shall I fear?
PSALM 27:1 KJV

BERLIN, NAZI GERMANY
DECEMBER 14, 1936

I am afraid. It is raining when I step out of the taxi. Now the terrible red swastika banners of the Third Reich flutter from the windows of my father's store. I sense I am being followed—observed, as I walk into the building and through the bright holiday decorations of our department store. When I stop at the perfume counter and pretend to sample the scent of Chanel No. 5, a man watches me with cold, dull eyes. I know he is Gestapo. He scribbles notes in a small notebook as I climb the stairs and walk toward Papa's office. I pretend I do not notice him. I pretend he does not matter. But I feel a heavy dread in the pit of my stomach. I did not expect the danger would come so soon.

Mama and my brothers have gone ahead to Kitzbühel in Austria.

Once we're home, Papa says he is glad they are safe. We must leave as well. Three hours until the train. Papa opens the window, and I play my violin for the last time for him in our beloved home.

I ask, "Oh, Papa? Can we ever come home again?"

He does not answer. He tells me I must take away only what I can easily carry. He selects from his library a first-edition copy of Goethe's *Faust*, the story of the man who sold his soul to the devil.

I think perhaps that Germany and the German church have become like Faust. For the sake of Herr Hitler's empty promises they have sold their souls to the devil.

3

LIVERPOOL, ENGLAND
SUMMER 1940

Sean and Rosie Murphy made the long journey from Pennsylvania, crossing the Atlantic on board a neutral American ship to take our children home with them to the safety of their dairy farm. Less than a month passed as we waited for my visa, so I could travel with them, but it didn't come.

My baby was sleeping when I laid her in Rosie Murphy's arms and kissed her farewell on the deck of the crowded ocean liner that would take them all from England to America.

"You know I'll care for the children like they're my own," my mother-in-law tried to comfort me. "Elisa, darlin', your Katie will be our little princess until you join us in America."

I nodded and, unable to speak, embraced her and my baby girl.

The ship's steward clanged the final warning bell. "All ashore that's going ashore!"

Murphy hoisted Charles and Louis up in his arms one last time and instructed our boys, "Be good lads, now. Take care of your baby sister. And help Grandma and Grandpa milk the cows too."

Charles furrowed his brow. "When are you coming?"

Murphy smiled, then mussed the boy's hair. "Soon."

Sean Murphy, my husband's iron-jawed father, plopped his fedora down on Charles's head. Sean was suddenly in charge. "So, you're Charles. In America we'll call you Charlie. You wear my fedora, like William Powell in *The Thin Man*. You like detective movies?"

Both boys nodded in unison.

Sean continued, "Great. And you, Louis—we'll call you Louie, eh? I'll have to get a second hat. To tell you boys apart." He stooped low. "What kind of hat would you like, Louie?"

Louis managed a crooked smile. He rubbed his upper lip where surgery had corrected a cleft palate. "Cowboy."

"Then a cowboy you shall be." Sean placed large square hands on the boys' shoulders. "But you mustn't switch hats unless you tell your grandma and me, eh?"

Murphy embraced his parents. We said tearful farewells, promising to come to America soon. Murphy took my arm, leading me toward the gangway. Had I ever known such emptiness as that moment?

The ship sailed, and the great White Star Line passenger shed emptied out. We lingered as the crowd of well-wishers dispersed. Small sounds

36

echoed beneath the vast shelter.

The band members put away their instruments. Janitors swept confetti and crushed flowers from the quay. Members of the press—Murphy's friends and colleagues—hailed him, then phoned in to their respective news sources the latest passenger list containing the names of great and small among the exodus of Americans from England.

"You heard me, Mac," one of Murphy's colleagues said. "Yeah, No kiddin'! The entire clan of American Ambassador Joseph Kennedy has just been shipped back home to America."

"Shipped? It was more like a stampede," Murphy said. "But who am I to point fingers? I send my kids home to my folks in Pennsylvania while Mister Ambassador Appeaser shivers in his bed at night for fear some stray Nazi bomb is going to land on the American Embassy. So Kennedy sends his kids back home to Hah-vahd. Bet he'll skedaddle home soon hisself."

I resisted the urge to comment how much going home to Harvard sounded like "going home to Tara." The world I had known as a child was quite gone with the wind.

After two years of marriage to John Murphy, I had mastered American, which is quite different than the language spoke in England. "I want to skedaddle. Okay, Murphy. I know your mother will take care of our babies. Little Katie. Every day is something new with a baby. And the boys. Charles and Louis. Growing so fast. I must get my visa soon and follow to America or my heart will break."

Murphy and I remained on the dock of the White Star Line and watched until the great ocean liner vanished into a fog bank. Had we done the right thing? Sending our baby and Charles and Louis to America with Murphy's parents? How long would it be before I saw them again?

I said quietly, "Churchill thinks people who evacuate their children to America are cowards."

"We know better, Elisa. The idea is to get the kids out of range of the Nazi bombers."

"I was in line for ration books—fewer rations now that the children have gone. A woman behind me asked if I'd rather have my children bombed in England or torpedoed on the Atlantic."

"Cheerful soul. What did you tell her?"

"I said I'd rather they celebrate Christmas on my husband's farm in Pennsylvania, where there are no ration cards and we can churn our own butter. But, Murphy, I'm scared."

"Everyone in England is scared for their kids, Elisa, and with good reason."

I pressed myself against him and wept against his shoulder. "Oh, Murphy! Why won't America grant me a visa? Why? First it was refugee quotas and now . . ."

"Now there's a war on. You came from

Germany, Elisa, and the Nazis hate you and your family. I mean personally. You're on a list. The kids need to be far across the water and out of harm's way."

I whispered through my tears, "I know. I just wish I could be with them."

"You know the drill. But here's the deal. My mother's got six days on the same boat with Rose Kennedy. And Mom is a Murphy, as Irish as the Kennedys. Rosie Murphy, she is. That's two roses on the same ship. Irish mothers stick together. No accident they're on the same ship. Mom'll put Katie in Rose Kennedy's arms and tell her all about Charles and Louis—and you, Elisa. A talented Jewish concert violinist on the run from Hitler who's stuck here in the UK because some pencil pusher delayed." He dabbed my cheeks with his handkerchief. "It'll be okay, honey. You and I will be together. Mom'll write every week. And when you get your visa . . ."

"Then you'll come too? Come home to Pennsylvania? To your parents' farm? With me?"

He did not reply, and sorrow passed through me like a sword. His arm remained around my shoulders as we left the empty passenger shelter for the drive back to London.

Yea, though I walk through the valley of the
shadow of death, I will fear no evil;
for Thou art with me.
PSALM 23:4 KJV

TRAIN COMPARTMENT 7A
GERMANY/AUSTRIA BORDER
DECEMBER 15, 1936

The shadow of death is dark tonight. Gestapo and SS everywhere on the train from Berlin to Austria. Papa is taken off the train for "questioning." What can I do? Oh, God! Papa is not with me as I cross the German frontier into Austria. Will I ever see my father again? What will Mama say when I come to Kitzbühel, and he is not with me?

An American news journalist named John Murphy, a young handsome man who has no fear, saves me from being arrested as well. Mr. Murphy crosses his arms and stares at the Nazi officials. He will not leave as the SS officers search my luggage. My clothes are dumped on the floor and trampled. The Nazis search the violin case I am carrying back to Vienna—the most precious Guarnerius violin belonging to Rudy Dorbransky— but miraculously they do not damage the instrument. Finally they find this diary.

I am a fool for writing down any names in this book before being safely out of Nazi Germany.

Eben Golah and my uncles' names are written within. Yes, I am certain I have put everyone in peril by writing down their names and the things discussed at our holiday party. I can hardly breathe as the man opens this diary and frowns and reads aloud this Bible verse, then throws the book hard against the wall. See, the red roses on the cover are scuffed by the force of his rage. John Murphy's presence as an American reporter intimidates those who threaten me. Mr. Murphy tells them he is going to interview Hitler. They believe him. Mr. Murphy's fierce, mocking questions directed toward the Gestapo agent, Herr Müller, prevent the officers from taking me off the train. And perhaps there is also something more. I think it is as if the Gestapo agent is blinded by the power of the verse on this page from the *Heilege Schrift*, the *Holy Writ*. He hates God's Word and hurls it away as if the words are fire to burn him.

I passed through the valley of death. I know now I must never return to Hitler's Reich. What Eben said is true. What will come upon Jews now is worse than the Inquisition.

John Murphy is my angel in compartment 7A, watching over me tonight. But what shall we do about Papa? I pray Mr. Murphy can use his American connections to help us. I leave the train in Kitzbühel. He travels on. I have given him my address at the Musikverein in Vienna.

4

A week had passed since Rosie and Sean Murphy sailed. No word came of their safe arrival, and a sense of dread knotted my stomach.

My ill-fitting, out-of-date clothing was picked from the charity barrel at St. Mark's, North Audley. Murphy and I slept each night on cots in Loralei's church office while more permanent quarters were being arranged.

Before each night's air raid sent us scurrying for cover in the crypt, I dreamed I watched U-boats just beneath the surface of the Atlantic stalking the liner carrying my loved ones.

That same week Loralei and I said good-bye to Mama and Lori.

Lori, pale and drawn, stood between Mama and Loralei on the Number 2 boarding platform of Paddington Station.

Loralei embraced Lori. "You must rest, Lori."

Lori nodded. "I keep thinking I'll wake up." Her eyes scanned the crowds of soldiers and fellow passengers as though she was looking for someone. For her mother, I wondered? For her baby boy? Did she hope she was dreaming? that she would turn and see them emerge from the midst of the crowd? Did she still hope the nightmare of her loss would come to an end?

Mama touched my cheek. "You must go on performing. Do what God has called you to do, Elisa, and when you can, come to Wales."

"Pray for us, Mama."

Mama hugged me tightly. "Maybe Christmas? Surely by Christmas all will be well and we'll be happy again."

"Oh, Mama! I pray we'll all be in America for Christmas with Murphy's family."

It was a hopeful thought, but not likely. Instead of welcoming refugees, the U.S. seemed to be slamming the gates to those in need even tighter.

Loralei and I remained in the train shed for a long time after the locomotive chuffed away with Lori and Mama aboard. The smoke cleared, and still we stared down the empty rails in a mix of relief and longing for those who could escape the hell of London.

We cousins walked to the bus stop. Loralei promised she would do what she could to help me get my American visa and join my children. Kissing me on the cheek, she returned to her job at St. Mark's, and I headed back to meet Murphy at the BBC.

It began to rain as I hurried toward the studio. I had forgotten my umbrella so covered my head with a scrap of the London *Times* that reported the sinking of several merchant vessels bound with supplies from America. I worried about Katie and Charles and Louis. Had their ship made it safely to America?

Murphy was waiting for me beneath the portico of All Souls Church, Langham. He hailed me as I splashed through puddles on the sidewalks.

"Elisa!" He smiled as I jogged up the steps and fell into his arms. "They made it off to Wales, then," he said.

"Yes. Only an hour late."

"It will be good for Lori. Poor girl. Your mother will be a comfort."

"I'm worried about the Luftwaffe targeting the rail lines."

"Not today. Good thing it's raining. May put off the bombers for a while."

"Poor Lori," I replied. "Hardly a word. She's still hoping it isn't true, I think."

"I've got news." He pulled a yellow slip of paper from his pocket.

Telegram. Was it good news or bad? His crooked grin told me everything I longed to hear.

I gasped and tried to focus my eyes. The pigeons cooed like angel song high in the eaves of the church. "Tell me. Tell me, Murphy. I can't read it." Tears mingled with the raindrops.

He scanned the telegram. "From Mom. From New York."

"Oh! Oh!" Pressing my cheek against the rough wool of his coat, I squeezed my eyes tightly and saw visions of the Empire State Building and the Statue of Liberty as he read.

Safely home STOP All's well STOP Pray you will come home by Christmas STOP Love MOM

"By Christmas!" I sighed, barely able to speak as images of Christmas trees and a world without rubble and death flooded my mind. "Oh, Murphy, if only!"

He gripped my shoulders and kissed my tears. "Main thing is, they're safe now. Mom and Dad will take the kids to see the sights and then by Thursday . . . home. A little train ride to the farm and we can sleep again without worrying about them."

I glanced at my pendant watch, opening the case to gaze into the faces of our children. Only then did I notice the time. "Murphy! I'm late for rehearsal."

He popped open his umbrella, and we stepped out into the downpour. "Come on, then." We hurried toward the studio. "And a bit more good news . . . sort of."

"I don't know if I can take any more good news. My heart is racing!"

"I said sort of. We've got temporary housing. It's a seedy little rooming house a few blocks from here—a shared bathroom with a half-dozen roomers. Sorry, honey. Only until the office can find us something better."

"I'm just thankful we'll have a bed," I replied, feeling the weight of the world lifted from my shoulders.

We kissed one another good-bye at the BBC's front door and agreed to meet for supper after the evening broadcast. He left the umbrella for me and pulled his fedora low over his brow.

Just as I had watched the train until it was out of sight, I stood and watched Murphy stride away. I was mindful that every parting could be a last good-bye. I memorized his jaunty walk and the tilt of his head against the rain. In truth, I memorized every detail about him in case I would be left with only memories of love to sustain me.

My friendship with Irish actress Mariah Fitzgerald and the Spanish flamenco dancer Raquel Esperanza was first forged in flames of the Blitz and later sealed on the high seas of the North Atlantic.

For the sake of morale on the home front, singers, musicians, and actors continued to perform and broadcast daily at the BBC. Many of us had fled the Nazis. We were thrown together through triumph and tragedy, and our hearts were knit. An American correspondent writing for the *Times* called the BBC performers "living national treasures . . . as precious to freedom's heritage as the paintings in the National Portrait Gallery."

We were very much alive, though Hitler had pursued us and wished us dead. Those of us who had escaped the tyranny of the Third Reich could tell the truth about the Nazis and help besieged Englishmen keep their heads up. We could also bring an occasional smile in the midst of heartache. Our effective witness to the horrors of National Socialism became a problem for the Nazis. The Third Reich wanted the keepers of truth dead. The BBC building on Langham Place made a fine fat target for the Luftwaffe.

The bombing continued and intensified as Hitler determined to flatten London before invading England.

After my children arrived in America, and Mama and Lori left London, I felt the pangs of loneliness. I was glad for the safety of my loved ones but missed the company of those most dear to my heart. After I had embraced Mama and Lori for what we knew might be the last time in our lives, the worst bombing raids in history began.

I returned to work with a new determination that I would not fear no matter what was to come. The siren wailed, interrupting our rehearsal. Carrying our precious instruments, we tramped down into the bomb shelter of the building. The heavy steel doors were closed, sealing us in. We all knew that a single bomb on target could flatten the building and kill us in a moment, yet we were determined that if we were killed, we would go out playing the music of the Jewish composer Mendelssohn, as the highest act of musical defiance against the Third Reich. Members of the BBC staff, from janitors to typists, gathered round us in the gloom as we performed *The Scottish Symphony*, with its strains of "A Mighty Fortress Is Our God."

Aboveground, almost a thousand German aircraft crossed the Channel. The sky over England was darkened by this airborne armada, and, up to that moment in history, the Nazi force sent against us was the largest collection of aircraft ever seen.

Fighter Command had not expected raids on London but now attempted to intercept the waves of bombers. A huge dogfight developed over London and the Thames Estuary.

The country was put on the highest alert. Convinced that the German invasion of Britain was imminent, the signal of the impending offensive went out from the BBC. The code word *Cromwell* was relayed to military units. Church bells clanged to the crash of bombs. We felt the deep vibrations of the concussions all around.

We paused in our playing. I wondered what destruction we would find if we lived to ascend into the open air.

Suddenly I thought I heard a faint, frantic hammering on the shelter door.

Our conductor tapped his baton. "All right, ladies and gentlemen, let's now play, 'There'll Always Be an England.' "

As we raised our instruments, I heard the banging again.

"Do you hear that?" I asked Martin Warrick, the cellist beside me.

The *boom! boom! boom!* of a nearby stick of explosives made us involuntarily duck our heads.

Moments passed. Our conductor stood erect and said again, "Always . . . Be . . . England."

But this time there was no mistake. I was certain I heard someone pounding on the shelter door. Had someone been locked out? left aboveground?

I stood and declared, "Wait a minute. Listen. I think someone's out there!"

Every movement froze. We held our breath. In a moment during the lull the voice of a woman was accompanied by clanging from without.

Martin's eyes widened. "Dear God!" He thrust his cello into my hand and, with two other men, dashed up the flights of metal stairs.

We did not move as the fire door crashed open and the smell of cordite and the roaring of explosions suddenly filled our safe place.

The voices of two women mingled with the exclamations of the men who had gone to their rescue.

I recognized the soft Irish accent of the red-haired beauty, actress Mariah Fitzgerald, and the Spanish inflexion of the dark-haired Spanish dancer Raquel Esperanza. As we listened to their excited words drift down the stairwell, it was like hearing a dramatic radio broadcast.

Martin slammed the heavy shelter door closed. "What were you doing?" he chastised.

Mariah was breathless. "On our way back from lunch. The alarm sounded . . . we were . . . point of no return."

Rachel's voice trembled. "Too far to go back to the tube station. The whole sky is dark with Luftwaffe. We decided to try to make it here. Ran for it. But the door was sealed. We've been trying to make you hear us."

Mariah finished, "Too awful! Fires everywhere. Everywhere! Bombs started fallin' when we reached the front step. Saw a church go up like a house of cards. The Hun'd like to knock the BBC down first—make no mistake!"

Martin said, "Elisa Murphy heard you. All the rest of us—we were, well, it was Elisa who heard you through all the clamor, or you'd still be out there."

As the two beauties appeared before us, covered in dust, carrying their shoes to aid their flight, we began to applaud.

Mariah stretched out her arms to me, and Esperanza followed. The two women, weeping with relief, rushed to embrace me.

Once again we raised our instruments and began to play "There'll Always Be an England." This time Mariah and Raquel joined their exquisite singing voices in harmony with the orchestra as the bombs resounded like a kettledrum.

*"May this dear land we love so well
In dignity and freedom dwell."*

BOOM! BOOM! BOOM!

*"Though worlds may change and go awry
While there is still one voice to cry
There'll always be an England."*

BOOM! BOOM! BOOM! BOOM!

Every person in that bleak, stifling shelter began to sing as London burned above us.

*"Surely you're proud; shout it out loud,
'Britons, awake.' "*

BOOM!

*"Freedom remains. These are the chains
Nothing can break.
There'll always be an England."*

There was not a dry eye among us that day.

Mariah, Raquel, and I became three sisters from that moment on.

Though German bombs fell on the Thameside docks, many fell on the residential areas around them. East and southeast London were devastated. Firestorms that ravaged the city served as signal lights directing the second wave of bombers in the evening.

Buildings all around the BBC were hit, yet the studio remained intact.

The next day, Mariah and Raquel broadcast to the world the story of what it had been like to be locked out of the shelter during the raid. Then they told what it had felt like to be brought into safety and welcomed. That terrible hour on the outside while destruction rained down seemed to be a parable for so many of us who had escaped from Hitler and found refuge in England. I was called to the microphone and shared the story of my escape from Berlin and Vienna and Prague and my hope that America would open its gates to refugees who had no place left to go.

The BBC conductor told how music of the Jewish composer Mendelssohn was forbidden to be played in Hitler's Reich. Then the orchestra performed Mendelssohn's "Scottish" Symphony.

We ended the broadcast with Mariah and Raquel singing "There'll Always Be an England" while I played solo violin.

"And England shall be free
If England means as much to you
As England means to me."[1]

We three could not imagine that our voices and our music would reach halfway around the world.

Winston Churchill visited the studio to speak to America after our performance. He shook our hands and told us our testimony to America might well help change the course of the war by awakening hearts to our peril.

Mariah, Raquel, and I stood outside the radio room to hear him defiantly announce: "Hitler has lighted a fire that will burn with a steady and consuming flame until the last vestiges of Nazi tyranny have been burnt out of Europe."

---

[1] "There Will Always Be an England," Ross Parker and Hugh Charles, summer 1939, popularized by Vera Lynn.

And when they were come into the house,
they saw the young Child with Mary His mother,
and fell down and worshipped Him.

MATTHEW 2:11 KJV

CHRISTMAS EVE, 1936
HOME OF THE WATTENBARGER FAMILY
KITZBŰHEL, AUSTRIA

The presence of the Lord is here in this little house in the Austrian alps—Kitzbühel. The Wattenbarger family with whom we are staying are people of deep faith. They are simple farmers and woodcarvers. Beside the hearth is the most beautiful hand-carved crèche I have ever seen. It is not hard for me to imagine that the hymn "Silent Night" was first written and sung in these mountains.

Frau Wattenbarger asks me to play my violin. I remember Christmas past in our beautiful home in Berlin. Music and laughter. Snow falling on the ground. A whispered secret and knowing glances. The scents of pastries and the Christmas goose filling our house. The midnight chiming of the tall old clock in our foyer.

And then I remember my last moments in the house with Papa: *"Your great-grandfather traded a matched team of horses for the old clock. I wish I could carry it away in my pocket.*

Wish I could carry away your mother's piano too. Glad you play the violin, Elisa dear. It is small enough to carry out of Germany."

Mama and I are so worried about Papa, but we cannot speak openly about it. Where is Papa? I wonder what will become of us. I must return to my work with the orchestra in Vienna. Mama and my younger brothers cannot ever go back to Germany now. What will become of other Jews who have not been able to leave Hitler's Reich?

I look at the Christ Child lying in the manger and remember there is more to the nativity story than the one, beautiful silent night of Christ's birth. More than shepherds. More than wisemen. More than the bright star. More than angels singing "Peace on Earth!"

Herr Wattenbarger opens the Bible to the Gospel of Matthew and begins to read, coming to this last part of the story:

"Then Herod, when he saw that he had been tricked by the wise men, became furious, and he sent and killed all the male children in Bethlehem and in all that region who were two years old or under. . . . 'A voice was heard . . . Rachel weeping for her children; she refused to be comforted, because they are no more.' "[2]

---

[2] Matthew 2:16, 18 ESV

I lay down to sleep beside Mama, but I hear her quietly weeping and the peace of the season is not in my heart.

Like Herod the Great, Adolf Hitler is a butcher and a madman. What, then, will become of all the Jewish babies left within his power?

5

I steeled myself to get back to work.
    The strains of Beethoven's *Fifth* drifted
from the practice room as I hurried down the
corridor with my violin.

Raquel and Mariah poked their faces round the
corner of the women's dressing room and
snagged me as I tried to pass.

"I'm late!" I cried.

"Come on now, darlin'!" Mariah did not let me
avoid them. "Don't tell me you're unfamiliar with
Beethoven, now."

Raquel flicked the lapel of the ragged dress I
had rummaged from the charity barrel at St.
Mark's. "So sad, eh?" She linked her arm in
mine.

"We can't have you performin' in rags." Mariah
covered my eyes with her hands.

"What? What are you two up to?" I laughed.

"Steady, now!" Mariah removed her hands to
reveal a half-dozen dresses on display.

"What's this?"

Raquel explained, "We brought them for you to
borrow. Whatever you want, eh?"

"Whatever fits," Mariah agreed proudly. "And

not very out of fashion. Hardly out of date at all. Not like the dreary rag you're wearin' now."

Three dresses each made up the entire apparel of Mariah and Raquel. My friends also offered an extra pair of shoes to me as well. They had literally laid everything they owned at my feet.

The rehearsal went on without me as I tried on every item and received an honest critique of my improved appearance. I chose one modest navy blue day dress with a white collar from Mariah and one bright red dress, suitable to wear to the cinema, from Raquel. The shoes did not fit, so I remained shod in stolid black pumps that had been out of style for ten years.

That evening I wore Raquel's red dress to meet Murphy at Simpson's.

He took one look at me and said, "You look like a million bucks, you know that? Let's celebrate."

We ordered Simpson's famous roast beef and Yorkshire pudding, costing the handsome sum of two dollars a plate. Then Murphy hailed a cab, and we rode through the blackout and the storm to our temporary quarters in the dreariest boardinghouse in London.

Even in the darkness I could see that the place was scorched from the near miss of a German bomb. Windows were boarded up. Our room was on the second floor, reached by climbing leaning stairs that groaned with every footstep.

Murphy threw open the door. A single lightbulb

hung from a wire above the bed. "It ain't the Savoy, but it's got four walls and we can sleep together."

Rain sluiced from the eaves. A dark water stain spread across the ceiling plaster, and drips clanged musically into a tin pot on the floor.

"I'm glad for the storm, Murphy." I turned and raised my face to his. "The planes won't come tonight, will they?"

His eyes devoured me hungrily. "It seems like . . . it's been awhile, Elisa."

For the first time in weeks, we made love without fear of interruption.

Mindful of the other boarders behind paper-thin walls, I was grateful for the drumming torrent of rain.

We had lost everything. Again and again I found myself wearing borrowed clothes and wondering where I would be sleeping. Yet a sense of contentment settled over me as I drowsed in Murphy's arms. That night I did not dream of funerals or farewells to dear friends. I saw no visions of the marching ranks of Hitler Youth or of German U-boats pursuing my loved ones. I did not hear Jewish children crying out for me to save them.

The pelting of raindrops sang a sweet lullaby. My little ones were with their grandparents now . . . safe . . . safe . . . safe on the far side of the world!

61

I awakened before dawn when the rain stopped suddenly. I traced Murphy's features as he slept beside me, then awakened him with a kiss. I knew, through every loss, I was home as long as we were together.

Beneath the flaking plaster of the dismal little room, we made love again sweetly, as if there was no war. As if the Dorniers were not, even then, starting their engines and lining up for takeoff on the runways of conquered France.

Hear, O LORD, when I cry with my voice:
have mercy also upon me, and answer me.
PSALM 27:7 KJV

VIENNA, AUSTRIA
DECEMBER 28, 1936

My only prayer when I step off the train and hurry home to the flat I share with cellist Leah Feldstein is that there will be some word that Papa is safe.

Leah meets me at the door and tells me the American John Murphy has come looking for me. I think perhaps he has news of Papa. Leah tells me Mr. Murphy is staying at the Sacher Hotel. I go there alone to see him.

In the taxi I convince myself Mr. Murphy has somehow arranged for Papa's freedom, that my father will be at the hotel waiting for me.

I am crushed when Mr. Murphy tells me I am wrong. I try to stay composed, but I know I am a mess. Tears run down my cheeks and my heart pounds.

Then things get even worse. Mr. Murphy prepares himself to deliver unsettling news. He has seen my father.

My brave Papa has stolen a plane and flown out of Templehof Airport in a terrible wintry storm. Mr. Murphy says he helped with the escape.

No one knows where Papa is now . . . or even if he survived the flight.

He must be alive! He must! I won't believe anything else.

Mr. Murphy says my father wants me out of Vienna—out of Austria altogether. I don't believe him. I don't believe Papa ever said that!

We have a terrible argument. I say I will not leave unless there is no more Austria.

Mister American-Knows-Everything Murphy says Hitler is coming to the Ringstrasse. Get all the Jews out of Austria, he says.

I thank him for his concern. He stops me from leaving by asking about our holiday concerts. I tell him all the tickets are sold. Try again next year.

If there is a next year, he says.

I return home and tell Leah everything that has happened. She is not surprised. I think she agrees with Mr. Murphy that Hitler will enter Austria and do to the democracy here what he has done in Germany. Leah and her fiancé, Shimon, are trying to get visas to Eretz-Israel. It is the only place left for a Jew, she says.

6

The women's dressing room at the BBC studio was littered with copies of *Picturegoer* magazine. We aspiring performers studied the hairdos of rich and famous Hollywood stars. We imitated the fashions and mannerisms of our American idols in preparation for our performances in hospital wards.

After a full morning of broadcasts, Mariah, Raquel, and I were set to entertain at the Children's Hospital. We had an hour for lunch. I carried my violin case into a teashop, where I met Mariah and Raquel at a table in the crowded room. I noticed red-haired Mariah being carefully scrutinized by a trio of women.

A copy of *Picturegoer Film Weekly* was open in the onlookers' hands.

The women twittered among themselves.

"I know it's her!"

"Oh, can't be!"

"Herself? Here on Oxford Street?"

"Just looks like her."

I glanced at the magazine cover, and the lovely face of twenty-year-old Maureen O'Hara smiled at the world. I had noted on occasion that our

Mariah really did bear an uncanny resemblance to the Irish beauty. I said softly, "Mariah, they think you're Maureen O'Hara."

One of the fans exclaimed to the rest of her group, "No! It IS her!"

"But she's Irish. What would Maureen O'Hara be doing in London during the Blitz?"

"Maybe making a fillum?"

"But who are those other two with her?"

Raquel leaned close to Mariah. "If you're Maureen O'Hara, who am I?"

The movie fans approached us timidly, shoving one another forward, nudging the boldest among them to speak first. "Pardon, Miss . . . Miss O'Hara, is it? May we have your autograph?"

Mariah beamed up at them, playing her scene to the hilt. She took out her pen and graciously signed the copy of *Film Weekly*. "Lovely to meet you."

"Oh, thank you!" one of the fans gushed. "I loved you in *The Hunchback of Notre Dame*."

"Thank you, Miss O'Hara!" A small, excited crowd of shoppers began to gather. The trio showed the freshly inked autograph to others.

"Maureen O'Hara!"

"Look! It's HER!"

"See! I told you it was herself!"

"And who are those women with her, then? They can't be just nobody. That one there." A young teen pointed at Raquel. "It's Carmen Miranda."

Raquel gave a quick grin, a wink, and a tiny wave as if she was embarrassed to be found out-and-about without her tutti-frutti hat.

"But who's the other one? The blond with the violin?"

I whispered to Mariah, "Quick, who am I?"

Someone in the crowd piped, "Did you hear that voice? that accent? It's Hedy Lamarr! I'd recognize her voice anywhere, I would! She's from Vienna. That accent. Oy! Hedy Lamarr, it is!"

Someone argued, "Hedy Lamarr ain't a blond."

Another exclaimed, "You never heard of hair dye? In Hollywood they dye their hair to avoid being sussed out."

Mariah winked at me. "Sure, Elisa, you're Hedy Lamarr. Go for it."

Suddenly a long line formed out the door of the teashop as word swept through Oxford Street that Maureen O'Hara, Carmen Miranda, and Hedy Lamarr were using their ration coupons to have a scone and a cuppa tea right there in the neighborhood.

The questions began:

"Oh, Miss Lamarr! I saw you in *Algiers*!"

"Miss Lamarr! What do you think of that Frenchman, Charles Boyer?"

"Ain't he just dreamy?"

"Did you really go with him to the cazzbah?"

"What *is* a cazzbah, anyway?"

Scraps of paper and film adverts from the newspapers materialized, and we began to sign autographs.

BEST WISHES . . . Hedy Lamarr

More questions tumbled out.

"If you're Carmen Miranda, where's your fruit-bowl hat?"

Raquel pounced on the answer with an exaggerated Latin accent, "You know how many ration coupons it weel take to buy even one banana to wear in my hair in Lohn-deen?"

A roar of laughter and applause replied.

An elderly woman shouted, "Whatcha doin' in London?"

I answered truthfully in my legitimate Viennese accent, "Performing on the BBC, and irritating Herr Hitler." As proof, I produced our BBC performance schedule with broadcast time slots circled. "Incognito, of course."

From the back of the crowd I heard a familiar voice shout, "Play your violin for us, Hedy!"

I spotted Murphy's fedora waving above the mob. We were caught.

I heard an incredulous Cockney voice cry, " 'Eddy Lamarr plays fiddle?"

Murphy replied, "She's from Vienna, isn't she? Haven't you ever heard of the 'Viennese Waltz'?"

Another confirmed it. "Of course all of 'em

plays the fiddle. From wee tykes. I read about it in *Picturegoer.* Stands to reason 'Eddy Lamarr plays the fiddle."

In an instant everyone began to clamor for a performance. Maureen O'Hara must sing. Carmen Miranda must dance. And Hedy Lamarr must uncork her fiddle and let everyone hear her play in public for the first time ever.

We performed the same show we had planned for our visit to the Children's Hospital ward and, as Murphy said, "We wowed 'em!"

I do not know how many shoppers saw us perform that afternoon—somewhere in the hundreds. We had to move outside the teashop for the sake of our impromptu audience. The applause was deafening, and the crowds spilled out onto Oxford Street, stopping traffic. A London bobby rerouted cars and buses.

After thirty minutes, Murphy pushed through the mob, introduced himself as our manager, and said he had come to escort us to the Children's Hospital for our scheduled engagement. As we stepped into the taxi, the good cheer among the Oxford Street shoppers was palpable. They compared autographs and scurried home to tell their neighbors about the chance encounter with Maureen, Carmen, and Hedy.

The cabdriver also got autographs of the famous Hollywood film stars and declined to accept a tip because he was so honored to drive such esteemed ladies of the stage and screen.

Someone snapped a photo of the three of us and, though fuzzy and a bit indistinct, the faces of Maureen, Carmen, and Hedy made the entertainment page of the *Times*. The caption read: "Delicious even without the tutti-frutti hat!"

I do believe we humble BBC performers did a lot that day to promote the UK careers of those three beautiful film stars. The children whom we visited in the hospital did not care what our true names might be. They just enjoyed the show.

The *Times* also reported that several children born in London that week were christened with our adopted names. These unsuspecting newborns included a boy burdened with "Hedley" and one set of triplets.

Teach me Your way, O LORD, and lead me on a level path because of my enemies. Give me not up to the will of my adversaries. . . . I believe that I shall look upon the goodness of the LORD in the land of the living!
PSALM 27:11–13 ESV

LONDON, ENGLAND
CORONATION OF KING GEORGE V
MAY 18, 1937

England is the land of the living. Churchill says the English are still free and unafraid of the Nazis. He challenges the government to stand up to Herr Hitler.

I travel from Vienna with Leah and the Viennese Chamber Orchestra to perform at the garden party at Buckingham Palace for the coronation of King George V. Last December in Berlin, Lori and Loralei and I were swept up with the romance when King Edward gave up his throne to marry a commoner. I find I am no longer so impressed by the love story as the world becomes more violent and uncertain. Now my heart is moved by the duty and courage of George, the brother next in line to wear the English crown his brother scorned.

Among the international press corps at the coronation festivities I see John Murphy again, but only briefly. He tells me he has been in Spain and seen with his own eyes the strafing of women and children by German fighter planes. He takes my hands in his and searches my face tenderly. I feel a stirring for this ruggedly handsome American. He asks about Papa, and when I tell him there is no news about my father, he says I would be smart to stay in London and never go back to Vienna.

Leah and I also perform Bach with the string quartette on the BBC, and the broadcast director asks if I might like to return to London and join their orchestra. I answer that so many musicians are leaving the continent that I may be one of the few left in Vienna. I had seen him speak to John Murphy and suspect Murphy has put him up to inviting me.

Leah takes me to a private meeting of Christian Zionists and the Jewish Agency as they discuss how best to get Jewish children out of the path of danger. And not Jews only, but gypsies, who are the new target.

Eben Golah, dear friend of my father, is among those at the meeting, and remembers me from Christmas at our home in Berlin. He tells me he continues to make inquiries about my father. He says he prays for all my family as they stand firm against the Reich, but he also says I must consider moving to London. Leah speaks to him about Shimon and herself and their hope to get visas to British Palestine. Eben promises he will do what he can. He asks me to consider escorting Jewish refugee children out of harm's way. I tell him I will do what I can.

The great surprise for me is meeting Mama for tea at the Savoy. She has come all the way from Prague for the coronation festivities and to hear me play. She says that she feels strongly she will come to England soon unless there is word about Papa. I am saddened by this. I ask, can we not stand our ground against the Nazis?

Mama says they are stealing the ground inch by inch from under all that is holy, and that we must not be fools and remain where there is danger.

That night I tell Leah I feel I have been running away my whole life. I will return to Vienna and play out the season while we pray the Nazis will honor Austrian sovereignty.

7

LONDON BLITZ
SUMMER 1940

I had come to believe the words of Psalm 91: "A thousand may fall at your side, ten thousand at your right hand, but it will not come near you."[3]

In the midst of danger, my heart was at peace in the belief that every step I took was ordered by the Lord. When I rose in the morning and lay down at night, I asked God to keep me and my loved ones within the palm of His hand.

Lori Kalner, her heart broken, wrote me often from Wales, where she recuperated with the help of my mother's loving care.

Day and night, the Luftwaffe reduced whole city blocks of London to rubble by their relentless pounding. As the numbers of dead and wounded grew, so did the numbers of us who were left homeless.

I made the Evensong service at Westminster Abbey a part of my daily worship. It was at the Abbey, during one such air raid, when I first was officially introduced to seven-year-old Connor and the choirboys I came to know as "The Four Apostles." I could not have imagined that

---

[3] Psalm 91:7 ESV

afternoon how intertwined our lives would become through tragedy.

The warning siren blared as Murphy and I left the service at the thousand-year-old church and began to walk back toward our boardinghouse.

Murphy pointed skyward where the first rank of Luftwaffe fighters preceded the bombers. High above the greenswards of London, in a sort of imitation of medieval jousts, outnumbered RAF Spitfire pilots engaged in combat against swarms of German planes.

Murphy and I paused to watch the life-and-death drama played out among mountainous clouds. A Spitfire dove out of the high reaches directly toward a German Messerschmitt. They seemed destined for a head-on collision.

I shut my eyes. When I opened them again the ME-109 was limping away eastward, trailing a plume of white vapor.

"Coolant," Murphy said knowledgeably. "Got him! Bet he'll have to bail out over the Channel. Go on, boys, give it to them!" My husband shook himself as if suddenly recollecting that we were in danger. "We've only got moments before the Dorniers arrive," he remarked. "There's a shelter in the Abbey crypt." Murphy took my arm, and we hurried back into the ancient house of worship.

SHELTER THIS WAY. The fresh yellow paint was stenciled on the venerable stone blocks of the ancient church. It seemed altogether right to me that we would take refuge in this place. The Abbey had been a spiritual refuge since a monastery had been established there in the seventh century.

A Thames fisherman had a vision of St. Peter on the north bank of the river. This was the spot where the Collegiate Church of St. Peter at Westminster was established. Over the centuries it had been expanded and remodeled. Kings and queens, poets and playwrights were buried there. It was a magnificent edifice in which the sound of angelic voices rose to the vaulted ceilings.

How many prayers had risen from this holy place since the first Christians had laid the cornerstone? I was surrounded by a great cloud of heavenly witnesses whenever I entered the Abbey. The earth, foundations, the building blocks, the high vaults of the sanctuary, the tombs of the saints, must surely be saturated with God's presence. The air seemed to echo with generations of hymns and the Word of God spoken daily for many centuries. Westminster Abbey seemed to me like an earthly gate opening into heaven.

I considered that a German bomb might fall upon this holy ground today. I might never leave this place alive. And if I were killed in that hour? Surely many believers who had gone before would be waiting beyond this portal to welcome me.

Murphy and I joined the steady stream of choirboys, still dressed in their red and white choral robes, as they tramped down the worn stone steps into the dark bowels of the crypt. As I was surrounded by the laughter and excited chatter, it was though we had been transported into another century.

"I feel so safe here," I remarked to Murphy.

The cherubic faces of the boys in the choir stalls had become familiar to me. I knew their voices well and had asked the docent for a roster so I might learn their names. The Westminster choir school provided the finest education for boys from all ranks of British society. Selected for their singing talent and academic potential, they received full tuition, room, and board in return for agreeing to a rigorous schedule of rehearsal and performance. Westminster Abbey Choir School existed solely to educate and care for the thirty or so boys who sang as choristers in the Abbey choir. The purpose-built school, set in the heart of the Abbey precincts, offered a superior education tailored precisely to the needs of choristers. Like many schools in the great cathedrals of Europe, academic lessons, musical tuition, sports, activities, and games were carefully arranged around the boys' various singing commitments.

In Berlin, Vienna, and Prague I knew of several parochial choir schools that had been dissolved and the boys forced to become part of the Hitler Youth. Among the thirty choristers of Westminster Abbey I recognized two brothers with Czech surnames: Peter and Tomas Svitek. Both had the strong features of Ashkenazi Jews. A musician friend who knew the choirmaster confirmed what I had guessed. Eleven-year-old Peter seldom smiled. I had never heard him speak; he had never uttered so much as one word that I had observed. When Peter sang so clear and rich, his eyes seemed haunted with memories too grim for one so young.

In contrast, Peter's younger brother, nine-year-old Tomas, shone like a bright penny. His countenance was always joyful as he tilted his chin slightly upward and filled the dusty vaults of the Abbey with lilting song. Tomas stood next to Connor Turner in the stalls. I often saw the two nudge one another in unguarded moments before or after the services. They put their heads together and shared the comedic plotting of best friends who longed to slip a toad into the pocket of some unsuspecting girl.

Connor soloed in a clear, high soprano. He had tousled blond hair, fair skin with a sprinkling of freckles across his nose, and bright blue eyes that danced when he saw me. His ears protruded, and I once heard an older boy call him "Teapot." Connor took the teasing with good humor. He and Tomas had one another's backs.

John and James Warne were brothers—English from head to toe. John, with straight brown hair and serious brown eyes, was about thirteen and sang contralto. He had the swagger of an athlete about him, as if wearing his red and white choir robe was a thing only to be tolerated. I saw him frown with disgust, clench his fists, and lift his chin defiantly at his own reflection in a mirror.

His younger brother, James, age ten, looked very much like John, except that he wore wire-rimmed glasses that continually slid down the bridge of his aquiline nose as he read the music.

In my mind I called John, James, Peter, and Tomas "The Four Apostles."

As the Abbey choristers processed past my seat for each day's Evensong, they had come to recognize me as a regular attendee. Perhaps they could sense I was a musician as well. After services I had often lingered to speak with the organist about a piece of music or a composer. I had twice met the choir director through friends in the BBC Orchestra.

Over time, though I had never spoken to the boys, our eyes met and furtive smiles were exchanged when, at the end of each service, I gave them a surreptitious thumbs-up of approval and appreciation.

Today Connor and Tomas whispered behind their hands as I walked down the steep stairs.

I overheard Connor say in his best imitation of American cinema dialogue, "What a dish!"

Tomas added with a low whistle and a slight Czech accent, "I'll say! She's some tomato, you bet."

I had never cherished a compliment so highly as the wolf whistle from those boys.

And so it was, on the day of the air raid, I found myself in the midst of these darling schoolboys whom I had admired at a distance. I was pleased and comfortable as their excited chatter filled the dark, low confines of the crypt.

I introduced myself as a fellow musician and told them how much I had enjoyed their music. Connor replied that some of the chaps had noticed me in the choir stalls, and some even had a crush on me. All of them liked it when I came to Evensong to hear them sing.

In the moment of Connor's cheerful candor, a lasting friendship was welded.

On the landing above us, the air raid warden scanned the long, empty corridor, then called, "Everybody in?" He hesitated, waiting for an answer. The distant crump of the first bombs replied. We were silent. Breathless. I imagined someone outside, hurrying to get to safety as the barrage began.

"All right, then. Last call!" A moment more and then, "We're closing the door now." The massive timber door swung shut.

The warden remained on the top step in case some frantic latecomer arrived.

The *boom, boom, boom* of ordnance penetrated the thick stone walls. All eyes turned upward as the dust of centuries was shaken loose.

I held Murphy's hand.

"That was close," he said hoarsely.

Connor piped, "Ah, it's ours. Nothin' to worry about. It's the ack-ack guns in St. James."

John, drawing himself up and jutting out his chin in a manly posture, declared, "It's our boys all right. Hope the war isn't over before I get a chance to have a go at a Jerry."

James, who blinked rapidly with every concussion, reprimanded his older brother, "You know Mum don't like you saying such a thing, John. Don't wish it lasts a day longer than this."

Peter was ashen, as gray as the stone upon which he leaned. He could not hide his stark fear.

I hung back in the shadows and prayed as the explosions came nearer.

Murphy spoke quietly in my ear, "That boy's lived through something . . . look at him."

Tomas overheard Murphy's remark. "My brother can't talk well. Not since we were strafed on the road in France. Our mother was killed. Our father is in America. We will go there. We have been practicing American songs. Learning to sing like Americans."

An enormous concussion shook the foundations. Instinctively, we covered our heads. Murphy held me tightly.

Peter cried out.

Tomas consoled Peter in the Czech tongue. I understood a bit. "Don't worry, brother. The RAF will knock them out of the sky. You'll see. It's ours, not theirs. Peter? Peter! I think we have just felt a Dornier crash. We will come up and see we have knocked a Dornier right out of the sky. Peter? You understand, Peter?"

But Peter did not answer. He crouched. His wide, terrified eyes were fixed on the ceiling as he waited for the blocks to come crashing down on us.

Tomas said to Connor, "He's so scared. He dreams about the bombs. About our mother and our sister in the ditch. He relives what happened in France. He thinks now is then . . . every time."

Connor covered his teapot ears with his hands as the next stick of bombs made the floor tremble beneath our feet. Then, as if by some miracle, Connor raised his face, smiled slightly, and pulled out a tin penny whistle from beneath his robe. He raised it to his lips and began to play an introduction as sweet as the trill of a nightingale.

In awe, Murphy said to me, "He's playing 'Shenandoah'!"

Tomas began to sing along in a perfect bell-like soprano, *"Oh, Shenandoah, I long to see you . . ."*

John and a dozen others joined in: *"A-way, you rolling river . . ."*

Peter raised his eyes and stood erect. I saw his lips move. "America!" Then he opened his mouth and began to sing the tune so full of longing for the New World. The melody overcame the roar of explosions that ripped through the earth so close to us.

"Oh Shenandoah, I long to see you . . .
Away, I'm bound away,
'Cross the wide Missouri."[4]

For more than an hour the battle raged far above us, but the boys of the Abbey sang song after song while Connor accompanied them on the tin whistle. The terrible hours passed without terror. Music sustained us.

It was deep night when, at last, the all-clear sounded. We bade one another farewell and promised to meet again at Evensong tomorrow. We emerged from the crypt to a sight both terrible and beautiful. The night was as bright as day. Smoke and ash from the great city stung our eyes and filled our nostrils.

All of London was ablaze.

---

[4] "Oh Shenandoah" or simply "Shenandoah," a traditional American folk song of uncertain origin, dating at least to the early nineteenth century

You have made us like sheep for slaughter
and have scattered us among the nations. . . .
Awake! Why are You sleeping, O Lord?
Rouse Yourself! Do not reject us forever!
PSALM 44:11, 23 ESV

VIENNA, AUSTRIA
DECEMBER 1937

I wonder sometimes if God is asleep. Why has He been silent? Why do my prayers go unanswered? It is the Christmas season again, and "Silent Night" has taken on a new meaning for me. A year since Papa disappeared. Still no word of his fate. Nor any further word from John Murphy or Eben Golah about Papa.

The year 1937 is a terrible one for the world. The Spanish Civil War still rages. Franco's nationalists are backed by Nazi warplanes. Some people say what is happening in Spain is the rehearsal for what will come. Germany is practicing in Spain, perfecting the art of death.

I hear John Murphy is reporting from Spain.

Mama and my brothers remain in Prague. She has taken a house. Since Prague was Papa's last destination, perhaps she feels closer to him there. She may move to London in the spring.

The orchestra is readying another round of holiday concerts, but all of us have an edge of uneasiness. So many of us with German-Jewish heritage. In Germany it grows worse each day. I remember what happened in Berlin. Now signs like I saw there are appearing in Vienna: *Juden Verboten.*

After the German airship *Hindenberg* crashes, we go to the cinema and see a newsreel about it. Leah is recognized as Jewish by the doorman at the cinema and refused entry! I almost slap him, and I do tell him to go back to Germany and stay there.

Leah and her Shimon save their money and wait for visas to British Palestine.

I tell them not to worry—that Austria is not Germany. Everything will still turn out all right. I don't want them to go.

Shimon looks sad. He tells me Hitler is sending more and more Nazis into Austria, and he points to the JEWS FORBIDDEN sign across the street as proof. He says, with or without visas, they are going to Eretz-Israel. I think he means it.

I show Leah a copy of the *Berliner Zeitung* newspaper, the one with a picture of Hitler standing next to his friend, the Muslim Grand Mufti of Jerusalem. "Vows to banish Jews from Holy City forever," the caption reads.

See? I demand. Why do you think it's safer there?

Because it's our homeland, Leah says.

I house Jewish children passing through Vienna on their way to France and then to Palestine. I see the forged papers they carry. For Leah and Shimon and me to be caught helping is to risk prison.

If not for John Murphy's help on the train, I would be in prison already. Still, he is an American. It was no risk for him at all.

What will 1938 bring?

LONDON BLITZ
SUMMER 1940

Our masquerade as three Hollywood stars on Oxford Street became an act suddenly in demand. As performers we were called on to "do our bit" for the morale of our adopted country, so Mariah, Raquel, and I performed our routine on the BBC. One day after, we were recruited to join an organization called Entertainments National Service Association, or ENSA for short. Our troupe was made up of professionals, as well as well-meaning amateurs, and was such a mixed bag that among the public the ENSA show was also known as "Every Night Something Awful"

We patriotically entertained as Hedy, Carmen, and Maureen impersonators for hospitals, home-front factories, and for the armed forces. We were first introduced to our fellow ENSA artistes in a dusty little theatre on Drury Lane. The manager was a wiry fellow named Nobby, who wore a brown-and-yellow plaid suit. He never removed his hat for anyone, and this was the only signal he was Jewish. It was rumored Nobby had once managed strippers in a Bronx burlesque theatre. We lined up on the stage and he paced before us, explaining that he alone had been charged with putting together entertainment troupes to keep the morale of England high. His was the grave and daunting responsibility to send us forth between broadcasts to lift the spirits of an entire nation. How was he to accomplish this? It would take a miracle, because many of England's finest actors and performers had left for the States before the war and would not be returning.

"You'd think Hollywood could have picked an American actress to play Scarlett O'Hara in *Gone with the Wind*. Eh? You'd think they could, but no. The Hollywood big shots gotta raid England's treasures. Vivien Leigh's gotta learn to talk like a Southern belle! London burns, and the whole rage in the London cinema is watching Scarlett O'Hara flee as Atlanta burns. Okay, so we've got to make it good, ladies and gentlemen. You're what's left of British talent after the American raid on the West End."

Nobby sighed, closing his eyes dramatically. When he opened them again, he was staring at Raquel. He appraised her in a this-is-strictly-business way. "So, girlie, great gams. Aside from impersonatin' Carmen Miranda, and singin' South American torch songs on the BBC, what's your story? You're the one from Spain? Right?"

From the end of the row, the famed classical concert guitarist Pablo Garcia leaned forward and gaped furiously at Nobby in disbelief at what he was hearing. "Sir, please! You are addressing the premiere flamenco dancer of Spain—Raquel Esperanza!"

Nobby was unimpressed. "Is that supposed to mean somethin' to the ordinary chap in a munitions factory, I ask you? I gotta put a show together here!" Hands on his hips, he asked, "So. How'd you get here, Miss Esperanza? Lemme hear your story, because the common people will want to know."

Raquel smiled at Nobby with her Mona Lisa smile. He was the only one in the room who did not know who she was.

Her reply was dignified and without emotion. "I was a professional flamenco dancer before the war in Spain. The German Fascists practiced for bombing London by first bombing Madrid. I lost my husband and my child. God sent to me three young girls—two Jewish sisters and a gypsy girl like me—orphaned on the same day my family was killed. We fled from the Fascists to Paris. There I danced in the opera *Carmen*. The Nazis conquered France. A million refugees on the roads. We managed to escape on a fishing vessel out of Calais. I have friends here in the opera in London. They remembered when I danced the *Segurilla* the night my family died. They helped me and my girls. I also have friends in American opera. I hope to go to New York and dance again at the Metropolitan Opera House. *Carmen*."

Nobby nodded and rubbed his chin. "Lemme see what you've got." He inclined his head toward the guitarist. "Can you give her a hand?"

Pablo unsheathed his guitar like a sword and began to play the ancient *cante jondo*, awakening the suffering soul of Raquel. As he played and sang, she became again the woman among the dead and dying of her homeland.

"I climbed the wall;
The wind cried to me:
'Why these sighs,
When there is no remedy?'
I wept, the breeze,
To see wounds so deep,
Deep, deep in my heart."

Raquel danced the dance of mourning. Our cast line, touched by the fierce breeze of her dance, stepped back and gave her room. Dust rose up from the dormant boards.

"I've no fear of rowing,
If I want to I will.
I fear only the breeze
From your bay blowing still."[5]

---

[5] A traditional Gypsy song, recited in a lecture entitled "Deep Song," by Federico Garcia Lorca in Granada, Spain, on Feb 19, 1922, and translated by A.S. Kline, © 2008. http://www.poetryintranslation.com/PITBR/Spanish/DeepSong.htm

The tapping of her feet on stage transformed those mediocre planks into the bloody cobblestones of Madrid where her husband and child lay dead.

When at last the guitar fell silent, we were silent too. Then all of us who understood the meaning of Raquel's dance began to cheer and applaud.

Nobby stood with his head bowed and his arms crossed. At last he raised his eyes and declared, "Well, that was bloody depressing. None of that. None of that in this troupe, girlie. You'll stick to the Carmen Miranda material or we can't use you to tour, see? We're meant to *lift* up the spirits . . . you get it?"

Pablo looked as if he might strangle Nobby. Raquel simply smiled sadly, bowed slightly, and resumed her place in the lineup.

Each of us was made to audition. Top billing went to a young girl with a big voice. Miss Julie Andrews sang the most popular tunes of the day, such as "You Are My Sunshine."

We put together a show that opened with a medley of American tunes. Nobby bashed away at the honky-tonk piano. A trumpeter belted out old familiar vaudeville tunes. Our performances made a great noise in factory lunchrooms as hundreds of knives and forks clattered. Nobby's experience as the manager of a burlesque house paid off as our performances both entertained and lifted morale. I continued to be introduced onstage as a blond Hedy Lamarr. I waited stage right with my violin as Nobby and Pablo performed a comedy routine:

Nobby: Anything I can do for you while you're visiting England?
Pablo: I hear Hedy Lamarr is here, and I'd love to meet her.
Nobby: Hedy Lamarr, eh? Okay. Get on a train.
Pablo: A train? Why?
Nobby: 'Cause the line forms in Scotland!

I came out onstage to thunderous applause and laughter. Mariah sang Gershwin tunes, I played my violin, and Raquel tap-danced.

The highest compliment we could receive was when Nobby declared, "Well, girlies, you wowed 'em again!"

Late one afternoon I emerged from an air raid shelter and hurried toward our shabby boarding-house as the fire brigade clanged past. As I rounded the corner, I suddenly realized that once again I was homeless. Incendiary bombs had hailed down fire and brimstone on our street. Flames leapt from every window of our dwelling. Our landlady stood weeping on the sidewalk.

"Are you all right?" I asked.

"Awl-right? Awl-right! Me precious lovely 'ouse is up in flames an' m'lady wants t' know if I'm . . . what?"

"Is anyone injured?" I tried again gently.

"Anyone? Anyone injured! No person, if that's what y' means. But me little cat . . . aye! Me little sweet kitty! Ohhhhh! Poor Tabby! Look! Look! I'd give me 'ouse an' gladly for the sake of me little Tabby!" She wept profuse and sincere tears. I knew she meant what she said about trading the house for the cat. But I knew that nothing could survive in such a fierce blaze.

"I'm so very sorry." I patted her shoulder. "It is good no one—no human, I mean—was killed."

"Me Tabby! Poor, poor little dear. I found 'er abandoned in the rubbish heap an' nursed her from a tiny kitten. She was like a child. Like a child!"

The frantic search for undamaged water mains was useless. At last the officials simply turned and began to warn the spectators to stand back before the walls collapsed. My landlady wailed on in grief for her cat.

I did not mention that I was once again without clothes to wear. Even the loss of Raquel's red dress was nothing compared to the death of the tabby.

On the opposite side of the perimeter, I recognized Murphy standing near a policeman. I waved, hoping he would see I was uninjured.

In his arms he cradled something small and orange. I yelled, "Murphy, hold onto that cat!"

He raised his head at the same moment the landlady shrieked like some sort of horrible banshee and waved her arms. "Me Tabby! He's got me Tabby. Oh Lord! Lord have mercy! Bless my soul, she's alive. Alive!"

Cupping my hands around my mouth, I shouted, "Meet us round the corner! Bring the cat! At the White Hart Pub!"

Someone relayed the message to him, and he set out down a side street, while I clasped the arm of our blubbering proprietress and we hurried away from the collapsing building.

We rounded the corner at the same moment as Murphy spotted us a block away. The cat was snuggled safely in his arms as he approached the White Hart.

"Lord love you! LORD! Love you! You've saved me darlin' girl!" cried the woman, breaking free and running toward him. She smothered the cat in kisses and wrested her from Murphy's arms. "I raised her from a kitten, I did. Found her in the rubbish heap and nursed her meself . . . now look! Not even the Nazis can kill her. It's true indeed what they say about a cat and nine lives and all that."

She left Murphy and me and wandered off.

"Well, then, you're a hero," I said to Murphy. "Saved the cat."

"She was out wandering about when I walked up. I scooped her into my arms, and she began to purr."

"You have that way about you."

"Glad she made it out. Glad no one was in the bonfire."

We watched the landlady stagger off, whispering in the yellow cat's ears.

"No one killed," I repeated. "But I'm left with the clothes on my back, I'm afraid. Mariah's blue dress and nothing more. We've lost the umbrella too."

"Elisa, you know I will always love you . . . even with no clothes."

"Thanks. But . . . Raquel's red dress." I mourned slightly. "I won't be able to borrow anything from anyone anymore."

"It's becoming a problem."

"And where shall we sleep tonight? Back at St. Mark's? Loralei's office?"

"No. I've got good news, Elisa. TENS has found us decent lodgings."

"I wish I could have got the red frock out of the other place before it burned down."

"If ever a building needed renovating, that was it. Come on. I've already got us checked in to the new hotel." He dangled a key.

"Is it better than the last?"

"It's still standing."

"As long as I'm not sharing the WC with twelve other lodgers."

He eyed me from under the brim of his fedora. "How would you like your own bathtub?"

"It couldn't be possible in London. And I know I'm not in heaven yet!"

"Well, then? How do you feel about the Savoy?"

That evening in the posh Savoy River Room I danced the conga in Mariah's plain navy day dress. In the powder room, I explained to a wealthy American woman in furs that I had twice lost my wardrobe to bombings. I could see the awe and admiration in her eyes.

When the siren sounded, Murphy and I tramped down among the rich and famous to the reinforced steel and concrete bomb shelter. Hours passed. The hotel orchestra improvised jazz numbers as the barrage raged above the Thames.

The all-clear sounded, and we made our way back upstairs. Miraculously, the Savoy was undamaged, though buildings all around were stricken.

It was after midnight. The elevator was out of service, so we set our faces to the long journey up six flights to our room.

Murphy, in a move he had practiced with the landlady's cat, scooped me up and carried me over the threshold and laid me gently on the bed.

"I am purring," I whispered.

"Just what I hoped to hear." He kissed me,

turned out the lights, and opened the blackout curtains. The golden glow from enormous fires on the river flickered against the wall like soft, romantic firelight. Murphy turned on the radio and searched for mellow music while I undressed.

"I told you." He turned down the sheets. "See . . . I love you even with no clothes at all."

We made love fiercely, then lay back exhausted and content after the most horrific day. How could it be, I wondered, as I heard Judy Garland's voice from the radio?

London burned as she sweetly sang "Somewhere Over the Rainbow."

Deliver me from my enemies, O my God;
protect me from those who rise up against me;
deliver me from those who work evil,
and save me from bloodthirsty men.
PSALM 59:1–2 ESV

VIENNA, AUSTRIA
DECEMBER 21, 1937

How things have changed in Austria in only a year. Disguised Nazis stream over the border at the same steady rate as Jews fleeing from Hitler in Germany and refugees from the Spanish Civil War. There are protests about Jewish musicians from Nazi sympathizers in the Austrian government. I pray that what happened in Germany will not happen in Vienna, yet I am beginning to feel it is inevitable.

I am so proud of Rudy Dorbransky. He is our concertmaster, the leading musician of our orchestra. Tonight he proves his leadership.

We are all onstage, waiting for the performance to commence. Just after Rudy steps out of the wings some madman in the upper gallery shouts, "No Jews on our stage! Heil Hitler!" and "Germany for Germans!"

Then he shoots at Rudy!

The bullet strikes the stage and more shots

follow. Through the fusillade Rudy protects the Guarnerius.

Rudy is not hurt, but someone calls for a doctor. Someone has been wounded.

A dozen men beat and wrestle the shooter to the ground. He is hauled away shouting, "Germany and Austria are one! Death to the Jews!"

"A crazy man," I say.

Leah is crying and hugging Rudy. She says to me, "If Hitler comes, he'll have forty thousand crazy men just like that one with him."

Rudy raises his violin and the auditorium falls silent. "Herr Wertheim is wounded. A flesh wound only. He will recover."

Applause from the concertgoers.

Rudy continues, "The criminal is behind bars. We pray he will never recover."

Much clapping and tears of joy.

Rudy flourishes the violin. "Our instruments are undamaged. Let the concert continue. It is the *Biedermeier* thing to do."

Biedermeier: simple and graceful. In Vienna, it means we are family and we pull together.

Wild applause and cheering.

We play as never before and receive six curtain calls and a continuous roll of applause. Austrian spirit as displayed by Rudy will never fall to Nazi oppression.

Leah is wrong.

John Murphy is wrong.

He is in the audience and sees it all.

He meets Leah and me at the stage door after the concert. He offers to buy us coffee at the Hotel Sacher. He says he has bought tickets for every performance until the sixth of January.

I remember last year when I sent him away, telling him the concerts were all sold out.

Leah, pleading the excuse that Shimon is home ill, deserts me.

I ask Mr. Murphy if he is a music lover.

He asks about my father and my mother and tells me again I should not still be in Vienna. He says what happens tonight proves it.

Then he grows very forward. "I feel responsible for you," he says. "Like I need to look after you."

This after I haven't seen him for a year!

When he teases me about how we met on the train, I slap his face. When he apologizes and says, "Good night," I correct him and say, "Good-bye." Then, with great dignity, I depart and leave him frozen there on the sidewalk.

But secretly, I wish he would follow me. . . .

8

LONDON BLITZ
SUMMER 1940

There was a saying that the only way a man could get out of the infantry was on a stretcher or six feet under. That was also the only way civilians could escape the front lines of the Battle of Britain.

In those difficult days there were more civilians wounded during the Blitz than soldiers on the battlefield. Hospital wards overflowed into great houses of private estates, where volunteers were recruited to fill in for the lack of medical personnel.

On our days off from the BBC, Mariah, Raquel, and I continued to do our bit. Our performers auxiliary often traveled outside of London to military and civilian hospitals.

Raquel was the custodian of the three young girls with whom she had escaped from Fascist Spain, and then from Paris just ahead of the Nazis. Mariah lived with her widowed sister, Patsy, and Patsy's two small children. Raquel's three girls stayed with Patsy when we traveled out to entertain the wounded.

At least one day a week I kissed my darling Murphy farewell at Paddington Station and set off to perform in person for the wounded and the heartsick.

Mariah's sparkling green eyes, copper red hair, and Irish sense of humor made her a favorite among the young soldiers when she sang.

I played wild gypsy tunes on my violin while voluptuous Raquel danced flamenco on drab, disinfected linoleum floors between the beds of crowded wards.

A doctor was overheard to say, "If that dance doesn't make them rise up and walk, nothing will."

Our little trio was a hit, always ending our schtick with a Barcelona-Dubliner-Viennese version of "There'll Always Be an England."

At first I spoke very little to the patients for fear my German accent would make them uncomfortable. But I smiled a lot, and smiles begat smiles.

On our last tour we had a lineup of sixteen engagements in three days. The night before our first performance we were in Cambridge in our hotel room. Mariah determined she would help me speak English to the soldiers with a correct accent.

"Like this, darlin'." Mariah flashed her perfect white teeth at me as we sat cross-legged in our nightgowns on the bed. "You look a lad straight in the eye and say, 'Now tell me where you're from, darlin' boy.'"

I tried to capture her lyrical Celtic inflection while continuing to smile sweetly.

"No. You'll be terrorizin' the poor lads. They'll be thinkin' they've awakened in enemy territory."

Raquel interrupted my poor recital, her smoky Latin voice thick with disapproval. "Eleesa! You have such an ear for music! Yet you cannot hear the words is not correct? No, no!"

I tried again, smiling ever more sweetly, attempting to soften my heavy Teutonic consonants.

Mariah's thick mane wagged. "It'll never do! Y'sound like Marlene Dietrich tryin' t' blend in at a Galway pub."

Raquel agreed. "*Sí*. Most unappetizing accent. The Germans. All of them. Speak of love like they are clearing their throats."

Mariah nodded. "Right. Clearin' dere troats."

Raquel instructed, "Eleesa, you must try to speak like this."

Mariah sniffed and cocked an eyebrow at Raquel. "Hush now. Don't you be tellin' her how t' speak proper English, Raquel. Sure, you'll be havin' her soundin' like Carmen Miranda. We'll have to put your frutti-tutti hat on her head."

My accent was hopeless in those days. I was too freshly escaped from Vienna to fit in comfortably in any English conversation. "I'll just smile and play my violin."

Mariah clucked her tongue and surrendered. "Hopeless all right."

Raquel narrowed her eyes and reached into her bag for a red blouse. She held it up to me for size. "Yes. Wear something low-cut, eh? A little off the shoulder. Like a gypsy. You wear this. Men will not notice your accent. Tell them you are Hungarian."

"May I say Czech?" I giggled. "Prague. One of my passports was Czech."

Mariah agreed, "Sure, darlin'. Hungary. Prague. Whatever y'like, then. Smile and bat your eyelashes. They'll never know the difference."

As Mariah and I howled with laughter, Raquel hiked her gown, showing her gorgeous legs, and sashayed around the room in demonstration of the proper way to greet a wounded soldier. "See? He will throw away his crutches and follow you out of the hospital."

My lessons in proper pronunciation came to an end when a knock sounded at the door. Had we been too loud?

Mariah opened it a crack.

The innkeeper's wife peered in suspiciously. "There's a trunk call. London. A man, American sounding."

Mariah tossed her hair. "Well then, for one of us, is it?"

The woman replied, "Are you Missus Murphy?"

Mariah swept her hand toward me. "Murphy.

Such a nice Irish name, isn't it? Elisa darlin', you're bein' paged."

I smiled and, without uttering a sound, threw a dressing gown over my nightclothes and followed the dour woman down the narrow stairs to an old-fashioned telephone on the wall beside a cluttered desk.

It was Murphy on the line, sounding very far away and very excited. "Elisa! BBC just contacted me. Looking for you. Something's up, honey! Big things. You and the girls get back down here to London on the two o'clock train tomorrow."

The bulbous nose of the BBC's headquarters pushed into Portland Place like the prow of a ship run aground right before colliding with Oxford Street. "More like a wedge of cheese, if you ask me," Murphy intoned irreverently.

Armed soldiers parading out front confirmed the fact the British government believed Broadcasting House was a top priority target for sabotage, but it was also in German bombsights. The amount of destruction in the surrounding neighborhoods supported this opinion. Even before air raids on London became common-place, Broadcasting House was attacked. A nearby block of flats had been leveled by an explosion that narrowly missed a crop of moviegoers watching *Gone with the Wind*.

Above the entryway, statues of Shakespeare's Prospero, the magician, and Ariel, the spirit of the air, peeked out of sandbag colonnades like typical Londoners of the day. The stone images from *The Tempest* showed brave faces and stiff upper lips but still sought shelter as needed.

We were led through a series of recently installed steel blast doors and down multiple flights of stairs to the third sub-basement. Stiff upper lips were all very well for public morale, but the actual business of broadcasting went on from belowground.

The air was fetid and reeked of the aroma of over-boiled cabbage drifting from the cafeteria sadly misplaced one floor above us. "How the Brits can turn somethin' as delightful as cabbage into this," Mariah waved her hand around her head, "is beyond me."

"It is not altogether their fault," Raquel said, touching a perfumed handkerchief to her nose. "Proper cooking of cabbage requires a window, I think."

We assembled in a makeshift conference room. It was furnished with a threadbare camelback sofa, a desk apparently rescued from a reformatory from the amount of initials carved into its scarred surface, and a half circle of mismatched chairs.

One of the chairs was occupied by Cedric Barrett, a playwright for both the London stage and BBC radio dramas. The author, in tweed coat and spectacles, smoked a pipe that challenged the cabbage odor, and thankfully was actually an improvement.

Mariah, Raquel, and I took the sofa. Where had Murphy gone? He disappeared without warning at the last turning in the subterranean maze.

When he reappeared moments later he apologized. "Ed Murrow is setting up a broadcast down the hall. I had to say hello."

Opposite us, across the table, were two men: Eugene McDonald, assistant chairman of ENSA, and another figure I did not recognize—American from his tan complexion and well-tailored clothing.

McDonald, with his suit coat not quite able to button across his paunch, his unshined shoes, and his rumpled hair, was a sad contrast to the carefully styled American, introduced to us as Gerald Snow. From that moment on, the American took charge.

"You three ladies really shook things up! You did indeed. Mister Goldwyn is very impressed."

"Mister . . . Goldwyn?" Raquel repeated.

Murphy's grin extending from ear-to-ear made me want to punch him.

"Yeah, Samuel Goldwyn. You know, MGM Studios? I'm sorry, I thought you knew."

"Some miscommunication," I said, frowning at

Murphy, who grinned impishly back. "Please, continue."

"Mister Goldwyn loved the impersonations of Lamarr, O'Hara, and Miranda. Thinks it's a scream. But it's more than that. Mister Goldwyn thinks you are great representatives of the refugee plight. Think of it: Spain, France, Austria, Germany . . ."

"Ireland?" Mariah noted.

"Yeah, that too," Snow continued undeterred. "So here's the deal: Hollywood first. Newsreels for sure. A short feature with the three of you gals. We get Barrett here to write a script. Then he stays in Tinseltown to work on the feature Mister Goldwyn wants: Europe crushed under the Nazi jackboot, England fights on alone, bloodied but unbowed—that sort of thing—while the three of you go off on a speaking tour. Raise American awareness about what's really going on here. Plight of the refugees. What do you say?"

Mariah, Raquel, and I were stumped, which was saying a lot for the three of us. Finally I managed to ask, "Mister Goldwyn asked for us . . . personally?"

"Yeah, well, I saw the newspaper reports on your exploits first," Snow admitted. "I encouraged him. 'S.G.,' I said, 'you gotta give these gals a chance. They're boffo.'"

From Raquel's expression she was still translating *boffo* when the studio executive grew unexpectedly serious. "My last name—Snow—don't let that fool you. Couple generations back it was Schneemann. Jewish as it gets. My wife and son . . . wait'll you meet Robert. Six years old and already a handful. We're going back to America on the first boat after I get all my business settled. Anyway, I thank heaven my great-grandparents got out of the old country when they did. But more bad things are gonna happen if more folks don't get the chance they got, and that's where you come in."

"My children are in Pennsylvania," I said.

Snow was ready for that objection. "Another month out of your life, tops, and MGM will pay all the expenses."

"I have three little girls I'm responsible for," Raquel suggested. "I can't abandon them. And Pablo, my accompanist."

McDonald volunteered, "Pablo Garcia. Famous guitarist."

"Bring 'em," Snow offered. "Same deal. Real refugees."

That left only Mariah. "There's me sister," she said slowly. "And her two babes. She wants to go to America in the worst way. Always has."

"Bring 'em." Snow was smiling now, certain we had all agreed. "Had me worried for a minute," he admitted. "Mister Goldwyn said 'all or none.' That's what he said: 'Those three or find me three other ones.'"

Knowing how eager Snow seemed to be to have the matter settled allowed me to ramp up my courage. "One more thing," I said. "Real refugees? All right, there is one more requirement. I met a group of Westminster choirboys. Five of them. They sing like angels, and they've been working on American folk songs. I want"—I favored Mariah and Raquel with inquiring looks and received confirming nods in return—"we want them included as well."

"Five boys, eh? All right. You drive a hard bargain, but bring 'em on. What's S.G. gonna say? 'Send 'em back?' So, we're agreed?"

We were.

Hours after news of our upcoming journey to the U.S. was announced, Murphy received a phone call from Eben Golah asking for us to come to a meeting at St. Mark's, North Audley. Murphy and I arrived at Grosvener Square a few minutes past eight in the morning, following days of the worst bombings of the Blitz. Loralei and Eben greeted us when we stepped off the bus. Concrete tank barricades, mountains of sandbags, and barbed wire surrounded the buildings on the leafy square.

Loralei hugged me, looked deeply into my eyes, and placed a hand on my cheek. I knew that something big was underway. Murphy shook

Eben's hand and shared news as we made our way up the street toward the church.

I spoke of our experience in the shelter of Westminster Abbey and my concern that all the boys must surely be in great danger.

Loralei confirmed my belief. "The damage around Parliament Square is no accident. The Germans are targeting landmarks. The Abbey school has been closed. Boys sent home. Several have lost parents and are on the list of evacuees. At least you have managed to gain a place for five on the list of entertainers."

Eben spoke quietly. "The Blitz has done more than burn down the East London docks. It has awakened those who have been sleeping in the halls of Parliament these many years."

Loralei held my hand. "Awakened them to what Jewish children and parents went through trying to get someplace safe . . . anywhere."

Eben added, "The intent of the Nazis is to bomb England into submission. To make her surrender."

"It won't happen," Murphy replied, staring up the block toward the church's sandbag-shielded portico and the blacked-out, stained-glass windows. "Not with Churchill finally at the helm of this ship of state. It's going to be sink or swim here."

"Then Hitler will do all he can to sink the ship. Many thousands of innocents will be killed as he carries out his plan."

I thought of Katie and Charles and Louis, safe in America, and how soon I would be seeing them again. Unlike parents stuck in this island under siege, I was free from the worry about my children's safety.

Neither Loralei nor I spoke as Eben and Murphy sorted out the facts.

Murphy stepped around a broken sandbag on the pavement and asked, "Official word on the numbers of dead?"

"There'll never be an accurate count. East End. Whole families killed. Today's casualty list is filled with the names of English schoolchildren from the poorer parts of London. Meanwhile your American newspapers publish photos of wealthy British children posing happily on country estates on Long Island."

"And sightseeing in New York," Murphy added grimly.

Eben held Murphy in his gaze. "Your children? In America? Is this correct?"

Murphy answered. "We're lucky. My folks made the crossing from America before things got bad, then took the kids back home with them to Pennsylvania. And Elisa, going on an ENSA junket to Hollywood."

"What about you?"

"My work is here. I've decided to stay on a while. Got a job to do now that the fireworks have really started. Someone's got to report what's going on. America may have her head in the sand, but I mean to kick that ostrich in the rear, hard as I can."

"Time is short. Soon it will be too late for anyone else to leave. I mean, if America is drawn into the war." Eben's gaze rose to fix upon the white clouds sailing across the sky.

Murphy drew a deep breath. "Trouble is, American isolationists are too strong to let that happen easily. Roosevelt is committed to keeping us neutral. There's lots of sentiment for America to stay out of a European war this time."

"America's interests are in the Orient. Japan will not let your country live in peace."

"It would take something pretty big to blast the U.S. off the fence."

Eben nodded, but I knew he did not agree with Murphy's assessment. "As long as that is the case, American shipping remains neutral. There is opportunity to carry refugees—children—away from all this."

Murphy shrugged. "Okay, Eben. So you're thinking . . . maybe I can help. Along with Elisa's tour. More publicity in America for the kids. If transport can be arranged from England." I could see the wheels of determination turning in Murphy's brain. Newspaper articles about the civilian devastation in England, broadcasts to America about homeless British children—all these things might open the floodgates for immigration. America had been deaf to the pleas of Eastern Europeans. What if the cries for refuge came from English-speaking children?

Eben nodded. "We know Elisa's trip will help promote American support. Famous concert violinist. But we're wondering: what if she is also an escort on board an evacuee ship? Photographs of British children in the American newspapers. This week, the Blitz has put the British government to the question. Why should the son of a rich man sleep in the safety of a New York hotel while the son of a poor man dozes in a tube station below a dangerous city?"

"How does Parliament answer?"

We slowly climbed the steps of St. Mark's. "Churchill has agreed something must be done."

Murphy's eyes narrowed. "Better late than never."

The enormous double doors swung wide on the black and white marble floor of the foyer. Early morning light beamed through stained-glass windows taped against bomb blasts. Aromas of hot porridge, tea, and toast mingled with the clamor of refugees eating breakfast on tin plates.

"Come on, then." Loralei led us to the back of the auditorium.

Something was different in the makeup of the crowd. St. Mark's was more jammed than I had ever seen it. The usual babble of foreign languages was laced with Cockney accents from dust-caked Londoners who had lost everything in the bombing. The din of voices and tin spoons against tin bowls was deafening.

Eben shoved his hands deep into his pockets. "Every center in London is the same this morning. Filled to capacity. Each refugee center would fill the cabins on every ship." He waited for the sight to imprint upon our minds.

"There's someone you must meet." Loralei led the way beneath the solemn faces of stained-glass saints to a walnut-paneled meeting room. Mr. Geoffrey Shakespeare, newly appointed chairman of the Children's Overseas Reception Board, called CORB, awaited us. At his side was Miss Lucinda Pike, hatchet-faced headmistress of a closed London girls' school.

Mr. Shakespeare explained, "The task of the board is to select children of all classes, organize their passage overseas, and to see to their supervision on the passage and their reception and education until the war is over."

Miss Pike eyed me sternly through thick spectacles. "We have received 100,000 applications within a few days. An impossible number, of course."

Shakespeare continued, "No parents, relatives, or guardians are allowed to go. The children, ranging in age from five to fifteen, cannot travel alone. It has been decided to place them in the care of escorts, who will look after them on the voyage."

Miss Pike lowered her chin and studied me. "Your name has been offered by the Jewish Agency as a possible escort." She gave Eben a cursory nod. "We understand your expenses are already underwritten by . . . some Hollywood person. Your musical expertise and experience with the BBC might prove to be of benefit to the children in the crossing."

Mr. Shakespeare quickly added, "And you have some public notoriety in the musical field. This will certainly be of benefit in publicizing the need of British children being placed in American homes for the duration."

"I'll do whatever I can to help," I offered. "I want to be a voice for refugee children, regardless of their nationality."

Mr. Shakespeare glanced at Miss Pike as if to ask if I would be suitable.

The woman pressed her thin lips together. "We are attempting to have a fair representation of various ethnic groups among the CORB children and their escorts. Yes. You fill a slot adequately, Missus Murphy. Or do you prefer your stage name—Linder, is it?"

"Please, call me Elisa." I smiled.

She looked away. "Missus Murphy, we shall remain at all times on a professional plane. Your married name is Irish, but you're actually . . . Jewish, aren't you?"

I felt Murphy tense. He shifted uneasily beside me.

I said, "The crossing will only be six days."

Miss Pike intoned. "We'll hold religious services each day. You'll be in charge of the music. And a musical hour . . . instruction . . . each day."

I offered, "I'll prepare a curriculum for the children."

Miss Pike sniffed with disapproval. "There will be foreign children among the roster. The Jewish Agency has insisted upon this. Children of Jewish persuasion. I assume with your ethnic background that you will be able to keep the Jews entertained as well?"

Loralei's eyes widened slightly at the coldness of the headmistress. She interrupted. "Well then, thank you, Mister Shakespeare, Miss Pike. It's settled."

Eben interjected, "As a member of the Jewish Agency, I grant my full approval of the selection. Elisa *Lindheim* Murphy will be sailing as an escort among the CORB volunteers. Perfect. Perfect."

I was certain Miss Pike remained unconvinced of my suitability. Murphy and I stayed behind as Miss Pike and Mr. Shakespeare took their leave.

The actual departure date and time of the

sailing would not be made public because of the danger of U-boats. Evacuee children would sail with us. I would be notified soon and must pack my bags for the journey.

I sent a wire to Mama with the news. Knowing I would be gone possibly for years, she traveled down to London to be with me one last time.

All that remained of my belongings was one black concert gown and pair of low-heeled black shoes that had been in my locker at the BBC. In my handbag were a few cosmetics: a precious bottle of Chanel No. 5 from prewar Paris, a compact, and a lipstick. Every other item of clothing, including my umbrella and raincoat, was borrowed from friends. What, I wondered, would I pack to take to America? And what would I pack in?

When my friends in the orchestra heard I was sailing for America, they took up a collection and presented me with a new leather valise with my name engraved on a brass plate, and a cheque with funds enough for a shopping trip to Harrods.

With a sense of celebration, Mama and I spent the morning together shopping the bargain racks for sensible traveling clothes. I selected three skirts: khaki cotton for warm days, a solid navy blue wool, and a black watch tartan. Three blouses, a heavy Aran cardigan, and a warm, double-breasted raincoat with a thick quilted lining completed my wardrobe.

Practical. Sensible. Durable. All these descriptive words made sense in my present circumstances. I was pleased.

Mama reviewed my purchases with satisfaction and possibly amusement. "Very good, Elisa. So sturdy you could hike across the Alps in such attire. And I see you've enough cash left over for a special gift for your husband."

"Something for Murphy—oh yes, Mama! He could use a new pair of warm trousers. A new tie."

Mama smiled and shook her head from side to side. "No, my darling. You and your husband will be apart for perhaps a very long time. I promise, John Murphy will need something more than new trousers to keep him warm after you have gone." Mama took me by the hand and led me straight to the lingerie department. She ran her fingers gently over the soft silk of a floor-length azure negligee on the mannequin. It was something Claudette Colbert might have worn in the movies. The low-cut bodice was trimmed in lace. Spaghetti straps were not meant to hold anything up for very long. Mama winked at me. "Elisa, you will look lovely in this. However briefly you may wear it. It is the wrapping only. Be sure to let Murphy open his gift, eh?"

I embraced my mother for the last time at Kings

Cross rail station, then hurried back to the Savoy.

That night I lay back in the warm water of the deep tub and closed my eyes. This would be my last chance for a good long soak in a bubble bath before I reached America, and I was in no hurry to finish.

Murphy called to me through the door, "Hope the Nazi air force will give you a little time before they come back. Otherwise it's going to be an interesting jog to the air raid shelter."

Steam fogged the mirror. My contented voice echoed in the pale green tiled bathroom. "I'm not budging even if the entire Luftwaffe buzzes past our room."

I heard him mutter, "Yeah, well, if they spot you through the window, they'll be parachuting onto the roof."

I glanced toward the green Harrods box containing the negligee. I smiled. Little did he know . . .

Mama was always right. She knew my last night with Murphy needed to be special.

Murphy fiddled with the dial of the radio in search of romantic music. Instead, war news blared the disaster of a passenger ship sunk by a U-boat, mid-Atlantic. Two passengers out of nearly four hundred had been killed. All the rest had been rescued after a few hours. Only two lost out of the entire ship's company seemed a victory of sorts. Never mind that the vessel was sunk, 398 souls had been rescued and would live to sail another day.

My mind was set on joining my children on the far side of the ocean. I was undaunted by the news of the U-boat attack, though Murphy seemed shaken.

"How did the torpedo miss the British navy and manage to sink a neutral passenger ship?"

"They were aiming for the British navy and missed," I consoled.

"Like they're aiming for factories and hitting churches. That's a good indication of Nazi marksmanship. I guess we should be consoled in a weird sort of way."

He paused and poked his head into the bathroom. Grinning at me through the steam, he gave a low whistle and cupped his hands around his eyes as if he were looking through binoculars. "One look at you on deck by a U-boat crew? It'll be up-periscope and the whole wolf pack full steam ahead."

I chucked a wet face cloth at him. "Out!"

He howled and dodged my missile, slamming the door behind him. We continued our playful conversation through the door panel. "Now I really don't want you to leave!"

"My goal is to make you want to come with me to America."

"Sooner or later? 'Cuz I'm ready to sail with you right now!"

"Patience. 'Eine kleine Nachtmusik first,'" I teased.

I slipped on Murphy's oversized, red terry-cloth robe.

"I'd feel better with you sailing away across the Atlantic if the British navy had managed to sink the U-boat."

"Turn off the news, Murphy."

He tuned in to Glenn Miller's "In the Mood." "Better?" he called.

I heard our room service meal arrive and the voice of the waiter discussing the day's air raid. I ran a comb through my wet hair and daubed my last drop of Chanel No. 5 on my throat. Discarding the robe and slipping on the azure silk negligee, I was determined that my last night in England with Murphy would be one he would never forget.

Cracking the door open a bit I said, "Close your eyes before I come out." I smiled again at Mama's insistence that I buy this extravagant, impractical nightgown and wrap myself in silk as a gift for Murphy. "I've got a present for you."

A single red rose in a water glass shone beneath the lamp on the bedside table.

Where had Murphy found a rose blooming in all of blasted London? I wondered. My violin case and the valise were packed and ready for my morning rail journey to Liverpool. The table was set with silver and fine china heaped with roast beef and Yorkshire pudding.

Eyes squeezed tight, Murphy slouched in the wing-backed chair, grinned, and steepled his fingers with anticipation as I emerged from the bathroom.

"When can I look?" he asked. Catching a whiff of perfume he added, "Is that the scent of dessert?"

Lamplight shimmered on blue silk. I stood over him, studying his hands, imagining his touch. "Okay. You can look now."

Murphy opened his eyes. His crooked grin dissolved, and his gaze filled with wonder. I felt him drink me in. Were those tears I saw brimming?

"Whew." He did not move from the chair for a long moment but simply caressed me with his eyes. Then he stood and wrapped me in his arms. He lifted my chin. Our lips met and lingered.

His voice was husky. "Elisa. Dinner will be cold, I'm afraid." Another kiss.

I felt the embers of desire warm me. "Oh, Murphy, darling. Tell me you'll come to me soon."

His cheek was moist against my face. His passion was desperate. "How . . . how can I ever let you go? How, Elisa?"

The wicked draw the sword and bend their
bows to bring down the poor and needy,
to slay those whose way is upright.
PSALM 37:14 ESV

VIENNA, AUSTRIA
DECEMBER 20, 1937

The voice of Vienna's concertmaster is forever
stilled. Rudy Dorbransky is dead. Murdered by
Nazis.

Rudy had called to ask me to come to the
Seventh District, the worst part of Vienna—the
district of cheap cabarets and brothels. His
voice frightened me. His breathing was hoarse
and halting.

When I located the address—Number 6, Flat
D—the room behind the thin wooden door with
the rusted knob was icy cold and stank. Rudy
lay on a bare mattress. His face was battered
almost beyond recognition, eyes swollen shut,
teeth broken.

But there was something worse . . . much
worse.

His left hand, the hand that caressed the
beautiful notes of music which his right hand
drew forth with the bow, was smashed and
mangled. The first two fingers were severed,
and blood oozed from the stubs.

He had been assaulted by the Nazis for secretly transporting false passports for Jews in his violin case. My mind leapt back over the months to when Rudy had pressed me to keep the Guarnerius for him, had urged me to take it to Germany with me. Even that had been a smuggling operation.

Rudy had insisted I retrieve the violin from its hiding place, of which he told me, and take it to Leah.

Through rattling breaths that produced fainter and fainter puffs in the freezing chamber, Rudy told me my own father had been part of the passport plot. That was why he had been arrested in Germany.

And then Rudy piled another shock on top of the rest. He told me my father is still alive! Imprisoned, nameless, in Dachau.

Then Rudy collapsed into merciful unconsciousness.

I left him there to die. There was nothing else I could do.

All this, and it happened one year after I overheard Eben Golah at my parents' home in Berlin, saying that all Jews must get out of the Reich . . . that horrors were coming. One year!

9

LONDON, EUSTON RAIL STATION
FIRST DAY OF AUTUMN 1940

The distance from London to the port city of Liverpool on the Irish Sea was 175 miles, but the Grand Arch marking the entrance to Euston Rail station was already awash in salt water. The tears of ninety evacuee children, their parents, siblings, and other relatives threatened to flood the capital with sorrow. Murphy and I had made our farewell in private at the Savoy. Words choked off in his throat as he shut the door of the black cab and sent me on my way. I had been told it was important for me to show nothing but good cheer and a positive outlook in front of my assigned girls. Weeping on my husband's shoulder, Miss Pike informed me bluntly, would be frowned upon. I left him standing, desolate, outside the hotel as the cab drove away.

I consulted the official CORB information sheet for the twentieth time. It assigned me and my little brood of children to Platform 7, Car 12, Compartment 3.

Squaring my shoulders and hopefully my emotions, I strode into a great hall the size and shape of Noah's ark. Founded over a hundred years before as the first intercity station in

Central London, Euston's train shed was sixty feet high and several city blocks in length.

Apparently Miss Pike's admonition to keep a stiff upper lip had not received wide acceptance. Arriving at Platform 7 was like witnessing the unveiling of a tableaux entitled "Grief, More Grief, and Still More Grief." Little knots of parents and children mingled with previously unknown families. They now shared the prospect of thousands of miles and untold months of separation.

Amid the throng were handfuls that were not grief-stricken. I spotted Raquel shepherding her trio of orphans. Fair skinned, with wild curls, the Jewish sisters, seven-year-old Yael and nine-year-old Simcha, looked wide-eyed but comfortably secure, tucked beneath Raquel's arms. The eleven-year-old gypsy, Angelique, dark-eyed, serene, and beautiful, drank in the scene as a poet or an artist might absorb the emotions of others to be brought out later in a truthful depiction of this moment of human longing.

Mariah likewise managed her brood without tears. Mariah's petite, plain-featured sister, Patsy, fumbled with her ticket, dropped it, stooped to retrieve it, and in the process dumped the contents of her handbag. Mariah placed her sister against a stone pillar. Patiently, she attached three-year-old Michael to one of Patsy's hands and five-year-old Moira to the other. Then Mariah regathered all the fluttering papers and rolling coins. In the midst of this cheerful, pragmatic care-giving, Mariah managed to catch my eye and smile. *America!* she mouthed and I bobbed my head in return.

Guitarist Pablo, tall and darkly handsome, was surrounded by his admiring choirboy charges. James and John were locked in an embrace with their parents. Tomas and Peter appeared excited. I reflected that where most of the others were leaving loved ones behind, the two Jewish-Czech brothers were going to rejoin their father.

Someone at my elbow cleared her throat with the sound of a watchdog barking. "Missus Murphy," observed Miss Pike sourly, "you're late. Where are your girls?"

"I'm looking for them now," I said.

"Follow me." She added something that sounded like "unreliable foreigners," but a train's scream obscured her words.

I did not ask her to repeat them.

Beneath a sign reading Car 12 I located my assigned covey. Miss Pike favored me with a withering glance designed to make sure I did not move another inch, then departed without waiting to hear my thanks.

I was fortunate that my duty involved children who were from outside London. They had already said their good-byes before traveling to Euston

Station with a temporary escort, so I was spared their ordeal of separation.

The girls who would be my responsibility from here to New York stood beneath the placard like a shipment of school uniform dressmakers' models. Each wore sensible shoes, a heavy fabric skirt, a jacket over a plain blouse, and each carried a single small suitcase. I wondered if the ship's manifest would read: *Style: Preteen English Schoolgirl. Quantity: Five.*

It was hard to dispel this image of goods in transit because each child had a tag affixed to her buttonhole giving her name and age. *Nan, 11 yrs. Margaret, 12 yrs. Alice, 12 yrs. Lindy, 11 yrs. Betsy, 9 yrs.*

I read each badge aloud, then introduced myself. "I'm Elisa Murphy. I'm your chaperone for our trip."

"We know all about you," Alice erupted. "You're a famous violinist, and you escaped from the Nazis. You're going to Hollywood because everyone thinks you're a ringer for Hedy Lamarr, but I think you're much prettier, really, I do."

"Alice!" Nan snapped. "Don't gush so. It's embarrassing."

Sensible Nan with her bobbed hair and black-rimmed glasses. Just when I was enjoying the unexpected notoriety too.

Though all five girls had previously known each other, of my temporary wards, only Betsy and Lindy were related. Cousins from East Sussex, Betsy was two years younger, spoke when Lindy spoke, and nodded when her cousin nodded. Lindy had bright blue, darting eyes. She missed nothing while taking in everything.

"Look," Lindy said, pointing at a small boy being led by the hand toward the first-class carriages. "There's Robin Hood again."

The reference was not hard to identify. Against the drab browns and blacks worn by most of the evacuee children, the lad in question had a forest-green cloak topped with a pointed hood. Amid the departing leaves of England's autumn, he looked like a moment of spring or a living illustration from a work by J. M. Barrie.

"Robin Hood?" I asked.

"Robert Snow," Lindy explained. "American."

"American," Betsy chirped.

Young Robert was accompanied by an attendant uniformed as a nurse, but a few paces ahead walked his parents: Gerald Snow, the MGM executive, and his blond, fur-collared wife.

"We all call him Robin Hood," Margaret insisted.

"Don't be rude," Nan said.

Lindy's brow wrinkled. "Poor little boy."

"Poor?" Alice retorted. "They're Americans. They're all rich as Midas."

"No," Lindy observed, "I don't mean that. Look how he's staring at his father. He wishes his father would hold his hand, instead of leaving him to the nurse. Can't you tell?"

I instantly liked Lindy and was certain that, though she was not the oldest of my group, she was the brightest. I could depend on her to help the others. "Are you all from the same town?" I asked.

"Three of us are from Hastings," Alice asserted. "Lindy and Betsy are from Lewes. That's with an *e*, isn't it, Lindy?" she asked. "Lewes. Oh, I suppose I mean, two *e*'s."

But Lindy's attention was fixed elsewhere. "Can't you just feel what they're feeling?"

"Who, dear?" I inquired.

"That boy, there."

I recognized my friend Connor Turner of the choristers. His Irish whistle poked out of his coat pocket like a sword. The face of the woman who knelt to Connor's height was streaked with tears. She hugged the boy fiercely.

"Alone," Lindy said. "Either his father is off at the war, or . . . ."

Connor patted his mother's back and smiled for her. *Don't worry,* I saw him say. From his inside jacket pocket the child produced and offered a handkerchief. Connor's mother dabbed her cheeks and made an effort to echo the smile.

"Liverpool. The train standing at Platform 7 is for Liverpool," the public address system announced, and the tableaux began to break

136

apart: half to board the waiting transport and half to remain behind, nursing their sorrow.

Miss Pike hustled down the length of the platform, demanding compliance with the announcement.

"Come on, Lindy," Betsy urged.

"Wait one moment more." Lindy gazed openly at Connor and his mother.

I stood beside the girl to witness the conclusion of Connor's farewell. The boy's mother pressed the scrap of fabric to her lips, then tucked it back inside his coat pocket. Kissing Connor on the forehead, she shook Pablo's hand, then hurried away. Guitarist chaperone and five choirboys entered the coach next ahead of ours.

"Wasn't that just too painful?" Lindy said.

"Yes," I agreed. "And sometime when Miss Pike isn't watching, you and I will let ourselves have a good cry for him and for all the good-byes."

Lindy nodded, taking me seriously. "It'll be our secret," she confided. "I'm keeping a notebook, you see. Poems and such. I'm going to write them for Mum and send her letters because she has no one but me. Perhaps one day I'll write a book. Share all my memories, lest they be forgotten."

I decided I liked this eleven-year-old poet very much. I prayed that our journey together would be a happy memory she could record to comfort her grieving mother.

Lindy touched my violin case. "I do hope you will play for us each night before we sleep. Mum and I have heard you perform on the BBC. Before Hitler, you played in Vienna. And last week, a Mozart violin concerto. Which one?"

" 'Concerto #3 in G major.' He wrote it when he was only nineteen."

"Very beautiful," Lindy said soberly.

"You like music, then? Do you play an instrument?"

"Piano. A bit. But I can sing."

"We all sing," Nan declared confidently.

Lindy clasped Betsy's lapel, pulling her along. "We should have a talent night."

Young Betsy echoed her cousin. "A talent night!"

"Like an Andy Hardy movie!" Alice was ecstatic at the prospect of Life imitating Art.

"No sad songs allowed," Margaret concluded. "We must keep morale high!"

Plans for shipboard entertainment were already underway as we boarded, scrambling to take our seats. Songs were selected for the performance even before the locomotive whistle shrieked and the train to Liverpool lurched into motion.

It was pitch-black when, thirteen hours after departing London, we reached a vacant boarding school in Liverpool. Lindy and little Betsy had become my shadows. Lindy, with her notebook open, jotted notes about her companions and our adventure.

It was almost 10 p.m. when we staggered into the girls' dormitory. Fifty iron cots were jammed into a space meant to house no more than twenty-five children. Most of the evacuees fell onto their beds and were asleep before they had time to think of home.

I shared a room with Mariah and Raquel. Patsy and her two little ones roomed with another mother of young children. Exhausted, we were ready to turn out the light when I heard a small knock on our door.

Raquel was already unconscious.

Mariah moaned and turned over, covering her head. "Wake me when it's over."

"Miss Elisa?" I recognized Lindy's voice.

Opening the door, I saw that Lindy and Betsy had now been joined by the gypsy girl, Angelique.

"What are you girls doing? Still awake?"

Lindy extended her notebook and pencil to me. "Angelique belongs to your friend Raquel. She told me about the last time she saw her mother. She told me that I should write my mother a letter and mail it before the ship sails. Because we'll be in the Atlantic after tomorrow and who knows how long it will be before my mum gets a letter from me."

Betsy and Angelique nodded in unison.

Through bleary eyes I replied, "An excellent idea, Lindy. But tomorrow is time enough."

"No," Angelique interrupted. "You must write at the bottom of her letter."

"Me?" I asked.

Lindy explained. "It will help my mum, you see? If you write a note and promise her that you'll take good care of me in the crossing. You'll tell her all will be well and that she must not worry."

Both Betsy and Angelique concurred.

Lindy continued, "You see, I'm the last. My brothers both killed . . . and my dad too. Mum was worried about torpedoes. Afraid to send me away to America. But afraid for me to stay. I've told her all about you. If you write a postscript and promise her you'll look after me . . ."

Betsy piped, "And me too."

"Yes. Of course." I nodded and took the notebook and the pencil. What could I write to assure Lindy's mother?

Opening the door I admitted the trio. I sat at a small wooden desk and, by the dim light, scanned the last page of Lindy's letter.

"Mum, tell Aunt Candice that little Betsy and I are staying very close to one another, sleeping tonight in a dorm with lots of other girls sailing to America. I have made friends with a girl my own age named Angelique—I

call her Angel—who fled from Spain and then France and now is sailing with the Hollywood entertainment group. There are also boy choristers from Westminster who will sing in Hollywood. We heard them singing in the next compartment on the train, and I asked them to perform in our talent program. They have agreed.

We have all heard there are navy men in great ships who will be sailing all around our ship to prevent U-boats from attacking us. We are eager to start off.

Please, Mum, do not worry, as all is well. The BBC violinist Elisa Lindheim Murphy is escort for our group, and we will have music lessons on board and a talent show. I will sing "Somewhere Over the Rainbow" with Betsy and my other friends. Now Elisa will write to you about me.

Please do not answer this letter, as I will be in the mid-Atlantic. Excuse the handwriting. The train was joggly, and so was the bus.

Good-bye for now from your loving daughter, Lindy, and the others.

Your loving daughter, Lindy
XXXXXX

Lindy wrote in the letters *P* and *S* for me. I opened my Bible to Psalm 91 and started my postscript.

P.S.

Dear Mrs. Petticaris,

What a lovely girl your Lindy is! She cheers us all up and brings such light into our midst. I am so blessed to have such a beautiful and cheerful soul as Lindy to help me with the others. My own children made the crossing to America, and I know how you must worry, but I know all will be well. I am comforted by this promise from the Psalms, "He shall give His angels charge over thee to keep thee in all thy ways" Psalm 91:11![6] God has placed His angels around your dear angel, and I promise I will also watch over her on our journey to America!

Sincerely, Elisa Lindheim Murphy

I returned the letter to Lindy, who read it aloud to her companions. She thanked me with a hug.

"That's for Mum. I know she will smile when she reads this."

We did not hear the approach of Miss Pike. The dour matron, clothed in a long flannel nightgown and nightcap, loomed in the doorway. "What's all this!" she demanded. "What! What! Don't you know it's past curfew?"

The trio of girls cowered.

---

[6] KJV

I rose from the desk. "I had an important letter to write to Lindy's mother."

"You could accomplish your task before curfew, Missus Murphy."

"It was past curfew when we arrived here, Miss Pike." I motioned the girls to hurry back to their dorm as I dealt with the tyrant.

"You are a representative of CORB—and as such you will obey the rules."

I countered, "I am a private citizen escorting these girls as a favor to your organization. Now I must ask you, Miss Pike: what are you doing up and about after curfew? Morning will come awfully early."

My question flustered the grim woman. She blinked at me through her thick glasses and then with a harrumph scurried off to her own quarters.

Grateful Lindy had come to me seeking comfort for her mother, I settled down on my groaning cot with the promise of Psalm 91 fresh in my mind: "A thousand shall fall at thy side, and ten thousand at thy right hand; but it shall not come nigh thee."[7]

---

[7] Psalm 91:7 KJV

Even though I walk through the valley of the
shadow of death, I will fear no evil,
for You are with me; Your rod and
Your staff, they comfort me.
PSALM 23:4 ESV

VIENNA, AUSTRIA
DECEMBER 21, 1937

I heard the bells of St. Stephan's Cathedral ring
as I set out to the music school today. Each
ominous, mournful clang marked a step I took
toward the Musikverein and the hidden
Guarnerius Rudy told me about.

Overnight, Nazi gangs have been busy. The
streets are plastered with posters. *Jews out of
Vienna!* the handbills shout. As fast as Austrian
police remove them, three more spring up.

I carried an empty violin case with me. I did
not think anyone was watching me or had
heard Rudy's dying request for me to get the
violin, but I was still fearful someone might
have followed. It would not do to enter the
building empty-handed and emerge carrying a
violin.

In the music school hallway echoing with the
emptiness of the holidays, I have found the
Guarnerius violin exactly where Rudy said:
behind the case containing the grinning jaws

and empty eye sockets of the skull of Joseph Haydn.

The presence of death seems a fitting metaphor for all that is happening around me. Jews are being assaulted. Rudy tortured and killed. My father confined in the living hell called Dachau. Austria is dying and will soon be as dead as Haydn.

I heard a piano being played somewhere in the warren of practice rooms. I think now it was the ghost of Haydn mocking all our efforts to snatch lives from the ravening Nazi jaws.

I switched the violin cases as Rudy told me to do. Rudy's broken body was vivid in my mind as I resisted running from the hall.

Tonight, Rudy's handsome face, battered beyond recognition, will not leave my thoughts. Was there a reason Rudy hid the violin case behind Haydn's skull? Perhaps the skull is a warning . . . or perhaps it is a prophecy.

Hear my cry, O God, listen to my prayer . . .
for You have been my refuge, a strong tower
against the enemy. Let me dwell in
Your tent forever! Let me take refuge under
the shelter of Your wings!
PSALM 61:1, 3–4 ESV

VIENNA, AUSTRIA
DECEMBER 1937 (CONTINUED)

A miracle this diary is still here. The police were waiting in my apartment when I returned home. The little Jewish man who lived downstairs let them in. I am certain he was too afraid to warn me they were there, even though he told me of danger to my friends in the Jewish Quarter.

The Shupos told me they were checking the stories of everyone in the orchestra and asked why I had missed the performance. I did not want to tell them I had seen what happened to Rudy. I repeated my tale of having been ill because of hearing the news that my brother was sick and my family would not come to Vienna for the holidays.

A nondescript man drew a nondescript notebook from a matching coordinated overcoat. Flipping over several pages, he advised that I had been reported as being away from home for several hours. The other man, with his scuffed shoes and shiny, dark blue suit, eyed me suspiciously.

"Of course," I said indignantly, "I had to make a phone call. You can check if you like."

I denied having seen Rudy that evening.

They tried to get me to admit being well-acquainted with Rudy, but I evaded it. I took a high moral tone and told them Rudy had brought trouble on himself. They said I had been seen at the concert hall. If I was well enough to go out, why wasn't I performing?

I extended my hands, which were genuinely trembling. "I'm a violinist. How can I play like this?"

Suddenly my stomach turned over, and I was genuinely nauseous too. When I looked at my own hand, I suddenly had a vision of Rudy's, all hacked and bloody.

They tried to suggest Rudy and I were lovers, but this was safer ground, and I was able to laugh scornfully. I told them that the American newsman John Murphy was my lover and that he would certainly be interested in hearing about their interrogation in my apartment. This shook them up a little.

They believed me, apologized, pleading the need to complete their routine investigation, and left.

After they departed, I began to shake in earnest from my toes to the top of my head and shiver uncontrollably. Had these men seen what had been done to Rudy—to that bright, talented, heroic life? And they were here, pestering me, instead of finding the Nazi thugs who killed him?

10

LIVERPOOL, ENGLAND
AUTUMN 1940

At daybreak Miss Pike rousted us out of the dormitory and onto buses. Every morning there was a lull in the Nazi bombing raids between when the last of the night squadrons departed for Germany and before the massive daylight attacks began. Taking advantage of this window of relative safety, we were hustled to the docks.

It was there we got our first glimpse of the SS *Newcastle*, which would be our home for the next week, as well as our passport to a world without war. She was eight decks high from keel to bridge and loomed over the dock like a floating block of London flats. Her two smokestacks puffed gently, as if welcoming us aboard.

The contrast to blacked-out and partially demolished wartime London could not have been greater. *Newcastle* was sparkling clean. Though her hull was gray, *Newcastle*'s superstructure was gleaming white and her funnels adorned with black and red stripes.

None of my girls had ever been farther from home than London. Alice claimed to have visited

Paris, but no one believed her. Memorable outings for Lindy and Betsy had been occasional trips to the pleasure pavilion at Brighton. Margaret's eyes were wide, and Lindy was hurriedly scribbling in her notebook. Betsy tugged at her cousin's sleeve. "Lindy!" she said urgently. "It's huge! Won't we get lost?"

"Not to worry," Lindy assured her. "Elisa will look after us."

I would not have to meet all their needs alone, I learned. *Newcastle* had a complement of two hundred officers and crew. Of these, over half were from India—*lascars*, they were called. Since there were only ninety evacuees with the CORB program, sometimes it felt as if each child had a personal servant.

Dressed in white cotton tunics, wearing slippers with turned-up toes, and sporting turbans in pink or orange or sky blue, the lascar stewards were also far outside my girls' experience. Margaret pointed and whispered to Alice: "Are they wearing their pajamas?"

"I think it's wonderful," Lindy breathed. "Like genies from the *Arabian Nights*."

The first steward to greet us at the top of the gangplank bowed from the waist to receive Lindy aboard. "Welcome, missy," he said. "May I show you to your stateroom?" For a girl from Lewes with two *e*'s, it must have been a most memorable moment.

My girls were bunked together, with me in an adjacent cabin.

As soon as the full muster of refugee children, chaperones, and paying passengers were accounted for, *Newcastle* got up steam, unmoored, and moved out into the channel.

Whereupon we dropped anchor.

"Why are we stopping?" Alice fretted. "Are we sinking? Aren't we going to America after all?"

The explanation, delivered by Pablo, was simple: "The *Newcastle* sails as part of a convoy. We cannot leave until all the other ships are ready. Tonight we wait here; tomorrow, we sail."

I was explaining this to my charges when there was a diffident tap at the door. A lascar in a pink turban bowed, introduced himself as Sanjay, and inquired if "the English misses and memsahib would like anything."

Nan blurted out, "Like what? We didn't have breakfast. Would there be any toast about, do you suppose?"

"Most certainly," Sanjay agreed. "And perhaps tea, yes?"

The girls nodded. Tea and toast would be very agreeable.

Then Sanjay stunned us all by adding, "And a selection of fresh fruit, perhaps?"

"Fresh . . . ," Lindy began.

"Fruit?" Betsy concluded.

"Dear me, yes. The young misses would like oranges, or would perhaps bananas be more to your liking?"

"Both, please," Nan returned, and Sanjay bowed his way out.

"Oranges!" Alice said. "I haven't had an orange since last Christmas."

"I love bananas," Betsy said. "That is, if you do, Lindy."

The wonders of shipboard life extended far beyond fresh fruit. At our first proper meal each table received a menu that offered chicken or fish, potatoes or rice, soup hot or cold, and a choice between pudding and seven flavors of ice cream for dessert.

"Is this real?" Alice wondered aloud, ladling a third teaspoon of sugar into her tea. "Back home Mum fixed me an egg two mornings a week. Tinned beef for supper . . . when she could get it."

"Too right," Connor said from the adjoining table of choirboys. "Watch this." Taking a slice of soft bread he plastered it an inch thick with creamy yellow butter. "Real, too," he mumbled around a mouth stuffed to overflowing.

When the meal ended with everyone, including me, replete, an officer climbed a small stage in the dining hall. "I'm Third Officer Browne," he said, "welcoming you aboard. We're very glad to have you. And now I'd like to ask some of our special passengers to favor us with a song. The

154

quintet from the Westminster Choir. Please. Will you indulge us?"

It was impossible for The Four Apostles and Connor to refuse. "What are we going to do?" Tomas whispered to John. "I can hardly breathe."

"Only one thing to do," the leader of the pack returned.

At a gesture from John, Connor drew his tin whistle with a flourish and played a single, clear note. Then the quintet sang:

"Praise God from Whom all blessings flow.
Praise Him all creatures, here below.
Praise Him above, ye heavenly host.
Praise Father, Son, and Holy Ghost.
Amen!"[8]

There was a round of applause from the other CORB children and the chaperones. Even Miss Pike looked pleased.

In all the wonder there was only a single jarring note.

The last order of business at lunch was for each child and adult to be handed a life vest and instructed in how to put it on. Instructions complete, the children were also informed they

---

[8] "Praise God from Whom All Blessings Flow," doxology by Thomas Ken, 1674, also the last verse of a longer hymn, "Awake, My Soul, and with the Sun"

must not remove the safety device until told to do so . . . probably three days' sail, when *Newcastle* was well beyond the reach of the U-boat menace.

"Sleep in them," Browne ordered sternly. "No exceptions."

Later, as the girls and I tried to walk off the effects of the overwhelming meal, we saw how far-reaching was the concern.

"Look," Lindy said.

Robert Snow—Robin Hood—still wore his forest-green cloak, but over it was buckled a forest-green life vest.

For thus says the Lord: "He who touches you (O Zion) touches the apple of My eye."
ZECHARIAH 2:8, PARAPHRASED

VIENNA, AUSTRIA
CHRISTMAS EVE, 1937

It was late afternoon before I boarded the streetcar heading for the Jewish Quarter. In the market squares the booths were empty, the proprietors gone home to their families or back to snug, secure villages like Kitzbühel. How I wish I were there right now, and Papa safely there with me.

It is the notion that I can somehow help him, rescue him, that drives me. I remember the time I saw Dachau's walls and imagined the helpless prisoners confined there . . . never knowing that one of them is my father!

Darkness fell early this close to the darkest night of the year. It was already enveloping me as I carried Rudy's violin. I stepped from the streetcar and headed off down a narrow lane toward Leah's apartment overlooking the Judenplatz.

In a few windows flickering Hanukkah candles told me of the bravery of those who live within. Fresh paint splotched on exterior walls must be covering Nazi threats and filth.

When I turned the corner and faced a synagogue, I saw that even tonight of all nights there is no peace on earth, no goodwill toward men. *Christ Killers!* is painted on the bricks, together with slogans and menacing promises. A large crimson-painted swastika floated in the twilight above the words *Jews! Your blood will again run in these streets!*

A statue of the Jewish playwright Ephraim Lessing has been vandalized. The marble fingers were hacked off, and the groin slashed with red paint. *Race defilers will be castrated!*

Like Rudy! I wavered in place. Putting my hand to the wall to steady myself, it came away wet with paint, as if with gore.

I stood too long trying to collect myself, and the delay almost got me killed.

From many directions at once came shouting waves of Nazi fanatics. "Jews out of Austria," they bellowed. "Kill the Christ killers," they yelled. Windows were smashed. Screams of terror and pain filled the night.

Then they grabbed me. I saw a rock thrown through Leah's window; then all I could see were boots and angry faces and waving clubs and menacing torches.

"Teach them a lesson," a thin-lipped attacker suggested. "Let these Jews know what it's like to have their women violated."

Hands clutched at my clothing, ripped off my

shoes, seized the precious violin case. More hands tore my cap from my head.

"Stop," someone yelled. "Blond. She's Aryan."

Someone pushed through the lusting mob, throwing men aside and yanking them away from me.

It was Otto Wattenbarger, the farm boy from our skiing holidays in Kitzbühel. Otto was wearing a Nazi armband. He returned the violin to me. He offered to help me, to protect me. He urged me to stay with him and I would be safe. I shuddered at his touch and refused.

"Don't come here again," he said. "Ever."

By now police sirens were blaring. Otto dropped the armband on the street and walked to a waiting trolley.

I had not known I was crying, nor that I was bleeding from the back of my head, until another streetcar driver asked if I was all right.

I thought of Otto Wattenbarger and his brother, Franz—how what had come upon us was tearing families, cities, the whole world apart. I remembered the place where Franz had shown me that two snowflakes, identical in every way, could fall mere inches apart. Yet one would melt to flow south into light and warmth while the other would join the black uniforms, the marching rivers of the north.

The division of families and hearts is that clear . . . and that permanent.

11

LIVERPOOL HARBOR
AUTUMN 1940

As we lined the rail of the SS *Newcastle*, Lindy was tucked close against my right elbow and Betsy even closer to her cousin's side. Beyond Betsy was Angelique, Lindy's new sister of the soul. On my left were Nan, Alice, and Margaret.

There were no tears now. It came to me that the children were excited about this adventure. Grief at parting seemed all left behind with the parents and the siblings who were too old or too young to make the journey.

It had rained overnight, and now the air of the Irish Sea was sun-drenched. Everything from the domes and towers of the Liverpool harbor, to the horde of ships clustering to become Outbound Convoy 217, glowed like burnished copper.

Lindy, notebook in hand, scribbled images. She pointed to an adjacent freighter weighing anchor a half mile away. "Do you see how sharp its outline seems?" she asked. "It's like it was painted by an artist with a palette knife. Things sometimes look like that on a bright morning after a rain, don't they?"

"Bright and shining," Betsy contributed.

"You're right," I acknowledged. "And I know another kind of artist. Authors paint with words, and Lindy, the paper is your canvas."

Lindy did not argue but instead offered a parallel thought. "And orchestras paint with music, don't they, Elisa?"

I felt the sun on my smiling, uptilted cheeks. "When it all comes together, yes. But don't try to tell that to a conductor when half the horn section is hungover and the percussion section missed the train."

The girls laughed, and Lindy jotted something into her notebook.

As *Newcastle* moved off toward the northwest, the convoy's core of a dozen freighters and ocean liners was ringed by four British navy vessels. These long, low, and lean ships looked dangerous, like animated harpoons, as they quested forward and back at twice *Newcastle*'s speed. One ahead, one behind, and one on either side, they flanked us.

It was reassuring.

Choirboy John pointed toward the nearest one and said to Angelique, "Destroyers. Here to protect us."

"How best to describe them?" Lindy wondered aloud. "They look and move like greyhounds."

"Greyhounds," Betsy said, nodding.

"That's good," I agreed. "But more threatening. Wolves?"

Cedric Barrett, the playwright, also stood at the rail, but his face was pallid and he was not smiling. Still, he tried to contribute to the discussion. "The subs are the wolves. The destroyers are our . . ." He put one hand over his mouth and the other to his stomach. We heard a muffled "Pardon me," as he stumbled into *Newcastle*'s interior.

"I think he was going to say 'sheepdogs,'" Lindy ventured. "You know, maybe Mister Barrett will write about us when he gets to Hollywood. Heroic British youth escape from bombing to adventure on the high seas. What do you think?"

"I think Mister Barrett doesn't think much of the high seas," Nan observed.

"He'll be better soon," I offered. "But if our adventure is merely about how well they feed us, there may not be much to write about."

As the destroyers shuttled back and forth, encouraging the laggards, we sailed up the east coast of the Isle of Man. I overheard Lindy say to Angelique, "You've had it quite rough, getting here. Much rougher than me. Tell me about it."

Angel spoke and Lindy's pencil traced her notebook with the artistry of words.

My music class for the CORB agency consisted mostly of singing. First lesson on my curriculum was folk songs from different nations representing the nations of the passengers on board. Raquel sang a gypsy tune with her girls. The choirboys were called to the front to teach the tunes and lyrics of American folk songs. Connor played his Irish whistle and I, my violin. I was awkward and stiff with the folk melodies. The surprise of the day came when Mariah asked to try out my "fiddle" and, for the first time, revealed that she was an accomplished Celtic fiddle player.

To my delight, Mariah fiddled while Patsy clapped and taught us all to sing "Whiskey in the Jar," an Irish rebel's song.

Miss Pike, wide-eyed and ashen, entered the gym and listened long enough to hear fifty happy children belt out, "There's whiskey in the jar-o!"

Charging to my side, she hissed that my allotted music hour had passed and was over. "And further, such dubious ballads are not what we at CORB expected from a concert violinist. I will speak to you later about this shocking display."

With admiration for Mariah's unknown talent, I returned my violin to its case and turned the class over to a recreation specialist on staff of the *Newcastle*.

The afternoon wind was crisp, stinging my cheeks as I walked briskly around the promenade deck with Raquel and Mariah. Lindy, Betsy, and Angel followed after us like impatient puppies. Simcha and Yael remained behind with the organized children's activities in the gymnasium. Patsy peeled off with her two little ones to nap before supper.

Lindy carefully transcribed the lyrics of "Whiskey in the Jar" onto the pages of her notebook as Mariah dictated. "Please, Mariah. Repeat it slowly, please."

Mariah sang the tune at half tempo and then Connor's Irish whistle joined in from behind us.

"Musha rig um du ruma da,
Whack for the daddy-o,
Whack for the daddy-o,
There's whiskey in the jar.

"I counted out his money, and it made a
pretty penny.
I put it in my pocket and I took it home to
Jenny.
She said and she swore, that she never
would deceive me,
But the devil take the women, for they never
can be easy!"[9]

---

[9] "Whiskey in the Jar," a famous Irish traditional song

Connor and John, flanking the austere playwright Cedric Barrett, jogged up beside us.

Barrett, whose color looked a bit better than the first day, eyed my violin case. "You are more than CORB bargained for." Then he quipped, "I surely must have the choirboys sing this Irish robbers' song in my movie!"

I said to Mariah, "I heard Miss Pike discussing how best to throw you overboard, personally."

Barrett concurred, " 'Keelhaul the Irish woman,' Miss Pike said to the chief steward."

Mariah replied, "I've never learned to swim."

Barrett gestured at the flotilla of convoy ships surrounding us. "There's only about a thousand sailors who would love to pluck you out of the water."

"Only if it helps morale, Mister Barrett." Mariah smiled and batted her thick eyelashes.

Lindy tugged at my sleeve and gestured first to her notebook and then to Barrett. I understood her unspoken question and introduced Lindy to the great author.

"Mister Barrett, I would like to introduce you to a very talented young writer who is a part of my contingent. This is Lindy Petticaris."

He removed his pipe from between his teeth and, amid a cloud of exhaled pipe smoke, bowed gallantly. "Miss Petticaris. A fellow scribe, eh?"

Lindy blushed. "Very . . . pleased to . . . to . . .

meet you. I know your name from the plays on *The Children's Hour.*"

This both surprised and delighted the writer. "You say what? My dear child, no one ever knows the writer."

"I do," Lindy declared. "You are Cedric Barrett. THE Cedric Barrett who wrote the *Christmas Pantomime* and *Beauty and the Beast.*"

He thumped his chest in mock amazement. "A clever girl. A brilliant girl! You will most certainly one day be a famous writer, Miss Petticaris."

Emboldened by his praise, she smiled and held up her precious notebook. "Would you . . . would you read my story? tell me what you think?"

"I would be honored." He took it as if it were a Pulitzer Prize-winning manuscript.

Lindy, delighted, declared, "A serious critique, mind you. One writer to another."

He held his pipe aloft as if to promise. "I will most certainly."

The seas kicked up once again, and the ship began to roll as we paraded up the deck and down again. Barrett let his pipe die. He pocketed Lindy's precious notebook and shoved his Homburg hat low on his forehead. His complexion turned sallow once again. Eyes darted frantically for a way of escape as seasickness swept over him.

"You'd better go," Lindy, ever observant, said to him quietly.

"In . . . deed!" He sprinted off down a corridor to his quarters just as Miss Pike chugged toward our group with fire in her eyes.

"Missus Murphy!" she demanded. "A word in private, if you please. A word about your music curriculum."

Mariah leaned close. "Don't let her throw you to the sharks, now, darlin'."

Miss Pike crossed her arms over her chest and stood to one side as my pleasant companions pressed on into the wind without me.

"What is it, Miss Pike?"

"You know very well what it is!"

"No. Sorry." I feigned ignorance.

"Inappropriate! I have received a full report of the foreign songs in this morning's music class. Foreign songs, and this is an English ship!"

"More precisely, it is an American vessel."

"Certainly not Irish. English speaking. English music."

"Like Mozart and Bach?" I nodded slowly.

"You know precisely what I mean. I want you to know I intend to report to the board that you and your Hollywood friends are a bad influence on the morale of . . . of . . ."

"Only you, Miss Pike. Yours is the only face without a smile. Oh, and except for poor Mister Barrett, who is terribly seasick. You might as well know that we have a talent show planned. Like an American Andy Hardy movie. We intend to feature a song from every homeland. That is twelve different nationalities, Miss Pike, who are now under the jackboot of Hitler. The songs forbidden by the Nazis we will sing freely."

"This is serious business, this voyage. And I want you to know I intend to report your frivolous music instruction personally. You are most unqualified to shepherd these children to America."

"Is that all?"

She pushed her spectacles up on the bridge of her sharp nose. "Indeed. That is all."

As she stormed away to the telegraph office, I knew Miss Pike had declared war upon me personally.

Jesus called them to Him, saying, "Let the children come to Me and do not hinder them, for to such belongs the kingdom of God."
LUKE 18:16 ESV

VIENNA, AUSTRIA
MIDNIGHT, CHRISTMAS, 1937

Leah is alive! When I returned to my apartment, she was there. There had been a premonition in the Judengasse that something evil was coming, she said, so she had escaped before I made my ill-fated attempt to seek her.

Nor was she alone. With Leah were three Jewish children: two boys, about seven and eight, and a little girl no more than five. Leah wants to help them get to Palestine. I made the children hot chocolate and had them sit in my kitchen while Leah and I reviewed the horrors of the night.

I told her not to try to go back to the Judengasse. From looking at the state of my clothes and the dried blood on my head, I know she understood why, without my giving those details.

When she saw me with Rudy's violin case, she also understood what must have happened to him. "He told me to take it to you," I said as I concluded the story of his tragic end.

From that moment on, the revelations all came from Leah. She showed me the secrets of the Guarnerius case: five passports and other papers in a false bottom, diamonds concealed within hollow tuning pegs.

Leah waved the passports sadly. "None of these will work for my three *Liebe Kinder* in there." She nodded toward my kitchen. "And I don't think Vienna is safe for them. If they were found, some officious bureaucrat would insist they be sent back to the Reich, and you know what that would mean."

Among the papers was something that touched me directly—the description of why and when my father had been arrested and his transfer to Dachau. "Your father is a hero," Leah said. "Seven hundred! That's how many false passports your father provided the funds to purchase. Seven hundred German Jewish children."

My father had kept his involvement in smuggling children a secret from me, when my best friend knew the truth? Was I hurt? Was I angry? No.

More than anything I wanted to find a way to free my father.

But that wasn't all. Tonight was the night the course of my life changed forever. Because I can pass as a non-Jew, with my blond hair and Aryan stage name, I have been on the sidelines far too long. I pretended that everything would be all right again if I simply closed my eyes to the truth.

What has happened to Rudy, what is still happening to my father, destroys that notion once and for all.

"I want to help," I said. "My papers say I'm Aryan, and I am a violinist. I am good friends with an American newsman. The Nazis will fear to trouble me again. I want to help."

"You already have," Leah insisted.

"No, I mean, I really want to help. And not only carrying papers, either. Let's start with your three babies. I know a place in the Tyrol where they will be completely safe. I want to be the one to take them there . . . and all the ones who come afterwards."

12

AT SEA
NORTH ATLANTIC
AUTUMN 1940

At twilight of our third day at sea a rising wind chased the setting sun into the west. Third Officer Browne passed by where Mariah, Patsy, Raquel, and I stood at the rail lifting our chins to the breeze. "Enjoy it, ladies," he said. "There'll be a storm before morning, and tomorrow should stay rainy all day." Tipping his hat, he continued toward *Newcastle*'s bridge.

"Isn't he a fine figger of a man?" Mariah suggested, watching Browne disappear.

"And a gentleman," Raquel added.

We four appreciated a moment's tranquility. Tonight was the children's talent show for which we had been preparing. The practice sessions had often been wild affairs. A few minutes ago Lindy and Betsy had volunteered to take little Moira and Michael to the playroom until time to dress for dinner.

I had fifteen minutes with no one asking me to help them find their sheet music or accusing a bunkmate of borrowing their favorite stockings without permission. Fifteen minutes without Miss Pike accusing me of treason and sedition.

It was bliss.

As the skies purpled overhead, signal lanterns began blinking rapidly from the escorting destroyers, replied to by the strobes of the passenger and cargo ships. "How can they be havin' so much to say to each other?" Mariah wondered. "What's it mean?"

The answer came when the destroyer that was the leading sheepdog of our seagoing flock peeled off in a wide turn to port. She heeled sharply with increasing speed, and the curve of her new course brought her across our bow. The lean, dangerous vessel was pointed back toward Ireland. Moments later I saw the flanking warships do the same. Like opening a banana, the convoy's skin of protection peeled down the sides, leaving the core of civilian craft headed toward America.

"What a comfort that is," Raquel declared.

Patsy looked a question at her.

Raquel continued, "It means we're safe now. The British navy would never leave us until we are clear of any threat, isn't that so?" Her last observation was directed toward me, but I deferred the question to Officer Browne, hurrying back toward us with a sheaf of yellow radio transmissions in his hands.

"Out of danger?" I asked him, pointing at the departing destroyers.

"Eh? Oh, quite. We're beyond the war zone now. Next stop, New York."

I felt a rush of relief. No more sleeping dressed and in life jackets. It had taken days of travel and uncomfortable nights, but at last the purpose of this voyage was realized: we had escaped from the war.

We and the refugee children were out of harm's way.

I would see my own children again soon.

My cheerful vision was interrupted by a foul stench. The pleasant salt air was tainted with a vicious smell.

The Polish diplomat, Podlaski, had ignited one of his vile cigars upwind of us. Cedric Barrett, unable to escape completely, still stood as far to one side of Podlaski as politeness allowed.

Like the noxious fumes, the Pole's words also floated down to us on the breeze. "Criminal," he said. "Leaving us defenseless here like this."

"The destroyers have to escort an inbound convoy full of supplies," Barrett said reasonably. "We're safe enough now."

"Safe enough?" Podlaski retorted, waving his cigar for emphasis. "They should remain with us all the way to New York. Even after seeing what the Nazis did to Poland, and after fighting them in France, the English still do not know them as I do."

Mariah sneezed. "Sure and it's time to go in, I'm thinkin'."

"I agree," I said. "Time to see who's ripped her costume and who can't find her left shoe."

"I feel sorry for whoever shares a cabin with that man," Raquel said, gesturing toward the diplomat. "I can't imagine being cooped up with Mister Podlaski in any space smaller than . . . than Spain! And even then, I'd want to be upwind!"

We had done all our practicing in secret. A relay of Lindy, Angel, John, and James had kept tabs on Miss Pike's whereabouts. Whenever she got too close to one of the clandestine rehearsals, each of the sentries would strike up some impromptu heel-tapping and hand-clapping, as instructed by Raquel. These antics generated some strange looks from the grim chaperone, but our surprise had remained undiscovered.

We also had to roll out our production at top speed.

After all, we had invited Captain Doyle to our dining room for the third night at sea. The performance commenced immediately after the supper dishes were cleared away. I sat at the table with the captain, Mr. and Mrs. Snow with Robert, and Cedric Barrett, now recovered from his seasickness. Also at my table was Podlaski. His cigars formed a single point of agreement between myself and Miss Pike: they were foul!

Mariah acted as mistress of ceremonies. "Your worship, Captain Doyle, sir. Miss Pike, and the rest of youse ladies and gentlemen, thank you for attending our little theatrical endeavor. It's in your honor, Captain dear, but truth to tell, it's also me friend Connor's birthday. Now what d'ya think of that? So without further eloquence, let's begin."

I stood at the side of the platform. The five Westminster choirboys trooped to center stage. At a nod from Connor I raised my bow and began a slow, dramatic introduction of sliding scales and glissandos, ending with a note picked up by Connor on his flute.

At which moment of high expectation the boys began to sing:

" 'Twas midnight on the ocean.
Not a streetcar was in sight.
I went into a boxcar, to get myself a light.
The man behind the counter was a woman,
    old and gray,
Who used to peddle shoestrings on the road
    to Mandalay.
I said, 'Good morning, sir.'
Her eyes were bright with tears.
She put her head between her knees,
And stood that way for years.
Her children, six, were orphans, except one
    tiny tot
Who lived in a house across the street
Upon a vacant lot!

Oh, ain't we crazy? Oh, ain't we crazy?
We love to sing and dance the night away.
Oh, ain't we crazy, oh, ain't we crazy?
We're gonna sing and dance all night today!"[10]

By the end of verse two the entire dining hall was singing along with the chorus, "Oh, Ain't We Crazy!" Of course, long before the end of verse one, Miss Pike's complexion had gone from pink to scarlet and was well on the way to purple.

When the number concluded to thunderous applause, Mariah introduced Connor again and borrowed my violin. I rejoined my table while avoiding Miss Pike's glower.

"Where I'm from," Mariah said, "we calls it a 'fiddle.' But I'll be takin' good care of it for you, Elisa darlin'. Now Connor, my dear. Are you ready with your fine Irish whistle thing?"

And the two sailed into an instrumental duet of "Whiskey in the Jar." Of course by now all my music students knew the lyrics by heart and all joined in on the chorus.

Captain Doyle thumped his meaty hand on the table in time with the music. On the third "Musha rig um du ruma da," he opened his mouth to join

---

[10] "Oh, Ain't We Crazy!" attributed to Harry McClintock, aka "Haywire Mac"

in singing, caught a glare from La Pike that would have done credit to Medusa, and nearly drowned himself while downing a glass of water to cover his embarrassment.

Cedric Barrett leaned across the table. "I believe it was Dickens who wrote, 'One may as well be hung for stealing a horse as for a pig' . . . or something to that effect," whereupon Barrett added his own unexpectedly precise tenor to the chorus.

Fearing Miss Pike might be on the verge of apoplexy, Mariah ushered in Lindy, Angel, and Betsy. With my violin again as accompaniment, the trio gave a very sweet rendition of "Somewhere Over the Rainbow."

Miss Pike's hue had returned from black to merely ochre as other relatively tame acts followed. Different groups of my music students sang ballads and popular contemporary numbers.

All too soon it was time for the grand finale.

At Mariah's direction the lights in the hall were doused. The Four Apostles, holding electric torches borrowed from the ship's emergency equipment, focused them on a side door as a makeshift spotlight.

The first actor to appear, blinking in the light, was Yael, followed by Simcha, Angel, and finally Raquel. The chuckle that began for the littlest cast member increased to a chortle, then to a guffaw, and finally to a full-on, gasping-for-breath explosion of laughter.

Each female was attired in robes made of the floral print bedspreads borrowed from their cabins.

But it was the headgear that provoked the greatest reaction.

Each performer wore a turban made from a towel to which was attached oranges, bananas, mangos, and, best of all, atop Raquel's head . . . a pineapple.

As Pablo leapt upright and began to strum his guitar the girls sang:

"I yi yi yi yi I like you very much.
I yi yi yi yi I think you're grand.
Why, why, why is it that when I feel your
 touch,
My heart starts to beat, to beat the band?"

This much of the performance was probably already sufficient to get us hung as horse thieves in Miss Pike's opinion, but Raquel had only begun.

Swaying and singing, Raquel's little troupe encircled Miss Pike's table. As Raquel passed Captain Doyle, she extended her hand for him to join her . . . and he accepted!

"I yi yi yi yi I like you to hold me tight.
You are too too too too too divine.

If you want to be in someone's arms tonight,
Just be sure the arms you're in are mine."[11]

What started with Raquel, the girls, the captain, Cedric Barrett, and me soon picked up another hundred members as the conga line bumped and thumped around the room to the strains of *I yi yi yi yi I like you very much!*

Before long the human chain included everyone except Podlaski and Miss Pike, leaving her forced to endure his cigar smoke.

"Boffo!" MGM executive Snow pronounced as he juggled Robin Hood atop his shoulders.

From every doorway and passage, turbaned heads appeared. It seemed all the lascars on the ship had to find out what the crazy passengers were up to. It was like having pink and blue and yellow chrysanthemum blossoms festoon every entry!

Connor beamed. "Best birthday, ever," he shouted as we passed each other in a writhing loop of dancers. "Absolutely tops!"

"See you in the mornin', me darlin' girl." Mariah grinned over her shoulder. "Remember, in Ireland we believe you're never too old t' learn a new tune!"

I laughed and raised my hand in surrender,

---

[11] "I Yi, Yi, Yi, Yi" (I like you very much) lyrics by Mack Gordon, music by Harry Warren

deciding I would practice English vocabulary by singing in imitation of Mariah's lyrical Irish accent. And if I couldn't sing like Mariah, at least I would learn to dance and play the Irish fiddle like a true Celt.

I softly sang "Whiskey in the Jar" as I descended the steep stairs to C deck and the children's quarters.

Oddly, with the naval convoy ships gone, I had an increased sense of security. Surely we were out of harm's way by now, beyond the territory of German U-boats. By the time we reached New York harbor I vowed I would be playing a duet with Mariah as we sailed past the Statue of Liberty.

A few paces down the corridor the door to the boys' cabin swung open and Connor stuck his head out. Sunburned ears poked out from tousled hair. In spite of the late hour he was fully dressed except for shoes. "Halt! Who goes there?" His cheeks were ruddy from wind and from joy. His tie was askew. "Oh! It's you singing." He grinned and turned to the Apostles. "Never mind. It's only Missus Murphy!" A cheer rose up from his bunkmates.

"Still celebrating?" I paused before the door festooned with handmade birthday greetings and crayon drawings of Connor in the midst of ships and sharks and sailors.

"We were afraid you was Mizz Pike coming down the hallway. She's all about curfews, and such, don't you know?"

John called from the top bunk, "We'll not let her pass without a song!"

James seconded his elder brother's declaration.

Tomas cried, "A song! A song!"

Peter rubbed his cheek with his pale hand, then raised a finger for emphasis as he stuttered, "S–s–sing!"

I laughed and began my tune with the second verse.

> *"I went into me chamber, all for to take a*
> *slumber,*
> *I dreamt of gold and jewels and for sure it*
> *was no wonder.*
> *But Jenny took my charges and filled them*
> *up with water,*
> *Then sent for Captain Farrell to be ready*
> *for the slaughter."*

The boys joined me in the chorus:

> *"Musha rig um du ruma da,*
> *Whack for the daddy-o,*
> *Whack for the daddy-o,*
> *There's whiskey in the jar."*

We finished in perfect harmony and with a burst of applause and laughter that stirred the sleeping passengers of C deck.

"Will that do?" I curtsied.

Connor tapped his forehead, offering me a gallant salute. "Proceed, my lady."

I mussed his hair, though who could tell? "I hope you had a lovely day, Connor." Stooping, I kissed the top of his head. "A birthday kiss from your mother."

"She kissed 'im!" Tomas chortled.

"Ohhhh, Connor!" John teased.

"Did'ja see that?" James pushed his glasses up on his nose and howled.

Peter gave a wolf whistle.

The boys roared as Connor rolled his eyes and slammed the door in my face. Howls of glee, hoots, and catcalls followed me as I made my way down the hall.

Miss Pike, scowling and fierce in her purple plaid flannel dressing gown, emerged from her cabin and planted herself in the center of the corridor. Frizzy gray hair escaped in wild wisps from a frayed white night cap. Hands on broad hips, she blocked my path. Thick eyeglasses perched on her sharp nose. Lenses magnified pale, disapproving eyes.

"Good evening," I chirped, looking beyond her.

"Whiskey in the jar-o? What's all that, then? What are they up to?"

"The birthday."

"Past curfew!" she snapped.

"You know boys."

"I certainly do. Unruly. Incorrigible . . ."

I defended joy with a smile. "An eighth birthday aboard an ocean liner only comes once in a lifetime."

She made as if to storm the boys' quarters, but now it was I who blocked her path.

Her thin lips turned down at the corners. "Missus Murphy. Perhaps where you come from such antics after curfew are acceptable. But not among the English."

"Where I come from people are being arrested and imprisoned for breaking curfew. Let them celebrate, Miss Pike. They are only children . . . far from their families. For a very long time their world has been a hard place. A little fun can't hurt."

"Are we to set aside order for frivolity?"

I opened my mouth to reply.

My thoughts were suddenly shattered. The ship shuddered. A heavy, muffled thud was accompanied by the sounds of crashing glass and splintering woodwork. The lights went out. I was thrown against the wall and then to the floor.

"Torpedo!" I cried, knowing instantly what had happened.

Miss Pike had fallen near me. "Oh! We're hit! We're hit!"

The screams of children penetrated cabin doors. A succession of booms followed as I groped for some handhold by which I could pull myself up.

"Are you hurt?" I called to Miss Pike.

She breathed, "The Hun! The Hun has found us, I fear, Missus Murphy."

"We must . . . we must . . . the children! Lifeboat stations!"

"My glasses. Where are my glasses?"

The space was lit by a dim orange glow. Fires in the belly of the vessel? The corridor was cluttered with debris from wood paneling and shattered wall sconces. Yet strangely, Miss Pike's thick spectacles remained solidly in place on her nose. Blood streamed down her face and into her eyes from a nasty gash on her scalp. She did not attempt to rise.

"You're bleeding," I said.

"I'm bleeding," she repeated, touching her cheek. She peered closely at her hand to examine the blood. "Torpedo. Yes," she muttered in quiet amazement, as if the weapon had been personally aimed at her.

In those first few seconds I was certain the Nazis had scored a mortal blow against the *Newcastle*. The blast seemed to be directly beneath us. "The children! Miss Pike, we must . . . must . . . see to our children! Are you able, dear woman?"

She croaked a command. "Help me up, Elisa."

I heard Miss Pike's girls weeping and calling out to one another behind the door as I helped her stand. "Miss Pike, get them to the lifeboat station.

Life vests, Miss Pike! They'll need warm coats. Shoes," I commanded as I left her.

Her gruff voice, though a trifle slurred, cut through the sobs with no-nonsense orders, and the whimpering ceased.

With a sense of dread, I pushed my way through the wreckage toward my stateroom. Water lapped my feet. Though all was dark where I stood, the farther reaches of the hallway were bathed in amber light. Was the ship burning and sinking at the same time?

Let the groans of the prisoners come before
You; according to Your great power,
preserve those doomed to die!
PSALM 79:11 ESV

WRITTEN IN PRAGUE, CZECHOSLOVAKIA
ABOUT TRIP TO MUNICH, GERMANY
JANUARY 3, 1938

In the last few days I have been to Germany
again, God help me! The American John
Murphy once told me that a woman is like tea.
She will never know how strong she is until she
is in hot water.

When next I see him, I wonder if he will know
that I am in hot water over the neck now. God
must make me strong.

Before the New Year I traveled to Germany as
Elisa Linder, but now as a mother. With me
were passports for two Jewish children
described as Maxmillian and Celeste Linder,
"my" two-year-old son and infant daughter. I
was given the cover story of being a perfectly
Aryan German, raised in Prague, coming to
Munich on a sightseeing tour.

This very credible background was almost
my undoing. A Nazi officer accosted me and
asked if it was true I was Czech. I explained
my German heritage, which he believed,

whereupon he asked me for help.

It seems an elderly Czech man, who spoke no German, could not make himself understood to the increasingly impatient guards. I was asked to translate.

It was a frightening moment. I knew a native Czech speaker would see through my imposture. I could only pray he would be as sensitive to my plight as I was to his.

Thanks be to God, he was!

But even when that interview came to a successful conclusion, my dilemma was only beginning.

The German officer asked if I were alone in Munich. If this was some elaborate trap, I didn't want to implicate anyone else, so I said yes.

He asked to take me out to dinner! How could I refuse a member of the Gestapo?

My mouth was able to speak more heroically than my heart felt. "Oh, yes," I said. "I'd love to see the beer hall where the Hitler revolution began."

The *Oberleutnant*, who insisted I call him Alfred, took me into a world of thumping steins and pounding polka music, papered thickly with Nazi banners. The agent offered to teach me the Nazi drinking songs. As he said, "Soon you'll be singing them in Prague, yes? One People! One Nation! One *Führer*, eh?"

All the time I was keeping the forced smile

plastered on my face I kept wondering if this was one of the men who had interrogated my father. Was his preferred method of persuasion the rubber hose, the bare fist, or electric shocks?

And still I could not escape.

Instead of driving me to my hotel when we left the beer hall, he piloted the staff car into the countryside. I was more afraid than ever.

Then he parked on a hillside overlooking a brightly lit compound surrounded by barbed wire and guard towers.

It was Dachau.

My companion was proud of his work. "They die quite easily here," he said, his words slurred with too much drink. "The Greater Reich will be cleansed of all the *Untermenschen*."

I heard the savage barking of guard dogs and the rip of machine-gun fire. The Gestapo officer snickered. "Sometimes they kill themselves by crossing into the dead zone on purpose."

Papa, I thought. *Oh, Papa!*

My night of horrors ended at last because my companion had to catch an early train to Berlin. I let him think I had been inspired by the Nazi vision of the future by asking him to return me to the beer hall.

From there I could get a taxi to a hotel without revealing my destination to the Gestapo.

"Perhaps I'll see you in Prague," he suggested.

"Thank you for showing me what to expect," I said.

He kissed me. I kept the violin case between us as a shield. He saluted and drove away.

I became violently ill moments later.

The next morning I went to Munich's Marienplatz. With hundreds of other visitors I watched the famous animated figures on the clock tower perform their mechanical dance steps.

When I left the square I had three things I did not possess when I entered it: two small children in a covered pram . . . and the memory of a father's anguished face watching his children leave him, perhaps forever.

The children slept on the train ride from Munich to Prague. Dosed with cough medicine, they slumbered deeply. There was no danger at the border crossing.

It was a good thing. My heart sick for my father and my country, I have no heroism or cleverness left.

13

DEAD IN THE WATER
NORTH ATLANTIC
AUTUMN 1940

My eyes adjusted to the darkness. I discovered to my relief the orange flickers were not from a fire but from dimly glowing emergency lamps. In the days spent aboard the *Newcastle* I had never noticed them before this moment. Grateful for the faint illumination they provided, I knew how terrifying and bewildering those corridors would have seemed in the utter darkness of a cloudy North Atlantic night.

Newcastle's deck had an almost imperceptible downhill slope and a slight lean to the right as I staggered forward.

The ship still surged serenely onward. Our speed through the water did not slacken. I felt reassured. Was my first panicked reaction overblown? I took a deep breath and forced myself to calm down. My thoughts raced. *Maybe* Newcastle *isn't sinking, not at all! The water around my ankles must be from a broken pipe. Of course the children are frightened. Oh, Jesus! I'm frightened! Who wouldn't be?*

I prayed in that moment that my job was reassurance, not rescue.

Ahead the hallway curved outward before straightening again. I remembered my cabin was just beyond that bend. A few more paces and I would have my life vest securely belted on and could round up my young charges. *Like a drill,* I would tell them. *Part of the adventure.*

After six more steps my progress came to an abrupt halt. The passageway was blocked. The outer wall bowed inward; the floor buckled upwards. What remained of the corridor was jammed with fallen ceiling and splintered wood paneling.

My lips tightened with anger and determination to reach my cabin. Irrationally, I thought of the pendant watch Murphy had given me for my last birthday. His picture was inside the cover, as was the baby's. The watch lay on the night table in my cabin, and I meant to get it.

Seizing a chunk of paneling, I wrenched it free and tossed it behind me. A bit of ceiling tile followed, and some mahogany molding. A length of pipe frustrated me for a moment, but I managed to bend it out of the way.

I grasped a piece of jagged metal. The serrated edge sliced my palm when I tried to yank it free. Winding a pocket handkerchief around the wound, I concentrated on removing the trash blocking the inboard side of the hall. Though only half the height of the passage was clear, I managed to open a space wide enough for me to advance.

I don't know what made me poke my head into the opening. It would have been sensible and much easier to extend my foot through first.

What greeted my gaze beyond the wreckage was a void—a featureless emptiness that fell away into a pool of water and was open to the sea beyond. Waves lapped at the edges of the hole. White foam outlined the ragged remains of what had moments before been *Newcastle*'s smooth steel skin.

Where the corridor had been, where my cabin had been, and the one beyond that, and the rooms of the decks below mine, was now a gaping hole. If I had stepped unknowingly through that crevice, I would certainly have crossed the threshold between this world and the next. I struggled to reconcile the conflicting images. Behind me was the carpeted hallway of a comfortable passenger liner. Ahead was a crater resembling the wound left when a Nazi bomb shattered a block of London flats.

I trembled from the chill wind funneling up from the sea . . . and from the realization of what one more step would have meant. The crevasse was a canyon, stretching at least three decks high and two cabins wide . . . and included the space where my room had been.

Where I might have been.

The back wall and one side wall of my living

quarters were all that remained intact. No floor . . . no ceiling . . . no bed or nightstand or cupboard. No pendant watch.

If I had not stopped to visit with Mariah, if I had not paused to tell Connor good night, if Miss Pike had not detained me, I would have been directly above the strike of the torpedo, right in the path of the explosion.

Stark reality brought me, shivering, back to my duty. Seawater filled the space beneath where my cabin had been, and the level was rising. This was no minor alarm.

Newcastle was, indeed, mortally wounded, and our time was short.

Through a haze of acrid smoke I saw the door where my five girls were quartered. A mere twenty feet from where I stood, they were on the far side of a chasm filling with the seawater and rimmed by fire from the burning ship. I prayed they had not been blown away by the blast that demolished my cabin. Above the roar of gushing waves I heard faint cries for help. "Betsy! Lindy! Alice! Margaret! Nan!" I called their names, "Oh, Jesus! Help me!"

They began pounding frantically. Had they heard me?

I remembered the passage from Isaiah Mama taught me when I was a little girl terrified of thunder:

When you pass through the waters,
I will be with you;
and through the rivers,
they shall not overwhelm you.
When you walk through fire,
you shall not be burned,
and the flame shall not consume you.[12]

Was there ever a moment when the threats named in that verse were so real? Could God's ancient promise to His people be living and true for us on this terrible night? I knew somehow I must save my girls!

Muffled pleas reached me. "Help! Somebody please! Help us!"

It was not possible to go farther forward by the path I had intended to follow. There was no way to cross the yawning gulf. At first glance it seemed the only way to get to them was by retreating.

I stared into the void. Circling the inner edge of the abyss, like a ledge above a canyon, was a thin ribbon of deck. Six inches wide at most, the shelf tapered in places to the thickness of a slice of bread.

Could I do this?

"I'm coming! Hold on!"

"Elisa? What?"

---

[12] Isaiah 43:2 ESV

I turned. Miss Pike and her sniffling girls shuffled toward me. Like a bossy mother hen, she kept them close. Each was dressed in a warm coat with her life vest securely buckled over the top.

"Elisa?" she questioned again.

"Your lifeboat station is Number 6?"

"Yes. Why?" she demanded.

Her commanding manner had returned. It and the blood-soaked scarf knotted around her head gave her a distinctly nautical air, like a pirate queen.

The most direct route to Station 6 was forward. "The hall is . . . is blocked," I said. "The blast. The floor is gone."

Miss Pike caught the significant tremor in my voice.

"Your girls?"

"On the other side."

"Ah." She stooped and peered through the debris to examine the damage beyond. She gasped as her eyes swept across the devastation. "Oh, Lord! Lord have mercy!"

"My cabin. Gone."

Her face registered horror at how close I had come to losing my life. The frantic pounding from the children's cabin sounded again.

"How many lost in the blast?" she asked.

It was a question I could not answer. "My girls . . . I must join them. You can see I must. Miss Pike, go back the way you came."

"Yes, back. The stairs were open, and then up before we go forward to our station? But you?"

"You go," I said. "I . . . I'm going to them . . . the fastest way."

"Elisa, how?"

"A bit of a ledge remains. Like walking a fence when I was a girl. I can do it."

"My dear," she cried. "My dear girl!"

"I must try, Miss Pike. But please, send someone down. A ship's officer. Someone to help them . . . in case . . ." I swallowed hard. "Send someone to help me."

Miss Pike read the determination in my expression. Her eyes brimmed, and she muttered, "God keep you, Elisa." Then squaring her shoulders she instructed: "Come, girls. No dawdling. Follow me."

I was alone again with my fears, juggling the terrifying prospect of creeping along the tiny ledge against their urgent need. Taking a deep breath, I stretched my foot through the hole and planted it on the narrow rim. The metal shelf was solid under me, and my confidence grew.

Grasping the wreckage with my bandaged hand, I ducked my head, stepped into the opening, and made the mistake of looking down. Below me the sea surged and crashed. When *Newcastle* wallowed in a swell the steel canyon filled with streaks of foam and watery fingers stretched up as if to seize me. A puddle of burning oil gestured with tendrils of smoke. When the wave crest passed, the pulsing black mass receded, like a hideous monster preparing to spring. The air was filled with chilly, salt-and-oil-laden vapor.

I froze in place, unable to either advance or retreat.

God, help me, I groaned inwardly.

"Elisa. Elisa? Please hurry! We're stuck, and Lindy's hurt. Badly hurt, I think!"

"I'm coming," I yelled. "Hold on!" Relinquishing my white-knuckled grip on the last secure handhold, I inched forward. My cheek was pressed against the cold metal. My body might have been tattooed on the wall. I slid my feet sideways, testing each step. My arms outstretched to either side reflected the entreaty of my pounding heart for divine assistance.

The hall and cabins had been seared by the blast. Dangling scraps of paint hung like flayed skin, tempting me to trust their false support.

The ledge narrowed. Six inches . . . five . . . three . . .

My safety rested on my toes and fingertips. There were no further obvious grips. The bulkhead was as smooth as the inside of a well— and just as deadly. How could I go farther?

Newcastle creaked and growled.

From somewhere ahead and above me I heard the ship's whistle wail, a continuous, despairing moan. It was the sound of a death agony that reverberated within the chamber enclosing me.

Beyond my right hand, beyond an expanse of bare metal, just out of reach, was what remained of a wooden handrail. Right below that desirable goal the rim of deck on which I perched widened again. If I could lunge across the intervening blankness, I would have a renewed handhold and secure footing.

"Elisa! Are you there?" The cry was agonizingly frightened and desolate.

Saving my breath for what was coming, I did not reply. Lifting my right foot carefully, gently, I stretched my leg as far as I could, then forced my trembling, unwilling right hand to do the same. I waited for the swell to subside so the ship would be neither rising nor falling when I moved.

Now! My hand shot toward the rail, grasped it triumphantly. My toes touched the shelf of deck . . . and slipped off! My shoe fell away, spinning into the blackness to land with a distant splash. The ship rose again, corkscrewing sideways. I lost my balance and tumbled, digging my nails into the wooden bar. I managed to get both hands on the scrap of banister, but my feet flailed for purchase. I screamed for help as my own weight threatened to yank me loose and plunge me into the gaping maw of icy water.

Answering shrieks of alarm emanated from the

cabin as my terror echoed within the hearts of my girls.

And then my foot touched something solid. It was almost as if a hand were under my sole, steadying me. I pushed off the unseen step, and both my feet regained the ledge.

The next roll of the ship tossed me sideways again, but this time the motion threw me across the remaining space. I fell on my face, sprawled on carpeted flooring. When I got to my knees, I was outside the door of my girls' cabin.

I slapped the door with my uninjured palm. "Girls, I'm here! I'll get you out. Don't worry."

The doorframe was bent, the metal so twisted the door would not move when I shoved it and hit it with my shoulder. I hammered at it with my fists, and when it failed to yield, I kicked it.

It still did not budge.

A small, white hand appeared through a gap between the portal and the flooring. Nan's voice, hoarse from crying for help, floated out beside it. When I touched her imploring fingers, she seized mine like a lifeline. "It's Lindy . . . she's really hurt, Elisa. We don't know what to do."

"I'm here now," I repeated, my frustration at my own helplessness mounting. "But I've got to find something to pry the door open."

Nan's grasp squeezed even tighter. "No!" she implored. "Don't leave us."

"But I must."

A light flickered out of the darkness. I spotted a glass cabinet containing an axe, a flashlight, and a fire extinguisher. Cries for help had ceased, but the sniffling and sobbing had redoubled since I reached the door. "I'm going to fetch something to break open the door. Nan? Nan! Can you hear me?"

"Alice! Betsy! Be quiet," sensible Nan ordered. "Go on, Elisa. I can hear you now."

"I say, I'll be back to pry the door open. I'll have you out any minute. Now tell me: who's hurt and how?"

"It's Lindy. There was a big explosion. What happened? It threw us all out of bed. The lights went out, and there was a lot of crashing. We called out our names and everyone answered, except Lindy. She's . . . the bed tipped over on her. She hasn't spoken."

"All right, then." I was filled with resolve as I rushed to the fire cupboard and smashed the glass. Grasping fire axe and flashlight, I staggered back. "Listen, girls: I'm going to have to bash my way in. Are you all well clear of the entry?"

Nan's fingers fluttered a good-bye as she reluctantly said, "Yes . . . yes! Come ahead."

I prayed for strength as I swung the axe as if intent on felling an oak tree. At my first blow the center of the door panel splintered. At the second the axe head broke through. Three more sledgehammer-like strokes and most of the barrier ceased to exist.

I crawled through. Three weeping girls were pressed against the far wall of the cabin. Nan was huddled on the floor, shielding Lindy, who was trapped beneath the overturned metal-framed bunk. As I entered, Nan turned her face toward me. An expression of fearful anguish was imprinted there.

Nan moved aside and made room for me to kneel next to Lindy. In the yellow orb cast by the flashlight Lindy's cheeks were ashen. A trickle of blood came from the corner of her mouth. Her eyes were closed as if she was sleeping, but her breathing was labored and shuddering.

I ordered, "Nan, you're in charge. Take your life vests, coats, and shoes, and go at once to your boat station."

"I won't leave Lindy," Betsy protested.

What could I do? I had to get the others to safety but could not leave the girl pinned against the deck.

"I'll stay with her. Go! Nan, you and Betsy and Meg and Alice grab your things. Lifeboat Number 4! Like we rehearsed. Find Missus Pike. She'll get you properly stowed."

"What about you and Lindy?" Nan asked.

"Send help. Tell someone we need help. I'll be along soon," I said. "Go."

As the girls wove their way out of the skewed

confines of the cabin, only Nan looked at Lindy. The others kept their gaze away.

I heard an officer call to them, "Anyone else down here?"

Betsy shouted, "Miss Elisa is in the cabin! With my cousin Lindy. Cabin 22. Trapped!"

I could hear the officer's calm voice. "Do you know your lifeboat station?"

"Number 4," Nan replied.

"Get upstairs—quickly now!" he instructed.

Betsy demanded, "What about Elisa? What about Lindy? My cousin."

"I'll look after them. Hurry along now. Station Number 4. There's just time."

The bevy of refugee children tromped up the stairs. The officer progressed down the hallway, knocking on every door, directing stragglers up the dark steps.

I knew help had come too late for Lindy. She was ashen as she opened her eyes and looked up into my face. "Mummy?" she managed to speak. "Is that you, Mummy?"

I stroked her hair. "Yes, darling, I'm here." I tried to console the dying child. The thought of Lindy's last letter to her mother came clearly to my mind. I had promised to take care of Lindy. I wondered what the woman was doing now, still believing she had protected her daughter by sending her away.

"Don't leave . . . don't leave . . . me, Mummy."

I felt as though I had failed miserably. "I won't leave you, my darling girl. I'm right here." I stooped and kissed her forehead. I held her hand, stroked her hair, and prayed. What had her story been? I tried to remember. Somehow it felt important. I owed it to her to recall.

It came to me: She had been evacuated from the southeast of England because of the German bombing attacks along the coastal airfields and ports. She had been going to stay with relatives in Canada. She was her mother's only living child, sent away amid great heartache, because her mother loved her.

Lindy's eyes flicked open. She coughed, spraying me with blood. "Mum?"

"Yes, sweetheart."

"Mum," she continued, unheeding, "I've had the strangest dream. My chest hurts, Mum."

"I know, Lindy. Help is on the way."

The pitch of the ship had increased noticeably in the last few minutes. Forward was now significantly *down*. Back was distinctly *up*.

"In my dream, I saw Gramma. Only she wasn't old Gramma, like when she died. She looked young. She looked like you, Mum. She told me not to be afraid. Why . . ." A fit of coughing interrupted the girl's story. "Why did she say that? I'm not afraid, Mum."

"That's good, dear," I said. "Lindy? Can you hear me?"

The officer appeared in the doorway. A pool of light fell on me as Lindy shivered and took a few shallow breaths. *Too late. Too late!*

I looked up and spread my hands. "I won't leave her."

He squared his shoulders. "Elisa." He spoke to me as if I were a child in need of comfort. "You must go up with the others."

"I can't. I promised her . . . I *promised* her. And her mother. I can't." I began to weep. I stooped and placed my face against her brow. "I can't, you see . . ."

He picked his way through the rubble until he towered over me. "She's going home, Elisa. Do you understand me?"

"How can I leave her?" I sobbed.

The officer bent forward toward Lindy. "I'll take care of her. Go now, or you will die."

With a penknife he cut a lock of Lindy's hair, slipped it into a small book, and pressed it into my palm. "For her mother, Elisa. Take it and go." Suddenly he lifted me to my feet. "You must hurry. I'll take care of her."

He guided me to the doorway.

I begged. "Please! How can I?"

"I'll see to her now. There's no time left. You must run if you're to make it off the ship."

Then I thought of Murphy, of my own little ones. Their faces were before me, and I knew how much I wanted to live. "Am I too late?"

He gave me a stare that made my heart sink. "There are more who will need your help. Hurry along, Elisa. You've already done all you can here. I will stay with her."

"Stay?"

An accepting smile curved his lips, and I felt a terror unlike any I had ever known. He would stay? We both knew to remain behind meant death, yet this man made no move to flee. He knelt and caressed the hand of the child. "Just go."

I could not speak again. I pressed the volume containing Lindy's curl into my pocket. Then I turned and dashed out of the cabin. Groping toward the eerie glow emanating from the stairwell, I stumbled forward. Gasping for air, I struggled up and up the steep gangway to the panic and confusion of the sloping deck.

14

DEAD IN THE WATER
NORTH ATLANTIC
AUTUMN 1940

I still had one shoe on. Running and stumbling on a single heel soon proved more dangerous than the bits of shattered glass, so I removed it and tossed it behind me.

The deck sloped ever more sharply downward as I went forward. When I came to a set of stairs, I had to climb very carefully because of the odd angle; none of the steps were flat beneath my tread. Amid death and destruction I warned myself not to twist an ankle!

Rising from the relatively quiet lower decks onto the companionway of the first-class cabins thrust me into noisy, frantic chaos. It was like emerging from a London Underground train into the street-level pandemonium of Oxford Circus on the busiest shopping day of the year.

The corridor was jammed with people in all stages of dress and undress, moving in seemingly random directions. Despite all the evacuation procedures in which we had been drilled, confusion and consternation reigned supreme. Complicating matters was the babble of many languages. French, Spanish, Polish, and Russian refugees all seemed to have lost whatever English they commanded in the struggle to make themselves understood. They substituted shouting and hand waving. This was compounded when the lascar sailors gestured and shouted in their own language in reply to every inquiry.

My chief reaction was anger. Didn't these idiots know that a girl—one of my girls—had just been killed? I knew there were other children in need. If the adults couldn't be helpful, then couldn't they at least keep quiet?

Follow me, I gestured, no matter what language I heard, no matter what question was asked.

I pushed and shoved as I went, determined to rejoin the children. I struggled against the tide of humanity that threatened to carry me backward. The passengers presented enough degrees of unreality to fill the sideshows at a carnival. One man matched the rotund image of a snowman. I realized he was apparently wearing every bit of clothing he owned.

Another male figure was wearing top hat, tail coat, and . . . pajama bottoms.

A cabin door snapped open. A woman in bare feet, with her hair in curlers, wearing a silk gown and a thick layer of cold cream on her cheeks, demanded to know what we meant by making so much noise.

Where had she been in the minutes since the

torpedo struck? How could she still be so ignorant of the danger?

"Torpedo. Get dressed. Get to your lifeboat," I snapped.

"Impossible," the woman protested. "They told us we were safe. Besides, the steward promised he would alert me personally if there were an emergency. I shall certainly complain to the management of the shipping line." And she slammed the door.

There were many arguments about whether the emergency was real or not. Some thought it was a singularly inconvenient drill. Others said with authority that we had been struck by another ship in the blacked-out convoy, but that the damage was slight. One of these proposed returning to the salon to resume an interrupted game of bridge.

A white-uniformed steward added to the incongruity of the scene by striding along, striking a dinner gong. "Go to your lifeboat stations." *Clang!* "To your stations, please." *Clang!* "Have your life vests with you. Go to your stations, please." His voice was as calm as if he were announcing afternoon tea.

What cut through all the confusion at last is forever frozen in my memory. A mother with a girl and a boy huddled together berated her son for having left his overcoat in their cabin. "Now I'll have to go back and get it," she said with exasperation.

A ship's officer bellowed at her, "No! Under no circumstances may you go back anywhere. Get to your evacuation station. Don't you understand? We're sinking!"

With that official pronouncement there was a concerted movement toward the boat deck.

I came out into the wind and suddenly realized how bad our situation truly was. A 30-mph wind was whipping the sea into long streamers of white foam. Twenty-foot-high rollers crashed into *Newcastle* from an angle behind us, making the ship lumber and wallow. The dip toward the bow and the tilt to starboard continued to increase.

I reached the launch station for Lifeboat Number 4 . . . and it was already gone!

Peering over the side, I saw it. My imagined rescue was hanging near the end of its cables. The craft capable of carrying twenty evacuees to safety had been launched with only ten on board, and none of them were children.

I shouted at them to stop, to come back. Foolish of me, I know. Whether they heard me or not made no difference. They were intent on escape. Perhaps they could not have rehoisted the boat anyway.

Soon enough they must have wished they could.

One of the cables, the one supporting the stern of the lifeboat, jammed in its pulley, while the one on the bow continued to unspool. Angled steeply into the surf, with *Newcastle* still moving forward into the towering seas, the boat was dragged directly into the waves and instantly submerged.

All but one of those aboard was washed out.

The remaining occupant, a sailor, tried to save himself by climbing the hoist, but a wave slapped him and batted him against *Newcastle*'s hull. He sank out of sight.

There was no way to rescue any of those who went into the water and no way to retrieve the sunken lifeboat. All I could do was dash toward the stern in hopes of finding another place of safety.

Where were my girls?

The davits that suspended Lifeboat Number 6 were also empty. Despite my own urgent need to get off the *Newcastle*, I looked over the side of the *Newcastle* for Mrs. Pike and her charges. I spotted them at once in Lifeboat 6, recognizing the chaperone by the scarf still knotted over her brow. All around her clustered a bevy of smaller figures wearing life vests.

Were my girls also among them?

The frail boat bobbed just alongside. A sailor in the bow and an officer in the stern used oars to push Lifeboat Number 6 away from the doomed ship. I did not stop to count the girls. As Lifeboat 6 rode up the face of a twenty-foot swell and disappeared behind it, I could not be certain if they had all made it. Perhaps it was better to believe they were all safely aboard. Breathing a prayer for them, I lunged farther along the rail.

As I passed a stairwell, there came a cry for help. On the landing at the bottom was Robert, the boy everyone called Robin Hood. He was dressed in his forest-green life jacket and hooded cape.

Between Robert and safety was the lashing serpent of a live, severed electrical cable. With *Newcastle* corkscrewing in the surf, the thick wire appeared alive with malevolent intent. Its coils crisscrossed the steps. Each time the head of the snake hit a railing or steel support member it exploded with a shower of sparks. When the ship swung back to an even keel, there was barely a moment when the cable lay quiet.

"Jump over it!" I shouted to Robert. "You can do it."

"I'm scared!"

"I'll help you," I said, wondering to myself what I could possibly do. "Throw something across it to weight it down."

"What? I can't find anything!"

Beside me was the cabinet of a fire hose. I smashed the glass with my elbow, grabbed the heavy spiral of canvas-covered tubing, and yelled to Robert, "Watch out!"

Yanking the hose free of its housing, I slung it down the steps. The tube unrolled as it traveled, falling across the electrical cable and pinning it down.

"Now!" I yelled. "Jump over it."

Robert backed up, took a run at the stairs, and leapt over the angry, hissing wires with three feet to spare.

"What lifeboat?" I asked.

"Number 4," he said. "Mum and Dad must already be there. Can you help me find it? I'm all mixed up." His voice trembled, and he blinked rapidly.

I had to tell him that Number 4 had already left.

I did not tell him that all on board had been swept away. Perhaps Robert's family was safe on some other craft. "Come with me. We'll find them again later," I said.

He let me take him by the hand, and we set out farther toward the stern. *Newcastle* stood more and more upright, and I feared she would slip beneath the surface at any moment.

The davits for Number 8 were also empty, but Number 10 was still in place and being loaded. "Take any boat available," a man I recognized as Third Officer Browne shouted. "Women and children first. Here. Let me help you."

Sweeping Robert up in his arms, the officer lifted the boy toward the railing of the lifeboat.

A trio of lascar sailors rushed up out of the

darkness. One of them cannoned into Browne, sending him and Robert sprawling into me, and all of us to the deck. The native servants clambered into the boat and set about releasing the supports and paying out the lines.

Once again, rescue was slipping away.

"Stop!" Browne demanded. "There's room for many more."

The panicked group ignored him and continued their descent.

Robert's sharp eyes picked out a problem with the bow cable. "Look out," he called, "that end's loose." The front of Number 10 dropped rapidly seaward while the rear was still suspended high overhead.

The men in boat Number 10 heard his shrill cry and added their shrieks to the night as they desperately tried to catch the unspooling support rope. A lascar lunged for the free end, caught it, then was smashed headfirst into the pulley as the weight of the boat dropped free. His body cartwheeled into the waves.

With the bow now dangling straight down, all the occupants were pitched out except one. He stood upright, clinging to the stern support and shouting for help.

There was nothing any of us could do.

As *Newcastle* wallowed into another swell, the swing of the ship tossed the lifeboat against the steel hull like the clapper of a bell. The last man catapulted into the air and disappeared in the darkness.

"Come on," Browne said, grabbing me by one hand and Robert by the other. "We've got to cross to the other side. Quickly. No time to lose."

Third Officer Browne led us from one side of the ship to the other, using narrow service passages known only to the ship's crew. I would have been hopelessly lost in moments, but Browne's sense of direction was unerring.

We emerged again into the night air directly beside Lifeboat Number 7. Miraculously, it was still suspended at the proper height for boarding, and it was being filled in an orderly manner.

"Elisa," I heard Mariah cry. "Get in! Get in! You and Robert." I breathed a sigh of relief. Surely the worst was over now.

I boosted Robert into her arms. Though I needed no urging to hurry me along, a muffled explosion shook *Newcastle*, and she heeled ever more sharply to starboard.

"One of the boilers," Browne muttered. "Can't last long now."

Robert was pressed between Mariah and me. In all there were more than twenty passengers and crew crammed into the open, wooden-planked vessel.

"Where's your sister? Where's Patsy?" I asked Mariah, glancing around at the mix of children and adults. Instantly I clamped my mouth shut on my foolishness, but it was too late.

"We got separated."

"She . . . she and your niece and nephew must be on another lifeboat," I said awkwardly. How many times had I repeated that hopeful saying to myself and others? For how many hours had this tragedy been unfolding?

I spotted Raquel. Beside her was the oldest of the evacuee girls, but not the other two. Raquel was frantic with worry, standing up and leaning out of the lifeboat to call for "Simcha! Yael!" Then she added tersely, "Angelique, stay here. I must go look for the others." She put a foot on the gunwale in preparation for jumping out.

"No, you don't, miss," Browne corrected, barring her way. "We're about to launch. You'd have no boat to come back to. Anyone missing most likely got put into another craft."

Raquel sat back down, trembling in every muscle. Her eyes darted ceaselessly up and down the deck. Angelique hugged her fiercely.

"It's true," I said. "The officers are making a thorough search to make certain everyone is off the ship."

"You there, Wilson. Take charge of those boys."

The English sailor addressed as Wilson loaded a file of boys over the stern. Among them I recognized Connor, whose birthday celebration had saved me from death. With him were the

Apostles. I felt a rush of warmth at seeing them safe.

The sailor wore a wristwatch at which I could not help glancing. I thought it must be broken. Quarter 'til eleven? It had been only minutes past ten when the torpedo struck.

Forty-five minutes! Everything that had happened, from the instant the torpedo detonated, through all that had occurred since, had transpired in less than an hour. It did not seem possible.

Suddenly every light on *Newcastle* blazed into life. Like the last surge of energy in a dying beast, the ship poured its heart into that illumination. "No one else coming," Browne noted, scanning the brilliantly lit decks. "Right. Stand by to lower away."

Wilson, the burly crewman in the bow, and a lascar sailor at the stern, stood by the cable releases.

"Everyone hold tight," Browne added. "Carefully, now. Not too fast. Have to keep the angle right or we'll swamp her."

As we descended and all hope of anyone else joining us disappeared, I heard Raquel and Mariah both groan deeply, as if their souls were being wrenched from their bodies. Beside me Robert shivered, despite his cloak.

The back of Number 7 had to drop slightly ahead of the front to compensate for *Newcastle*'s angle. As the rear paid out too fast Robert shouted in terror before the sailor choked off the cable. The bouncing and jolting that followed were just as unnerving. I wrapped my arms around Robert and tucked my legs under the bench seat, fearful that what I had seen elsewhere would happen to us and we would be dumped into the sea.

"Gently! You in the middle there. Stand by with the oars to fend us off."

The center ranks of the lifeboat were occupied by lascar crewmen. Prompt to the order, they held the long wooden paddles at the ready to keep us from being smashed into *Newcastle*'s hull.

Under Browne's careful management, our lifeboat approached the waves on an even keel. Twice he ordered Number 7 hoisted partway back up until he was satisfied with the angle.

As we neared the sea, the wind whipped spray over us, and breakers coasted by beneath us like moving black hills. The momentary relief I had felt on reaching Number 7 and getting away from *Newcastle* dissolved. Being in a lifeboat in the midst of these towering seas and gale-force winds would be as terrifying as my earlier escape.

Because *Newcastle* was leaning toward us, we swung farther out from the side than other boats. The doomed ship drifted broadside to the waves, but her looming bulk provided some protection. Because of that circumstance and Officer Browne's careful attention to detail, we landed on the ocean with scarcely a splash . . . and were instantly jostled and rolled like a matchstick in a flood.

"Right! Cast off," Browne ordered. "Ship the oars and row us away from the hull." *Newcastle*'s towering hulk loomed over us, as if a city block had been turned on edge and was about to crush the passersby on the sidewalk beneath.

As we drifted away from the doomed ship, the inky, featureless night was suddenly punctuated with riotous explosions of color. From the bridge and the ever-rising stern, flares shot skyward. Orange and scarlet and brilliant blue-white signals of distress burst overhead. The howling wind instantly stretched them into streaks of color—banners illuminating the underbellies of the racing clouds.

Beneath the moments of glare I got fragmented glimpses of other survivors struggling to keep afloat. Bright amber life vests dotted the water with those who had fallen from capsized boats. A pair of sailors clung to a drifting raft. In the distance was a lifeboat sunken to its waterline, yet still afloat. The occupants sat stiffly upright, bracing themselves against the waves. As the flare's brilliance faded, they seemed to be sitting without support on the surface of the sea.

Blackness descended again as the beacon was extinguished. By the time the next one detonated above us a breaker had rolled across the swamped craft. Like a magician's trick, now it was empty . . . the survivors had disappeared.

15

LIFEBOAT NUMBER 7
NORTH ATLANTIC
AUTUMN 1940

I could not make out how all the flurry of escaping from belowdecks and shuttling from place to place fit into three quarters of an hour. Time must have been standing still for me. As we rowed farther from the side of the ship, it felt as if I must be among the very last passengers to get away.

Yet I was wrong. Robert, sandwiched tightly between Mariah and myself, waved toward *Newcastle*'s railing. On the deck there a lone man struggled with a heavy life raft that was the last resort now that all the boats were gone. Single-handedly he muscled the wooden frame attached to metal pontoons up to the barricade, then heaved it over. It tumbled into the water, disappeared, then bobbed up again.

"Hurry, man!" Browne yelled. "There's not much time!"

But instead of jumping for the raft, the man turned away and disappeared from sight. When he returned, he held a struggling, life-jacketed child under each arm, as if taking a pair of frenzied hens to market.

Raquel shrieked, "Simcha! Yael!"

In the two wrestling bundles I recognized the Jewish girls.

While we in Number 7 held our breath and prayed, the lone rescuer stepped over the rail with his charges and plunged into the sea. Even before they struck the surface our officer was yelling to the sailors to, "Pull, boys, pull!" He laid the tiller hard over to direct our course toward the trio bobbing between *Newcastle* and the raft.

Since I was neither rowing nor steering, I watched the man in the water with apprehension and hope. Mariah and I had to hold onto Raquel to keep her from jumping in the water.

The rescuer seized one child and tossed her onto the raft, then swam back and grabbed the other and did the same, before pulling himself onto the floating platform.

That was when I noticed the gaping hole in *Newcastle*'s flank, where the torpedo had entered and detonated. The rent in the ship's skin climbed three decks upward from the keel past where my cabin used to be. While narrowing at the top of the wound, it was as broad as the length of a double-decker bus at its base.

How did the ship still stay afloat? How had it lasted so long and not pulled all of us instantly to the depths?

How had I and my girls survived the blast?

Mariah screamed and pointed. The water

rushing into the cavernous mouth of the fissure had a tremendous suction. The raft with its three occupants was being drawn into the surging torrent and certain death!

We all knew death awaited the three on the raft. If they disappeared into the jaws of the cavernous chasm, they would either be dashed to pieces, crushed against the steel, or drowned when *Newcastle* slipped beneath the waves.

Raquel called the names of the children over and over again. While Mariah held Raquel's shoulders, and I her legs, we could not stop her from digging her fingernails into the wood of the lifeboat's gunwale.

Our officer urged the men to row harder, to put their backs into it, to break themselves with effort, but the waves breaking against *Newcastle*'s hull flowed backwards toward us, pushing us away.

I saw the man on the raft lift his head, facing the cauldron just before him. He knew the danger they were in. He was a strong swimmer; we had seen that when he retrieved the children from the water. If he abandoned them to their fate, perhaps he could save himself.

He made no move to do so. Instead he hugged the children closer and instructed them to wave at us. *Look there,* I saw him say, though I could not hear. *Look there. Rescue is on the way.*

Could we possibly reach them in time? Already

the raft had bumped one corner against *Newcastle*'s hull, bare yards from the chasm. The rush of water was sweeping them closer with each passing swell. With no oars and nothing to use for paddles, there was no way to maneuver out of danger.

An overturned lifeboat swept alongside the raft. What had happened to the occupants? There was no one clinging to the sharp keel or to the safety ropes floating from the sides. Whatever oars it had possessed must have disappeared when it capsized. Useless. Useless.

Then, as if drawn by invisible cords, the derelict craft pivoted toward the cavern of steel, making a precise turn. Angling directly into *Newcastle*'s side, the empty lifeboat passed the raft and plunged like an arrow into the opening . . . and jammed there on some jagged metal.

"Now! Now's our chance," Browne bellowed. "Give it all you've got!"

With the renewed effort Number 7 shot across the intervening space. Once more Raquel jumped upright, and this time we did nothing to prevent her. Her body extended far over the sides toward her children and she called to them. Yael spotted Raquel and leapt to her feet. The bobbing and surging threw the child off balance . . . right into Raquel's outstretched arms. Mariah and Raquel dragged Yael aboard.

Our boat collided with the raft. Now I finally recognized the rescuer. It was Cedric Barrett, the

British playwright. "Take the girl," he said, choking on a mouthful of seawater. He lifted Simcha to her knees and held her steady until a pair of sailors plucked her to safety.

"Look out! She's going," Browne cried.

I glanced up at *Newcastle*, expecting to see the great hulk crash down on us, but he meant the cork in the bottle. The capsized boat that had given the raft a brief respite snapped in two, and the pieces were sucked out of sight.

Immediately the raft was yanked away from us toward its own destruction.

"Jump, man," Browne urged Barrett. "Jump for your life!"

Barrett needed no further urging. Flinging himself upright, he leapt forward just as the raft smashed against *Newcastle*'s hull, but his jump was not far enough to reach Number 7. He fell in the water. Two oars reached out toward him. He grasped them both and pulled himself toward us as if they were the handrails of a bridge.

Moments later he was dragged out of the waves and Number 7 was rowed powerfully away from jeopardy, in search of others to rescue. Behind us the raft flipped up on end against *Newcastle*'s shattered side, waved a forlorn farewell, and disappeared into oblivion.

When Number 7 escaped the current jetting into *Newcastle*'s side, we were in an eddy of debris.

Lounge chairs, bits of wooden slats from the decking, empty life rings and . . . dead bodies.

It was a grim task: checking each and every floating corpse we located for the remote possibility of life. Each encounter was made even more grim because of the momentary hope of another rescue. Officer Browne made it extremely clear: we were not taking any of the dead aboard. The lifeboat was already near capacity.

When I saw those who had been alive only moments—at most minutes—before, bobbing away in the wake, I shuddered. I was grateful I recognized none of them.

Browne directed our course to anything resembling a survivor. We searched each scrap big enough for someone to be clinging to.

Where were all the other lifeboats? *Newcastle* had still been moving forward while boats were being launched. Were they scattered over miles of ocean?

Where was the rest of the convoy? How far away was rescue?

I hugged Robert close to me. Raquel was closely hemmed in by her girls. Mariah continued to scan the horizon. Above the creaks and groans of the sinking ship she called out the names of her sister and her niece and nephew.

Almost without warning we encountered another lifeboat. We rowed over the crest of a swell and nearly collided with it. It was barely afloat. Surrounded by frigid water up to their waists, there were four occupants. Two were elderly passengers. Both were dead.

With a cry of excitement Mariah recognized her sister, Patsy, and her niece, Moira. Both were alive . . . but barely. Patsy was in shock. Moira was icy cold and unresponsive.

We took them aboard. Mariah and I stripped them out of their soaked garments, shedding our own coats to wrap them in.

"Michael," Patsy murmured, when she could make herself understood past her chattering teeth. "Must find Michael."

Mariah rubbed her sister's feet and hands and fiercely promised to find the missing boy.

Sailor Matt Wilson commented, "She's going." My head snapped around. I was certain he knew Patsy was dying.

It was *Newcastle*'s final departure he meant.

Lights blazing, the ship's stern rose higher and higher into the air until her decks were almost perpendicular to the sea. Waves lapped against the first of the two funnels; the forward third of the ship was already underwater.

New sounds of destruction were blown to us on the wind. Bubbles of air and steam hissed and screamed from trapped cavities inside the ship. Raquel bundled the girls close against the nightmarish sound of souls in torment. The floundering wreck gulped great gouts of sea.

Mariah rubbed her sister's cheeks and patted her niece's hands. She worked feverishly, as if afraid *Newcastle*'s sinking might still somehow carry Patsy and Moira into a watery grave.

The ship heeled farther to starboard as she sank. The second smokestack aimed itself at us. The radio masts reached out toward us as if even now *Newcastle* would claim us to accompany her into the depths. Involuntarily I drew back, though I knew we were a safe distance away.

The lights blinked once . . . twice . . . a third time . . . and then the blaze winked out, leaving only a blacker silhouette against the impenetrable night. At the last *Newcastle* was no more than a blank expanse of canvas in the center of a portrait of white-capped waves. Then she slipped silently away and was gone.

Raquel gasped and pointed. Pablo's guitar drifted past.

I breathed a prayer for all those who had been lost in *Newcastle* . . . and for us.

As far as I could tell, we were alone on the vast, empty sea.

16

I felt the most intense silence. I do not know how else to describe it. There were still the rush of the wind and the patter of flying spray. I felt the thud when Number 7 crested a wave and her bow fell into the succeeding trough.

No more shrieks of alarm.

No more rending steel and tortured machinery.

The world was now cloaked in stillness and in night.

I think we were all stunned. I know I was. There had been no time to sort out terror from relief, grief from shock. I looked around the boat again. There were perhaps twenty-five with me. Were we the only survivors? Had hundreds perished?

My mind refused to accept this conclusion. I had seen other boats being launched. There had to be more still living than this handful.

The reality of loss was brought home to me by Mariah's expression of sheer desperation. She could not believe that Michael was missing. Perhaps she was afraid his death would kill her sister, who remained barely conscious. While the others looked numb, Mariah still exhibited frantic anxiety.

"We must keep looking," she demanded. "There must be others. We can't be the only ones left alive."

"We won't give up yet," Harold Browne agreed.

"Won't the other ships in the convoy be coming soon to pick us up and to help search?" Raquel asked.

There was no immediate reply and the omission was ominous. "No," the officer said at last. "Convoy procedure requires that if one ship is attacked, all the others scatter. Lingering to search for survivors would be to invite more U-boat attacks. No, none of the other ships will be coming back for us."

"So we're all alone?" Cedric Barrett, the playwright, queried.

"Not for long," Browne corrected, adding a brighter note to his earlier words. "I was near the radio room when the torpedo struck. I heard Sparks get off a message to Western Approaches Command. He gave our position exact to the last minute. Why, right now destroyers are steaming toward us. You can be certain they're coming at flank speed."

"How fast is that?" Robert inquired, lifting his green-hooded head.

"Thirty knots," the Apostle named James said with authority. "Thirty-five, the newer class."

"Right you are, mate," Matt Wilson confirmed. "And how long will it take 'em to get here if they start from three hundred miles away? A bit of figurin', eh?"

"Ten hours or less," John, James's older brother, calculated.

"By breakfast time tomorrow," Connor said cheerfully.

"So we'll keep searching," Browne said again. "Those of you who can, get some sleep."

There was much less debris around us now. On the featureless ocean, hemmed in by cloud and fog, I could not even point to where *Newcastle* had sunk, though I had witnessed it.

"How do we know where to search?" I quietly asked Wilson.

"That's all right, miss," he said, running his hand through his mop of shaggy blond hair. "Mister Browne there knows what he's about. Wind was out of the west when we was struck. It hasn't changed direction, so we just keep rowin' with the breeze to our faces. That'll help us stay near anyone who might have gone in the water, don'tcha see? It'll also keep us close to where the destroyers will come lookin' for us."

Wilson located a pack of blankets from a watertight container and passed them out. They were some shelter from the wind, but were soon soaked with spindrift.

The sailors plied the oars with long, even,

unhurried strokes. They pulled for several minutes; then Browne ordered them to stop while he called out in the darkness, "Is anyone there?" and listened for any reply.

After each pause, they resumed rowing.

I dozed a little amid that fruitless survey. I awoke when the weather turned still dirtier. Rain squalls added to our misery but flattened the waves some.

Mariah's gaze roamed over the blankness as if by intensity alone she could locate her beloved little nephew.

It felt tragically bleak.

Just as the rain storm moved off to the east she said, "There! I see something there!"

The direction toward which Mariah waved was at right angles to our course. I could not make out anything on the bearing she indicated. Her hopeful imagination was getting the better of her, I thought.

Third Officer Browne, who had been huddled in the stern trying to keep warm, stood upright and stared where Mariah pointed. "I don't . . . ," he began, then, "Wait! There is something there. Hullo! Is anyone there? Can you hear me? Hullo!"

Every ear in Number 7 strained for the response. "Hullo? Is anyone . . . ?"

"Yes!" came the emphatic reply. "Help! Help!"

"Pull, boys," the officer commanded. "Stretch out and pull!"

I shook off my drowsiness. Looking around me, I saw the lethargy that had engulfed everyone aboard Number 7 roll back. If we could save just one more life, it would be a triumph.

"Over . . . here," a male voice sputtered and coughed. "Hurry!"

As we drew near, a vague, bread-loaf shape on the waves resolved itself into an overturned lifeboat. Lying across its keel was a figure I recognized as Podlaski, the Polish diplomat . . . and he had one arm wrapped tightly around Mariah's nephew, Michael.

Patsy and her children were alive, but barely so. Raquel chafed Michael's feet and hands while I rubbed Moira's. Mariah concentrated on her sister. Mariah crooned to Patsy in Gaelic—lullabies of Connemara, tunes of comfort and hope.

Then the rains arrived in earnest. A solid-seeming deluge blotted the scene. The cold drenching from the skies piled misery upon misery. The lascars lay on their oars. The officer made no move to order them into renewed action.

"We must keep searching," Mariah insisted. "What if I had given up before we found Patsy?"

Browne shrugged. "If there are any survivors alive out there still, they will have to wait 'til daylight. I can't keep on any kind of bearing. Anyway, tomorrow we may need our strength for a real purpose."

His phrasing emphasized the finality of the loss of so many people we had known.

The officer's words were the curtain speech. The rainfall was the final curtain, ending Act One, during which we had rescued others.

The second act of the play brought the growing realization of our own great peril.

The first night after *Newcastle*'s sinking was, as Saint John of the Cross says, "the dark night of the soul" for many on board Lifeboat Number 7. Our prayers seemed to bounce off the drape of gloom and despair. They rose no higher than the height of the waves.

Harold Browne attempted to instill hope by making us believe some things were still in our power. "Women and children into the bow," he said. "You men rig the tarpaulin." His instructions caused a triangular canvas shelter to be raised as some protection against the spray and the cold. With four women and eleven children on board, it was not possible for the bit of canvas to shield all of us. "You'll have to take turns," the officer said. "And I insist that you do so. The risk from exposure is great. Even a few minutes' warmth may save your life."

Browne and Wilson gathered in the stern, together with Cedric Barrett and Podlaski. The nine lascar sailors occupied the seats between them and us.

The jostling required to maneuver in the confined space caused some irritation. The effort to get us organized allowed some sense of control.

It did not last.

Around midnight, one of the lascar sailors died. He had come aboard with a head injury and never fully regained consciousness. When his mate shook his elbow and slapped his cheek, there was no response.

What followed would have been unthinkable in the ease and civilized comfort of SS *Newcastle*.

What a difference two hours makes to basic human decency.

After determining the man was in fact truly dead, Browne ordered, "We are cramped for space. I'm sorry, but there it is. Put him over the rail."

"With no ceremony? No words spoken over him?" Raquel murmured.

"He is . . . was . . . a Mohammedan," Wilson noted. "Doubt if Anglican prayers'd suit 'im. If any of his friends wish to speak, they may."

No one did.

Since the dead body lay between his mate and the Apostle named John, the thirteen-year-old boy was called on to lift the corpse under the arms and help slip it over the side.

At this Raquel protested: "Why make the boy do it? Can't someone else?"

To which John replied, "It's all right, ma'am. I don't mind."

John was strong and sturdily built. The body was hoisted over the gunnels and deposited in the sea without a splash.

The silent farewell was not the end of the horror. The body floated alongside the boat, drifting with us in silent reproach.

Eventually a current eddied between us and the dead man, and he fell away astern. This experience was only one among the nightmares of that night. Worse was yet to come.

Would dawn never arrive? The sense of being abandoned, swallowed by inescapable gloom, permeated the boat. I prayed the coming of the sun would raise our spirits.

"Three in the morning," I heard James murmur to his brother. "Sunrise isn't until six thirty at this latitude."

More than three hours to wait. I continued massaging Moira's little hands and arms, trying to get some warmth and circulation back into the five-year-old's listless body. Beside me Raquel did the same with three-year-old Michael.

Patsy and Mariah were at the center of the canvas shelter. Behind the sisters, forming a living cocoon, were Angelique, Simcha, and Yael.

Raquel and I were next, but facing Patsy so she could see her children.

The boys made an outer ring around us, but they were outside the lip of the tarpaulin. Despite what the officer had said, we did not change places. John insisted, and the other boys agreed, that we females remain beneath or at least closest to the makeshift awning.

It worried me that Patsy and her children were so lethargic. All three had been immersed in the sea and had come aboard Number 7 soaked through. We dried them as best we could but had no way of restoring heat to their bodies.

"Look here, Aunt Elisa," Tomas said, touching my elbow to get my attention. He extended a glass jug. "The officer gave it to me. A bottle of tea. One of the men brought it but thought he'd lost it overboard. Just now found it. For the little guys and Mizz Patsy."

"Thank you, Tomas. But shouldn't everyone have a share?"

John said firmly, "Wouldn't even be a mouthful each."

Connor: "That's the right of it, Elisa."

The fragrant brew was barely warmer than our surroundings, but it was thickly sweetened.

I pressed the rim of the flask to Moira's mouth. She swallowed and licked her lips. It seemed to ease her. Some of the rock-hard tension left her body. I handed the container to

241

Raquel, who tipped it into Michael's mouth. Mariah did the same for Patsy. We passed the bottle back and forth until, all too soon, the contents were gone.

I scrubbed little Moira's hands, then rubbed the calves of her legs. Pressing her close to me, I tucked her cheek against mine and tried by force of will to send life back into her barely responsive form. I knew no Gaelic, but what I had I offered to her:

> "Golden slumber kiss your eyes,
> Smiles await you when you rise.
> Sleep, pretty baby, do not cry,
> And I will sing you a lullaby."

"I know that song," Tomas said, rousing himself. Though his voice quaked with cold, he sang the lyrics to the chorus:

> "Care you know not, therefore sleep.
> While I, over you, watch do keep.
> Sleep, pretty darling, do not cry,
> And I will sing you a lullaby."[13]

The waves smacked against the boat in a twelve-count beat, such as I had learned from

---

[13] Traditional lullaby, "Golden Slumbers Kiss Your Eyes," attributed to Renaissance Poet Thomas Dekker

Raquel. *THUMP, slap, slap; THUMP, slap, slap; THUMP, slap, THUMP, slap, THUMP, slap.*

The rhythm sounded familiar. What was it called? I could not make my foggy brain unravel the mystery.

Raquel wore her coat like a cloak buttoned up to the neck. She had Michael wrapped inside the garment with her. The coat's empty sleeves flapped in the wind like a scarecrow. Only Michael's forehead and nose protruded at the collar.

Raquel bent toward me. I thought she was adjusting her position, trying to ease her aching limbs. She hissed to get my attention.

I leaned close.

Her words felt warm on my ear but struck an icy dagger into my heart. "The boy is dead," she said. "I'm sure of it. He has not moved in an hour, and he's getting colder and colder."

Patsy's eyelids drooped, and her mouth was slack. Then I turned toward Mariah. Her gaze bored into mine like blazing coals. Somehow she knew!

"Yes, dear, the children are well. They're coming along fine," Mariah remarked to Patsy, more loudly than necessary. "Getting their strength back. You must do the same. Come on! Wiggle your fingers and toes for me. Just try, darlin'. Don't give up."

Her words were directed at her sister, but their meaning was for Raquel. The shock of Michael's death would sap the last life force from Patsy. Mariah's pointed speech conveyed we had to act as if Michael was still living, for Patsy's sake.

I was too dumbfounded to react at once.

It was eight-year-old Connor who raised high the banner of kindly deception. "Listen, Michael. Don't you like that song? Want to hear another? Do you know this one, Elisa? We learned it in choir: *Rozhinkes mit mandlen.*"

I swallowed hard, tasting bile and seawater, then made myself croak:

> *"In dem beys hamikdash*
> *In a vinkl kheyder*
>
> *"In the Temple, in a corner of a chamber*
> *The widowed Daughter of Zion sits all alone.*
> *As she rocks her only son Yidele to sleep,*
> *She sings him a pretty lullaby."*

"That's it," Connor encouraged. "Come on, James, Tomas. Sing with me."

"Go away," James returned. "Leave me alone. I feel sick."

John dug an elbow into his brother's side. "Connor's right," he warbled in a voice between man's and child's.

And in a clear, bell-like tone, Peter, whom darkness had freed from the restraining hand of shyness, sang:

244

*"In this pretty lullaby, my child, there lie
    many prophecies.*
*Some day you'll be wandering in the wide
    world,*
Trading in raisins and almonds.
And now sleep, Yidele, sleep." [14]

So we rubbed and patted and encouraged and sang, in the hopes of preserving lives hanging by even more tenuous threads than our own. At least I still had a living child on my lap to cuddle and encourage.

The sea continued to argue against our lullaby, insisting on their unvarying twelve-count pattern. At last I recognized the rhythm of the waves. It was a *petenera*—the form of flamenco never sung by gypsies in public because it foretells death.

---

[14] "Rozhinkes Mit Mandlen," traditional Yiddish folk song

17

LIFEBOAT NUMBER 7
NORTH ATLANTIC
AUTUMN 1940

The sky finally began to lighten. Pasty white faces were steeped in exhaustion. I saw the misted rings on James's eyeglasses as he levered them up on his nose. A strand of droplets rimmed the fringe of Robert's hood. I recognized where sky ended and ocean began. The dawn of the first morning after we had been torpedoed had arrived.

The waves remained monstrous in size. Rain fell in sheets. Daylight encouraged our spirits, since it meant we had survived the night.

It was only that and no more.

On my lap, despite my continued efforts to revive Moira, her small life ebbed away.

Raquel and the choirboys and I kept up the cheerful singing hour after hour. Our voices grew hoarse. Perhaps the men who occupied the back two-thirds of the lifeboat thought we were all crazy.

Perhaps they guessed what we were trying to do for Patsy.

Each time we paused, Mariah set us to our task again. Her features alternately conveyed pleading and demanding. She continued rubbing and encouraging her sister.

"Must you make so much noise?" Podlaski objected from the stern of the boat.

Officer Browne growled at him and he subsided.

I gave the Polish diplomat an angry stare. Hadn't he been rescued, hadn't he been plucked from certain death off the overturned lifeboat? Where was his compassion?

Podlaski's thinning hair was plastered on both sides of his head. Patches of gray stubble blotted his unshaven cheeks. He sneezed and patted his coat pockets, hunting for an undamaged cigar. To my relief, he did not locate one.

When we could not tolerate one more chorus, Connor responded by volunteering to sing "All the Pretty Little Horses."

"Hush you bye,
Don't you cry,
Go to sleepy little baby.
When you wake,
You shall have,
All the pretty little horses."[15]

Of course I knew Michael, and I feared Moira, would never awaken in this life. The horses they

---

[15] Traditional African-American lullaby

would have would be heavenly mounts ridden by angels.

"Is Peter next to sing?" Robert asked.

"N . . . not me. I d . . . don't want a turn."

"Listen, Patsy, *acushla*," Mariah said. "Don't your babies love the singin' altogether? Come on, love. Clap your hands with me."

Mariah struck her sister's hands, one against the other.

Robert, snug within his green jacket and hood, squirmed and asked, "Aunt Elisa, I'm hungry. When can we have something to eat?" His question frightened me. In the worry over Moira and Patsy I had forgotten that Robert was barely older than Michael, who had died.

Oh, God, I pleaded. *No more deaths. Give us the means to keep the rest alive.*

I posed Robert's question to the officer.

"Can't risk ruining all the stores in this rain and high sea," he said.

"Isn't there anything for the children?" I called back.

There was a whispered consultation between Browne and Wilson. The sailor bent over the floorboards of the boat and rummaged around.

I heard a metallic screech rise over the impulse of the waves without knowing its cause. Moments later a can of condensed milk was handed forward. A jagged hole had been punched in its top.

"Go on, Elisa," Mariah said, "give some to Moira first."

"Sure, Auntie Elisa. Little kids first," Connor said cheerfully. This from one who had just turned eight!

I touched the rim of the can to Moira's mouth. "That's it, honey. Little sips. That's it. A little more. Then let's give your brother a turn." There was very little reaction from the child. Her lips jerked reflexively in a sucking motion, but when I splashed a teaspoonful into her mouth it dribbled out again.

"Good girl," I praised. "That's it. Make your mama happy, sweetie. A little more. You can do it."

When I passed the can to Raquel she repeated the performance with Michael, though he was far past swallowing. "What a brave boy you are," she said. "Now you, Patsy. You have some too."

"No." The single syllable was the first sound I had heard Patsy utter in hours. But she could still hear us! Her eyelids flickered and she wagged the tip of one finger toward Robert. "Him next. He can have my share."

Robert shivered when the cold metal touched his lips, but he drank eagerly and asked if he might have another swallow.

"Let him take another," James said. "I don't feel like eating anyway."

"Me either," said Connor.

I marveled at the courage and fortitude of these boys.

And at that moment Moira gave the smallest shudder. It was no more than the vibration felt in a London flat when a tube train passes in its tunnel far beneath.

Then she died, and I felt her go.

"What shall we sing now, boys?" I asked, though my throat was so constricted I could barely breathe.

"Let me, Aunt Elisa," called a voice from behind Patsy.

In a haunting, lyrical voice, Angelique offered up "Durme, Durme," a Sephardic lullaby sung all around the Mediterranean, from Morocco to Turkey.

"Durme, durme hijiko de madre . . ."

Though her words were in Ladino I knew their meaning from concerts of Roma music I had played in Austria. It seemed a million years and a million miles ago.

"Sleep, sleep, mother's little one,
Free from worry and grief.
Listen, my joy, to your mother's words,
The words of Shema Yisrael."

When the chorus came around, Raquel's rich, husky voice joined in:

"Sleep, sleep,
Mother's little one,
With the beauty of Shema Israel."

"Wow." Connor sighed.

"Shh," John insisted. "Keep quiet." He stared at Angelique intensely.

And the surge of the ocean continued to count to twelve.

All through the day the rain alternated with periods of wind. The waves stayed mountainous. One moment we were walled in by masses of dark green water; the next we rode up the face of a swell. From each peak I could see for miles, but there was nothing to view except the threatening battalions of brine, looming rank upon rank.

Because of the driving spray there was no way to open the provisions stashed in the lifeboat. We were all hungry, but so miserably damp no one complained at the lack of food.

"My feet still hurt," Robert said.

Raquel straightened up, balancing Michael's weight within her coat. "I have an idea. Listen, children. Would you like to learn a gypsy dance?"

"What, here?" Connor queried.

"Why not?" Raquel returned. "It's called the *buleria*. It means . . . a joke, but sometimes it's a contest. Twelve beats and then repeat. Here's the first pattern." With her feet on the narrow strip of bench opposite she tapped a pattern that emphasized the third, sixth, eighth, tenth, and twelfth beats. "Can you do that?"

"Sure," Connor said. "Come on, Peter. No singin'. Just move your feet."

"I can do it, Aunt Elisa," Robert agreed. "See?"

It took some organizing before the chaos of many pairs of feet kept proper time.

When a level of success had been achieved, Tomas inquired, "Why'd you say 'the first pattern'?"

"Ah," Raquel responded. "This is where it gets interesting. Boys, the rhythm we just learned is yours. Can you remember it?"

"Sure," John scoffed. "Easy. Listen." And he demonstrated his mastery of the buleria.

"The second pattern is for the girls. Angelique already knows it."

"Me too," Simcha piped. "Me too."

"All right, Elisa and Mariah and Patsy. You too." Raquel again performed a twelve-count tapping, this time emphasizing the third, seventh, eighth, tenth, and twelfth beats. "Try it. It's harder than it seems."

It was hard to properly render the syncopated count. With Angelique and Raquel leading, we girls managed it. Patsy's feet barely moved. She bobbed her chin in time to the tempo.

"Here's the best part," Raquel said. "We do them both at once."

Chaos again! And then, "I say, that's wonderful," John exclaimed.

We were warmed. Feeling returned to toes and calves.

Soon the energy to keep up round after round of stamping subsided. Raquel and I continued the pretense of talking to and massaging Moira and Michael.

Only Mariah kept up a level of intensity. "Patsy, don't give up on me now! You hear me? There'll be a fine big rescue boat along most any time now. Hot tea for you and warm milk for the babes." Mariah patted her sister's face and stroked her hair. She massaged her feet and held a cupped palm of rainwater to her lips.

"A ship!" Connor said suddenly.

"Where away, boy?" Browne demanded.

"I saw it when we were on top of the wave. It's that way," he said, pointing.

When the lifeboat crested the top of the breaker all of us peered ahead.

"There's nothing there," Podlaski argued. "Stupid boy. Got excited over nothing."

"His eyes are better than yours," Barrett argued. "Shouldn't we try to row that direction?"

"And when he's proved wrong?"

"Then what difference does it make? Here, give me an oar. At least I'll be warmer than I am now."

At the next wave top Podlaski remarked scornfully. "See? I told you this was for nothing."

Browne was not so sure. "I thought . . ." He peered into the grayness.

I turned to look. Was there something in that direction that was darker than the vapor hugging the sea? Was there a more solid quality to that one patch of mist?

"Row!" the officer exclaimed. "Row like your lives depend on it!"

The lascars bent their backs into their work.

"Harder! Faster!" Podlaski exclaimed. "Can't you do better than that?"

"Are we rescued?" Robert asked me.

I was afraid to hope. "Pray," I said.

Hours of aimless drifting were succeeded by minutes of fearsome activity. "Pull! Pull harder!" It seemed everyone was shouting at once.

The reality of the phantom shape was revealed. It was some kind of cargo ship, smaller than *Newcastle*, with a single smokestack rising from its middle. As I watched, its outline changed from rectangle to inverted triangle as its bow swung toward us.

"They've seen us," Podlaski shouted. "What did I tell you? Keep coming! Keep coming!"

The wind was blowing from the direction of the rescue ship toward us. I heard the thrum of its engines and the rattle of machinery.

"Hello! We're here! Here!" the boys cried.

"Save your breath," the officer said. "But if you have something to wave, now's the time."

Instantly Number 7 became a float in the Lord Mayor's Day Parade. Coats and hats and Connor's pocket handkerchief erupted, festooning the boat in joyful anticipation.

We drew closer together. The bulk of the ship loomed larger and larger. Pale oval shapes lining the railing far above the level of our view almost, but not quite, resolved into faces.

Then I saw the oncoming form change from triangle to rectangle again. Next the ship showed us the bluff squareness of its stern and the words SS *Festung—Hamburg*.

Then, despite all our efforts at rowing against the wind, the ship dwindled into the mist and disappeared.

"What happened?"

"How could they not see us?"

"Why didn't you pull harder?" This criticism was from Podlaski.

"Aren't we rescued, Aunt Elisa?"

"They couldn't have missed us," the playwright said bitterly. "They left us here on purpose. Why?"

"Nazis," Browne said. "A sub-tender. A supply ship for the submarines. Stow the oars. That's enough exercise for now."

A low keening cry from the bow of our refuge.

"It's all right, Aunt Mariah," Connor said. "There'll be another ship soon. You'll see. We'll be rescued soon."

Dully, Mariah corrected, "It's Patsy. She's dead."

• • •

The rain and low-hanging shroud of clouds did not relent until the early morning hours of our second day adrift. The seas continued piling up hills and digging valleys. Half of us were seasick. I think all of us were heartsick.

Another dawn finally came. The clouds lifted off the water, but not off of our spirits. The endless parade of rolling swells finally subsided. It was time to think about living again.

On the morning of our second day aboard Number 7 I took stock of our situation. We were entirely alone on the Atlantic. There were twenty-seven people crammed aboard the lifeboat built for a maximum of twenty-two: two British members of *Newcastle*'s complement, two male passengers, eight lascar crewmen, six boys, three girls, three women . . . and three dead bodies.

There were so many issues we faced: Would we be rescued soon? If we weren't immediately picked up, what could we do to rescue ourselves? In the crowded conditions, all of us suffered from cramps. Our hands and feet felt pickled. We were unable to get clear of the water sloshing around the bilges. Our fingers and toes stayed numb.

Robert, the youngest of the boys, cried with the pain, though I rubbed and rubbed him. Peter was likewise suffering, but he bit his lip to bear it in silence. What could we do to relieve the aches?

Yet none of these are the reason I teared up that morning.

The biggest crisis was what to do with the bodies of Patsy and her two children.

Raquel and I avoided looking at Mariah's face. I feared for her life. She had invested so much hope, so much of her energy believing they would be rescued, that having them die anyway seemed to have utterly destroyed her. If we were picked up today, at least her loved ones could be taken back to Ireland for a proper burial.

How long should we wait to even raise the issue?

Mariah herself delivered us from our dilemma. Shaking her head, as if coming awake from a bad dream, she murmured, "Leastways I got them back for a little while, so I don't have to wonder about their fate. Perhaps some of youse carry that heavy burden on your hearts right now."

I thought then of my evacuee girls. Had they made it off *Newcastle* before she went down? Had their lifeboat survived its launching? Were they safe? Had they already been rescued, or were they adrift somewhere even as we?

Mariah continued, "Patsy loved the sea. She's been talkin' for years of leavin' for America. This spot is as close to America as she's goin' to get in this life, so let her and her wee'uns be buried right here."

Her request awakened my memory. In my pocket was the copy of the *Book of Common Prayer*. In it was the burial service. I passed the book to Officer Browne.

"I am the Resurrection and the life, saith the Lord: he that believeth in Me, though he were dead, yet shall he live."

With these words Harold Browne began the memorial. He brushed his graying moustache with his index finger and cleared his throat.

"We brought nothing into this world, and it is certain we can carry nothing out. The Lord giveth and the Lord hath taken away; blessed be the Name of the Lord."

At Mariah's direction we took the three life vests, Patsy's coat, and their socks. These things we might need, and they had no further use of them.

"God is our refuge and strength, a very present help in trouble. Therefore we will not fear, though the earth gives way, though the mountains be moved into the heart of the sea."[16]

---

[16] Psalm 46:1–2 ESV

I remembered sitting on a park bench on Primrose Hill with Murphy, looking out across London. I thought of the verdant hills of my youth and remembered how my papa had taken us on holiday to the Alps. I had grown up in Germany before Hitler. It was the most civilized, most modern nation in Europe. I had been part of a blessed family. I had all the comforts imaginable. I had found the love of my life in John Murphy.

Now here I was, floating on the expanse of waters. I owned the clothes I wore. I might live to be rescued and reunited with my family, but what happened to *Newcastle* and then to Mariah proved nothing was certain.

Truly, all the steady, trustworthy hills of my life had been uprooted and cast into the sea. Could I continue to rely on God? Could I escape from fear?

"Jesus said, 'Suffer little children, and forbid them not, to come unto Me; for of such is the kingdom of heaven.' "[17]

Number 7 was ballasted with bars of iron laid down next to the keel. Silently Matt Wilson dug three of these from beneath the floorboards and passed them forward.

---

[17] Matthew 19:14 KJV

We knew what he was suggesting.

Digging in her handbag, Raquel produced needle and thread. Mariah wiped away a tear and nodded her approval. Raquel and I began sewing the weights into the clothing of Patsy, Moira, and Michael.

"Let not your heart be troubled: ye believe in God, believe also in Me. In My Father's house are many mansions: if it were not so, I would have told you. I go to prepare a place for you."[18]

For twenty centuries these words comforted the grieving and gave hope to the brokenhearted. We would see our loved ones again; we would be reunited. Sometimes it felt as if that trust in a future reunion was all that kept us going in this tired, wicked world. Even while believing, our hearts' cry remained "How long, O Lord!"

Mariah, Raquel, and I and all the girls wept. So did all the boys except John, who had his arms folded and his chin tucked hard against his chest.

"Unto Almighty God we commend the souls of our dear departed, and we commit their bodies to the deep; in sure and certain hope of the Resurrection unto eternal life, through our

---

[18] John 14:1–2 KJV

Lord Jesus Christ; at whose coming in glorious majesty to judge the world the sea shall give up her dead.

"Almighty God, Father of mercies and giver of all comfort, deal graciously, we pray Thee, with all those who mourn, that, casting every care on Thee, we may know the consolation of Thy love. Through Jesus Christ our Lord.

"Amen."

And then there were only twenty-four aboard Lifeboat Number 7.

18

Angel looked into my face and asked quietly, "I saw all the girls from Lindy's cabin in the boat with Miss Pike. But I did not see Lindy."

"There was such confusion, Angel. She had to be with them." I imagined the lie was kinder than the truth on such a day.

I thought about the words of the officer as he compelled me to leave Lindy in the cabin or die. *"Lindy's got to go home now. . . . I'll take care of her. . . . You must leave now or you won't make it out."*

How I had run as I stumbled from that place of death! Without looking back, I had left Lindy in the hands of a stranger and had saved my own life. How would I ever face her mother? How would I ever tell the story of the final terrible moments of her daughter's life?

Reaching deep into the pocket of my coat, I felt again for the small volume containing the lock of Lindy's hair. I would at least return that treasure to the hands of Mrs. Petticaris. I would tell her that Lindy's last conscious thought was for her.

Raising my eyes I saw the steady gaze of Cedric Barrett on my face. What was that in his expression? Pity? Did he know I had left Lindy behind? Had he sensed I was not telling Angel the truth about her best friend?

I silently prayed, *O God! Please let me sleep without dreams. Give me an hour to rest so I can be strong!*

The sea grew calm. Mariah clasped my hand, laid her head upon my lap, and slept the deep sleep of grief. Stroking her hair as if she were a child, I sensed the warmth of the sun on my back. The only sound was the rush of the water split by the bow. I prayed for sleep, hoping that for a moment I would not be tortured by the memory of Lindy dying before me. Again the image of her sweet face appeared before me. Had I done all I could do for her? I could only think of her mother and the last letter she had written: *Do not write me because I will be mid-Atlantic and cannot answer.*

My promise to her mother that I would protect Lindy had followed. I had failed miserably. Was it my fault? Should I have stayed and died with her when the very angels had abandoned ship?

At last my head nodded forward and I dozed off.

I do not know how long I slept. It was not a dreamless sleep but filled with images of Murphy's face smiling above me. *"You're okay,*

Elisa. It's Evensong. Can you hear the boys singing? Can you hear me praying for you? for the kids? I'm at Westminster Abbey now. Everyone here is praying for you."

It came to me clearly that I was asleep and dreaming of a happier moment. I asked, *"But what about Lindy? All the others?"* I felt Murphy's hand on my arm. He shook his head sadly from side to side. *"What about Lindy?"* I asked and then spoke his name aloud. "Murphy!"

My eyes flew open, and I jerked awake. The sun was setting, and Cedric Barrett was framed by light. He was very close to my face. "Elisa? Are you all right?"

Nodding, I swept my hair back from my face. Poor Mariah was mercifully still asleep on my lap. "I was dreaming," I said quietly.

"Yes," Barrett answered.

Suddenly conscious that half a dozen children were staring at me, I managed a slight smile and said to Connor, "In my dream, my husband told me it was Evensong. He said that he was at the Abbey praying for us. He told me to listen to the singing."

Connor nodded as if it was a command. Taking out his tin whistle, he said to the Apostles, "It is Evensong."

At his direction, the boys began to sing the benediction in close harmony.

"Praise God from whom all blessings flow.
Praise Him all creatures here below.
Praise Him, above ye heavenly host.
Praise Father, Son and Holy Ghost.
Amen."

Barrett inhaled deeply and removed a battered notebook from his pocket. "Lindy's."

"Oh! Oh, Cedric! It isn't lost!"

"In my pocket all the time."

I touched the cover where Lindy had inscribed her name beneath the words *The Long Journey Home.*

"I was meant for Lifeboat 6, you see. I came to the station. No room. But your girls were there. All of them except . . ." He tucked his chin. "Well, little Betsy was there without Lindy. She told an officer you had stayed behind with Lindy—that Lindy had been hurt."

So Barrett had guessed the worst.

I looked at the gold reflection of the water. I thought of what I had heard . . . about the streets of heaven being paved with gold. I thought of Lindy's feet walking on water, walking on golden streets. "Yes. Yes."

"We want to take this home . . ."

". . . to her mother."

His eyes flickered with a memory. "She was quite a good little writer. I mean, honest critique, right? That's what she wanted and . . . well . . . she was, you know, wonderful."

He turned away, his back toward me when he sat. I thought I saw his shoulders shudder as he rested his head in his hands.

Angel did not turn her eyes from my face. "So," she said quietly. "Even so." Angel was too young to know about death and dying, yet she had lived through enough to know. *Lindy was not in Lifeboat Number 6. Lindy was not coming home.*

"Under your feet and in compartments below the gunnels are supplies for our survival. I want all of you to get busy checking to see what we have aboard and get ready to inventory it."

As soon as the committal service ended Harold Browne called us to a variety of tasks. His attempt to set our minds on life and take our thoughts off of death was transparent, but I was grateful.

I think we all were, except Mr. Podlaski. "What's the point? Either we're going to be rescued, or we aren't. If we are, we don't need to play games. If we aren't, none of your toys will matter."

"Shall I remind you of that when sharing the food, Mister Podlaski?"

"What? No, no!"

"Then make yourself useful."

In the forward compartments near where the women and children sat were tools. We found fishing line and hooks, a compass, rope, and a mirror, flares, and smoke bombs.

Beneath the floorboards we also located a mast and a sail, a can of grease, a bucket, and a hand axe.

"Like *Robinson Crusoe*," Connor said.

"Leave the mast and sail stowed for the moment," Browne ordered. "It's going to take some serious rearranging to uncover it and set it up. That can come later."

Of greatest interest to us all, now that the seas were calmer, were the food and water supplies in lockers and tanks at the stern. An entire canned-goods shop was on board, it seemed. There were tins of condensed milk, sardines, peaches, salmon, pineapple, and sealed cartons of ship's biscuit.

Peter's stomach growled and he looked embarrassed. "S–sorry."

"He's hungry," Tomas said. "We all are now."

I overheard Browne question Matt Wilson about the amount of water.

"Forty gallons," was the reply.

"Plenty," Tomas said. "And I'm thirsty."

I saw James staring at the sky. His lips moved without making any sound.

He caught me looking at him and grinned sheepishly.

"What are you calculating?" I asked.

"Forty gallons. Three hundred twenty pints. Thirteen and a bit more pints for each of us."

"That's a lot, isn't it?" Robert remarked.

James ducked his head and muttered something I didn't catch. "What was that?"

"I said, depends on how long it has to last."

John fixed his eye on Angelique. "That's no worry. Now that the weather's improved, the destroyers will be along most any time. They got slowed down yesterday, but they'll make it up today. You'll see."

"Unless they missed us already," Podlaski offered, chiming in, uninvited, into the conversation.

"Mister Podlaski," Cedric Barrett said, "I wish you'd take the advice offered by the great American humorist, Will Rogers: 'Never miss an opportunity to shut up!'"

Our first meal aboard Number 7 was issued around noon the second day after the sinking of *Newcastle*. It consisted, per person, of one hard ship's biscuit, about the size and thickness of a dime novel, topped by one sardine. Each ration had to be passed forward from the stern, where Browne did the sharing out. By the time a girl received her portion it had been handled five or six times but was no more chewable because of that.

"Hard tack," Connor said. "Like Admiral Nelson's navy. And I love sardines."

Yael turned up her snub nose at the aroma. "I do not like these little fishes. You have it, Simcha," she said to her sister.

"No, sweetheart," Raquel corrected. "You must eat it. It will make you strong."

There was some grumbling from the lascars. Though no one spoke in English, it was clear they did not approve of the small amount of food.

Water had to be distributed the same way, one eight-ounce measure at a time. The dipper was about the size and shape of one of Podlaski's fat cigars.

Before passing the first beaker forward, the officer held it aloft. "You should hear how I determined the amount," he said. "*Newcastle* was three days out of Liverpool when we were struck. For her, Ireland would be a day's steaming at most. For us"—Browne shrugged—"it depends on if we have favorable winds or have to go against them. With the sail drawing fully we could see Galway in six days."

"Please, sir," Connor asked, waving his hand as if in a classroom, "are we sailing back to Ireland, then? Are we not going to stay where the navy will be looking for us?"

Browne spoke quickly before Podlaski could remind us again how he was the senior political official on board. "The destroyers will do a box search. They will comb an area twenty miles across. Each pass will take an hour; then they move a mile or so and make another run. This searching they can do in a day and they will find us . . . if we are still inside that box. What I propose is that we remain here for one more day. I have apportioned our rations, especially the water, to last twice as long as our voyage should take, just in case. Are we all clear on that?"

None of us, not even Podlaski, had any comment to make. We were all sobered and thoughtful as we chewed salty, oily sardines and gnawed on brick-like biscuits.

The officer announced that supper and the next water ration would be shared at six in the evening. I tried not to count how many hours remained until then.

It was late afternoon of the second day afloat when Connor spotted another rescue vessel. This time no one, not even Podlaski, dismissed the claim. All strained their eyes toward the point indicated by the boy.

"I hope it's not the Germans again," John said.

"Will they take us prisoner?" James asked.

Peter began to tremble violently, as if with cold. Tomas hugged him and whispered in Czech, "Don't be afraid, my brother. No fear."

"Coming back to finish us off," Podlaski ventured.

"Them Jerries monitor our radio, same as we do theirs," Wilson said. "We'd blow that sub-tender out of the water was we to catch him. No worries, lads. They won't come near us again, 'cause they know the whole bloomin' navy is out hunting for us."

So not the Germans. But where was the rescue ship?

I held my breath with anticipation. Rescue! Safety! No anxiety about making a sea voyage to Ireland in an open boat on the North Atlantic.

"There!" Raquel exclaimed. "I see it too."

"Me too," Robert said, tossing back his hood. "Shall I wave my cloak, Aunt Elisa? Shall I?"

"Not yet, sweetheart. Wait a bit."

Beneath the low-hanging clouds a dark object rose against the horizon, hung there a moment, then disappeared again.

"I don't understand," Tomas said. "The big waves have gone down. Why do we see that ship and then not see it? Is it another submarine?"

A jet of spray shot upward where we had last marked the approaching vessel.

"It's a whale," Wilson remarked. "Whole pod of 'em, looks like."

Within minutes Number 7 was surrounded by a half score of whales, passing us on both sides.

"Amazing!" Connor exulted. "Look how fast they swim. Could we throw out a line and get a tow?"

"They're headed toward America," James observed, holding a compass in his hand.

"Isn't that where we want to go as well?"

The biggest animal in the pod rose no more than

twenty yards away. Carried by the breeze, his jet floated across us like another drenching rain. Immediately afterward he stood on his head and dove, giving a mighty slap of his tail that rocked us with the waves.

"I've heard tales they sometimes come up underneath small boats," Podlaski said. "One whip of such a tail will splinter us to toothpicks."

First fears of Nazis and now of malicious whales.

The lascar crewmen evidently took Podlaski's warning seriously. Jerking the oars up and down, they pounded out a warning to the whales intended to keep them away from us. Either the demonstration worked, or perhaps the animals were not really dangerous, but either way they disappeared into the west.

On board Number 7, disappointment once again reigned.

"The wind is dead against us," Browne noted, "so there's no point in raising the sail. But we'll row awhile, I think."

Somehow, without further discussion, the false alarm had determined our course. We were going to attempt to make it to Ireland. We would no longer wait for, or expect, rescue.

"Two men to an oar," Browne continued. "Fifteen-minute shifts. The exercise will do us good. I think all the men should take a turn."

"Not me," Podlaski demurred.

"I will," John offered. "If you'll let me."

"Glad to have you," Browne said approvingly.

There was muttering among the native sailors.

"Sanjay," Browne called to one of the lascars, "what are they saying?"

"They say the ration is too small. How can we row?"

Browne put his hands on his hips. "I already explained the amounts. Anyone want to question a direct order? Do they?"

There was a tense silence.

"One moment, Cap'n," Wilson said. "We won't be stopping again for a time, will we? If I've got a chance to warm up after, then I fancy a swim first."

Tomas and Peter exchanged incredulous looks, as did James and John. We had spent two days trying to remain dry and out of the clutches of the waves. Now this crazy man was going to deliberately jump in? Besides, we had just witnessed the power of the whales. What other great, sinister creatures of the deep were out there?

"Who's coming with me? Sanjay? Haji?"

Many turbans shook in response.

"I will!" Connor volunteered.

"You most certainly will not," I corrected. "You're staying inside the boat."

"Maybe another time, eh, old chap?" Wilson offered. "Anyone?"

John darted a glance toward Angelique, then dropped his gaze without speaking.

"Right, then." Shedding shoes and coat and stripping to undershirt and shorts, Wilson dove cleanly over the side. He executed three laps around Number 7 without stopping, then climbed back to his position.

"Bracing, that is," he said cheerfully, toweling off with a bit of burlap sacking. "Nothing better. Cheerio, Cap'n. What's our heading?"

And the oars began their rhythmic rise and fall.

The gray light dimmed toward nightfall as the choristers sang Psalm 136:

"Give thanks to the Lord of lords
His love endures forever."

I prayed as they caroled for us. James and John sang each verse while Tomas, Peter, and Connor offered the refrain.

"To Him who alone does great wonders . . .
His love endures forever.
To Him who by understanding made the
*   heavens . . .*
His love endures forever.
To Him who spread out the earth above the
*   waters . . .*
His love endures forever."

Here where there was no "earth above the waters," I wondered if I had ever really known the importance of this hymn.

The carol to the loving-kindness of the Lord was a regular part of the Evensong service at Westminster Abbey, so I had heard it performed many times. Had I ever really paid attention to the message?

> *"To Him who made the great lights . . .*
> *His love endures forever.*
> *The sun to rule over the day . . .*
> *His love endures forever."*

Even more to the point, did I believe that the Lord's mercy was unending? Could I take the words and apply them as balm to my fearful heart?

> *"The moon and stars to rule over the*
> *   night . . .*
> *His love endures forever."*[19]

When the psalm was finished, Third Officer Browne shared out our supper: another slab of hard tack. We were all calling it that now, convinced by Connor it sounded more nautical than "biscuit." For variety, we had one slice of

---

[19] Psalm 136:1–9 ESV, PARAPHRASED

canned peach, instead of a sardine, on top.

After we had prayed and sung and eaten, miraculously, there was still some left over.

"There's still the juice in the cans," Browne noted after the fruit had been served out. "I propose giving it to the children."

Podlaski opened his mouth in protest. Wilson on one side, and Barrett on the other, favored him with such threatening looks he subsided without speaking.

The grumbling was picked up amidships by the lascars. Hard looks were directed at Browne and at us. Something that had never happened before occurred: a portion of the syrup slopped out of the can as it was passed forward. Three native sailors licked their fingers—one of them defiantly.

Beginning with Yael and Robert, the sticky-sweet liquid was passed around the bow until only a half can remained and it was John's turn. "Let the ladies have it," he said.

Browne and Wilson agreed, so Raquel, Mariah, and I shared what was left. Mariah was hollow-eyed and barely spoke, but she thanked John for his thoughtfulness and straightened her shoulders. "And don't I have a duty to go home to me Da?" she said. "Bein' his only kin, and him expectin' grand news of our arrival in America."

The syrup tasted better than anything I had ever swallowed to that moment in my life. Before the

Nazi horror, when the orchestra traveled the great capitals of the world, we had been feted with champagne and caviar, Sachar tortes and roast beef from gleaming silver trolleys. Yet nothing in my memory reached the level of the juice of canned peaches.

Of course, then we were all terribly thirsty.

When the water ration reached Robert, I encouraged him to sip it slowly. "No more until morning," I warned. "Swish it around inside your mouth and make it last."

Since the breeze had swung into the south, Officer Browne proposed setting the sail. "During the night I want everyone to rest as much as possible," he said. "One man to the tiller and one as lookout 'til dawn. Two-hour watches. Me, Wilson, and Barrett taking turns with the helm. Naturally, Mister Podlaski, I assume your diplomatic duties do not extend to steering this ship of state."

"What is this nonsense you speak?" Podlaski protested. "At home I am a champion yachtsman."

He did not see the wink Browne gave Barrett. Podlaski insisted on taking the first turn at the tiller, leaving the others free to step the mast and rig the sail.

Soon after this operation, all was trimmed and order restored. Number 7 leaned slightly and the port rail dipped with the press of the wind. We ghosted along over the gentle swell. The compass heading indicated was east-south-east.

"Aunt Elisa," Connor said. "I'm not sleepy. Can we have a story?"

"Yes! A story, please," Robert echoed.

"Not tonight, boys," I said. "But perhaps a song?"

"Sure," Tomas agreed.

"What should it be?" James pondered.

While the choristers still debated the choice of selection, Peter's mellifluous tones floated around the canvas arch of sail and into the canvas-colored sky.

> *"The water is wide,*
> *I cannot get o'er.*
> *And neither have I wings to fly.*
> *Give me a boat that can carry two,*
> *And both shall row, my love and I."*[20]

From within the folds of his life vest Connor drew out his tin whistle. With Peter singing the lead, Connor piping the melody as interludes between verses, and the other boys harmonizing perfectly, the moment was like the juice of the peaches . . . the sweetest I had ever experienced.

---

[20] "The Water Is Wide," English folk song

I am my beloved's and my beloved is mine.
SONG OF SOLOMON 6:3 ESV

VIENNA, AUSTRIA
FEBRUARY 1938

I am married to John Murphy. He is not a knight in shining armor, but he married me so I might have the protection of his American citizenship. He does not love me and will be well paid for helping me. We will have the marriage annulled when I am safe with American papers.

I am sure he does not really like me, though for many months he came to performances and often asked me out for coffee.

I did my hair up like Katherine Hepburn in the movie *Bill of Divorcement*. I told myself that I would act my part and go on with my life, never seeing John Murphy again after the annulment. If I am arrested by the Nazis, my official link to the life of an American newsman may save my life. This is all I must think about.

Murphy's hands were shaking when we went to the American Embassy to fill out papers. He did not know how to answer the questions. His friend, who is a clerk there, asked him if he really knew me well enough to get married.

We laughed, but of course Murphy does not know me really, nor do I know him.

This is the record of my wedding ceremony.

Murphy to Harry the Clerk: "How long is this going to take?"

Harry: "Most ladies like the long-type ceremony."

Murphy: "You got a short one?"

Harry: "Sure. We can do it short. As short as you like."

Murphy: "How's thirty seconds?"

Harry: "It'll cost you extra."

Murphy reaching across the desk to grab Harry's tie: "You're charging me $500 bucks as it is, you little crook."

Harry: "That's because you want her passport in one day!"

Murphy: "I want a quick passport and a quick ceremony!"

And so it went. A phony wedding. A cigar band for a wedding ring. And then we kissed. His lips pressed mine, and he held me against him. Warm coils lit up inside me. I could not breathe . . . and then it was over. We said good-bye on the curb like two strangers.

I caught the streetcar and tried not to look back at him. It was a long time before my heart slowed to normal. I still feel that kiss.

19

The night brought no additional rain, but the weather turned dramatically colder. In the after-midnight hours the wind backed completely around so that it blew out of the north—directly from the North Pole, it seemed to me.

Some of the boys were proof against the chill. Robert in his forest-green cape was well protected. So was Connor in a heavy overcoat. "Mother made me promise to wear it whenever I went on deck," he said. "When the torpedo hit, I didn't have it, so I went back to my cabin for it."

The alarm bells of my maternal instincts clanged violently. By turning back, sweet Connor could have been trapped belowdecks. Or he might have missed his chance at being on Number 7 and been lost aboard some foundering lifeboat.

On the other hand, now he was warm and protected while Tomas and Peter, who had evacuated *Newcastle* in their pajamas, had one blanket between them, as did James and John.

Robert slept on my lap. Connor had his head

tucked against Mariah's arm. My Irish friend traded places with Raquel. The dancer and her three charges were tucked snuggly beneath the canvas canopy. Angelique snuggled inside John's overcoat. "I don't need it," he said. "I'm plenty warm in my sweater." John muscled in beside his brother, who knew better than to object.

It was the lascar crewmen who suffered the most. Their shipboard uniforms were of thin material. None of them had coats. Many were barefoot, while those who were shod wore only sandals. There were enough blankets aboard to provide one for every three men. The two on the outside of each bench were half warm and half frozen.

My nose and ears grew cold enough to wake me. Even through my drowsy confusion I saw black looks of envy from two shivering lascar sailors.

Untangling myself from Robert, I reached my hand up to rub some feeling back into them and saw that Peter was awake.

"Peter? Are you feeling all right?"

"Yes, Aunt Elisa," he replied in a soft, clear whisper. "I often wake at night to look at the stars."

I had not even noticed that the shift in the wind had rolled back the layers of cloud so that bright pinpoints of light glowed overhead. "Do you know their names?"

"Some." He indicated a bright blue-white star rising directly in line with the bow. "That's Rigel. He marks Orion's knee."

"I know Orion," I agreed. "That's his sword and belt."

I heard the smile in Peter's voice as he warmed to a favorite topic. "The orange one, just there? That's Betelgeuse. Sometimes I imagine heaven is up there. My mother and sister . . . you know? Surrounded by shining lights and no more war."

I thought about the children of our voyage who had not survived. Fresh grief welled up in my throat for Lindy and the others. *Why, God?* I silently asked.

I said aloud, "Heaven is a wonderful place, they say."

Peter answered, "When I look at the stars, I'm sure it must be true."

I realized Peter had not stuttered once in all this dissertation, nor did his speech impediment create any problem when he sang. It was only when he tried to speak in the daylight that his brother had to interpret for him.

"Tell me more," I said.

"Father was professor of physics at Charles University in Prague," Peter said proudly. "He had been there since before I was born. Then the Germans came."

When I said nothing he said bitterly, "They said

the school belonged to the Deutsche Universite of Berlin. No Jews wanted. My father went to work in a rail yard, shoveling coal."

I also knew about Jews being expelled from teaching positions and orchestras, but again I waited for Peter to speak. "Now my father is in America, working with Professor Enrico Fermi, studying atomic fission. At Columbia University. In New York. Do you know of it? We are supposed to see him there before we go to Holl-ee-wood-land." Peter carefully pronounced each syllable of the California film colony, naming it as if it were the title of a magical kingdom in a fairy tale.

"Yes," I agreed. I had not a clue what was meant by "atomic fission," but I recognized the prestigious university. "Columbia in New York. You'll like it, Peter. And your father will be so glad to see you and Tomas again."

The boy nodded, then yawned. "Father was very excited. He says Fermi is the smartest physicist in the world. Father says Fermi's wife is Jewish, like us. They had to escape from Mussolini, just like . . . like we . . ."

As if I could hear the voice of my father speaking, my mind was filled with the words of the first two verses of Isaiah 57 (ESV):

The righteous man perishes,
and no one lays it to heart;

devout men are taken away,
while no one understands.
For the righteous man is taken away from
  calamity;
he enters into peace.

Peter had nodded off to sleep. Moments later, I did the same.

In You, O LORD, do I take refuge;
let me never be put to shame! In Your
righteousness deliver me and rescue me;
incline Your ear to me, and save me!
PSALM 71:1–2 ESV

VIENNA, AUSTRIA
MARCH 10, 1938

The Austrian prime minister has been arrested and the government taken over by Fascists who favor Hitler. I am weeping now as I write this. What will come of us now? Surely Germany will annex Austria, and our small island of safety will be destroyed.

Since the first of January, I have escorted seventeen Jewish children from Germany to Austria, and then on to safety in Switzerland, using my American passport for cover and protection.

John Murphy unexpectedly came to my flat tonight. He seemed nervous when he told me why he had come.

"I want to warn you that you and your friends must leave Austria. It is very dangerous now. No more risks. I thought you should have a wedding ring. For appearances." He thrust a small box into my hand. I opened it. There was a blue lapis wedding band inside.

"Lovely," I said. "Blue."

"Like the dress you wore. Same color. The day we were . . . married."

I wondered if he used part of the money he was paid to marry me? I felt emotion tug at my throat. I had not forgotten our one and only kiss.

He slipped the band on my finger. "Just wanted to let you know. I was thinking about you. About us. Hoping you're okay."

Leah came to the door and Murphy left quickly, saying there were enormous political events he must witness and write about.

Leah says he looked back at me with longing as he left. I wonder if he remembers our parting kiss as I do.

I wonder if we will ever meet again. Leah and I made plans to leave for Kitzbühel. If Austria falls to the Reich, we will escape to Switzerland from there.

20

Our days aboard Number 7 quickly fell into a routine. When we awoke from our unsatisfying rest, there was much contorting of limbs to restore circulation, and many groans.

Officer Browne led us in The Lord's Prayer:

"Our Father, which art in heaven.
Hallowed be Thy Name."

When we came to the petition about "Give us this day, our daily bread," John's stomach growled.

No one laughed.

Everyone made conversation about the weather, the wind, and about how much we had progressed toward the end of our journey.

John: "Breeze is more from the west now. Good for us."

James: "But it's died away since the sun rose. Bad for us."

Angelique addressed her question to John: "How far have we come?"

I saw conflicting emotions cross John's face.

He wanted to sound encouraging, to give Angelique hope. At the same time he could not lie to her. Someone would certainly correct him if he gave a wildly wrong answer, and then the beautiful gypsy girl might no longer trust him.

John hedged. "It's hard to say, exactly."

James had no such hesitation. "Even when we had the breeze we can't have been averaging more than three knots." He paused to straighten his spectacles. "Probably less. I bet we haven't made—"

His brother interrupted. "Seventy-five miles. That's great progress. A third of the distance to Ireland."

"If we're even going the right direction," the Polish diplomat asserted. "How do we even know?"

"There's the sun, Mister Podlaski," Browne said. "We're sailing toward it, aren't we?"

Podlaski harrumphed.

"We couldn't miss something as big as Ireland, could we, Aunt Elisa?" Robert inquired, stretching one arm toward my nose and the other toward Mariah's.

"As big and green as ever it is?" Mariah offered. "Not a'tall, a'tall. Soon enough we'll be sailin' into Galway Bay to a hero's welcome. And what do you think we'll have to eat then, eh?"

This was also part of the routine. Contrary to

what I first thought, taking turns describing a desirable meal was not depressing. Instead it seemed to raise the children's spirits.

"Sausages!" Connor piped cheerfully.

"Scads of roast beef and potatoes," James suggested.

"As much soft bread and nice jam as I want," was Robert's choice.

"Sure, and won't it be Irish stew?" Mariah laughed. "And sausage and roast beef and bread with . . . with what sort of jam, Robin Hood?"

"Strawberry!" the green-clad miniature archer declared. "Unless . . ." He paused thoughtfully.

"Yes?" Mariah encouraged.

"Do they have rolls with butter and honey in Ireland?"

"For you, my dear, yes. Even if we was to have to import it!"

The time between waking and the first of our two daily meals passed very slowly. Food and water were distributed around noon and then again six hours later.

I soon learned the longer I stayed asleep the better.

It was on day four that we made a terrible discovery.

As the evening distribution of rations commenced, Matt Wilson passed out the first round of the hard tack, each topped with a small chunk of canned salmon. There was a longer than usual pause as Wilson broke into the second case of ship's biscuits.

He swore bitterly, bringing a stinging reprimand from Browne.

"Sorry, sir. It's because this second case is spoiled."

"What!"

"See for yourself, sir."

Browne bent down toward the locker built into the stern. "Rusted through the bottom!" he said. "Whole crate sucked up seawater from the bilges like a sponge."

"And that ain't all, sir," Wilson added, dropping his voice to a whispered level.

All conversation stopped as we awaited the news.

Wilson raised a cupped hand from below my vision toward Browne's face. The officer dipped his fingers, touched them to his mouth, and then spat over the side. He bit his chapped lip and frowned, then straightened his shoulders and raised his chin. "Ladies and gentlemen, besides losing one crate of biscuits, I must also report that the second water tank has split a seam. Instead of being full of drinkable liquid, it is full of brine. We must, therefore, go on half water rations immediately."

I felt as if I had been stolen from.

Others on board said as much. Podlaski immediately protested, "Four ounces twice a day? You've got to be joking! We can't live on that!"

"Would you rather run out before reaching Ireland and be without water altogether?" Browne said.

Once more there was murmuring from the lascar sailors. "Not even two swallows?"

"How can we manage on less than we are already?"

"How can this be?"

Podlaski echoed the accusing tone. "Mismanagement, that's what it is. We should never have sailed off into the unknown. We should have stayed near the sinking, where we could be found. Now we're lost and about to run out of water."

"Calm down, Mister Podlaski," Browne demanded. "We're going on short rations precisely because we don't want to run out. And we aren't lost."

"So you say," Podlaski retorted with a sneer. "Have we seen any sign of a ship or a plane or Ireland? We may be sailing toward Norway for all we know."

It was as if Podlaski poisoned the air with his doubts. I saw a cloud of resentment fall over the brown faces of the lascars. In the way they stared at us I recognized a common thought: *Women and children contribute nothing to rowing the lifeboat, yet they consume precious rations.* The crewmen would have a better chance of surviving this ordeal if they did not have us on board.

"Can't we at least have our full ration this once more?" Mariah asked. "We . . . it's very late for makin' this change, and we've been waitin' since noon already, so we have. Can't we start the new amount tomorrow?"

"I'm sorry, miss, but I'm afraid the answer's no. That extra half-day's ration might make the difference between . . . well, you understand."

When half a ship's biscuit and a glob of salmon reached Robert, he nibbled the salmon and licked up the juice. Then, holding the square of hard tack, he waited for the rest of the food to be distributed and the water to be passed out.

A half measure of water—four ounces—looks like almost nothing. Robert took a sip, then tried to gnaw a corner of the rock-hard biscuit. After three tries he handed me the hard tack. "Please keep this for me, Auntie," he said. "I'm not really that hungry now." Then he swallowed the water in one gulp and leaned back against me. Connor likewise handed me his bread ration "for safekeeping."

That night, for the first time since we had been adrift, there was no call for singing before bedtime.

Just as we had resigned ourselves to a miserable night in despairing silence, Matt

Wilson picked his way forward. Stepping carefully between sailors, he came and stood in our midst but addressed himself to the boys. "Buck up, lads," he said. "What's a shipwreck, anyway? Bit of adventure to tell your mates about when you get back to school, that's what. And what's half rations? Just a way to make the story that much better! Besides, don't you know the whole bloomin' navy's out lookin' for us? Why, they're bound to get here tomorrow. So cheer up. You tell your chums you was on half rations and see how that sounds. 'Course you needn't tell 'em it was just for one day, eh? Now I'm not one to lecture, but men, it's our duty to keep up the ladies' spirits, in'it? Now, where's our song, then?"

Obligingly, James roused up and began:

> *"I give you a toast, ladies and gentlemen*
> *I give you a toast, ladies and gentlemen.*
> *May this fair dear land we love so well*
> *In dignity and freedom dwell.*
> *Though worlds may change and go awry*
> *While is still one voice to cry."*

And then James croaked to a hoarse stop. He put his hand to his throat and rasped, "I'm sorry. I can't . . ."

At that moment Raquel's voice, always husky anyway, drifted out of the canvas shelter.

"There'll always be an England
While there's a country lane,
Wherever there's a cottage small
Beside a field of grain."

And so it went, adults and children, each offering what their voices could bear, with Connor tooting the penny whistle.

When we came to the final chorus, Wilson himself produced a rich baritone.

"There'll always be an England,
And England shall be free
If England means as much to you
As England means to me."[21]

The last notes hung on the nighttime air, which was already closing in damp and chilly around us. Wilson said with satisfaction evident in his voice, "There you are then. Well done, men. Well done."

We lapsed into silence as the waves lapped the hull of our fragile craft. I made my heart focus on hope. Gazing into the starry night I imagined sailing a stormy sea with Jesus asleep in the bow.

What use is there in the suffering of these little ones? I silently asked Him. *And what about the*

---

21 "There'll Always Be an England," English patriotic song

broken hearts of their parents? So You sail with us, Lord?

In the stirring of the breeze I thought I heard a whisper: *"Fear not. I am with you."*

We awoke already thirsty. It was still hours until the next offering of water. The lift given to our morale by Wilson's pep talk the evening before had long since evaporated. A morose stillness reigned.

Relinquishing his place at the tiller to Officer Browne, Wilson came forward again. "Got a trick to teach you," he said. With a jerk of his calloused fingers he grasped one of his shirt buttons and wrenched it free. It lay on his broad palm like a bit of gray shell when he extended it toward Connor.

"Go on, take it," he said.

"What for?" Connor returned.

"Put it in your mouth. Suck on it. It helps the moisture come. Your mouth won't be so dry that way, eh? Try it! It works."

Buttons popped off coats and shirts and into mouths.

"Careful not to swallow 'em," Wilson warned.

On my lap Robert fingered the fastenings of his cloak. "Mama wouldn't like for me to tear off a button," he said sadly.

Before I could debate it with him he brightened. Reaching inside his collar to pluck at a silver chain, Robert produced a small, round medallion depicting St. George slaying the dragon. "Do you think this would work?" he asked Wilson.

"The very thing," the sailor agreed. "Pop it right in there. Old Saint George would've done the same, was he wearin' a Saint Robert medal."

Officer Browne spoke from the stern. His words were also raspy and deeper than usual. "Wilson's gimmick is a good thing to know. Here's something else: you must not, under any circumstances, drink seawater. No matter how thirsty you get or how inviting it seems, don't do it! It will kill you."

The sail flapped listlessly against the mast. Browne ordered rowing to begin again, but Wilson asked for a five-minute reprieve. "Want my mornin' swim, Cap'n." Stripping to his shorts, he added, "Who'll join me today?"

John stood, removed a button from his mouth, and handed it to his brother. "I will," he said.

"Right-o! Good show. Three laps?"

"Three laps it is."

It was not a race, but there were comments made that young John showed better form than Wilson.

Angelique openly admired her champion, saying to Raquel, "See how strong he is." When the other girls teased her, the gypsy's eyes flashed, but she did not stop watching John's muscled back and strong shoulders.

When the men returned to Number 7, Wilson clasped John's hand. "That's the way." Then he addressed himself to Browne. "Now we're warmed up, Cap'n. How about if me and John here pull an oar apiece? Might make twenty miles before breakfast."

After that challenge all the men set about rowing with renewed vigor. The boat leapt forward like a horse out of the starting gate.

The hearty pace was maintained for about half an hour. Then the rowing returned to a more sedate rhythm. "Ho for Ireland," Wilson called. "Think I can almost see it from here."

I had lost track of what day it was. Wilson and John had just completed another swim, now reduced to a single lap around Number 7. They climbed back aboard, but no one spoke of being reenergized or ready to set a new rowing record.

The short rations and the small amount of water we were allowed were beginning to tell on all of us. My tongue felt glued to the roof of my mouth. When I spoke, my Teutonic accent was thicker than ever before.

The first indication there was anything wrong with one of the lascar crewmen was when he began talking loudly to himself. It was midmorning, a few hours before our next meal and water. Lifting his chin to the cloudless sky, the sailor raved, shook his fist, pointed at Officer Browne, then stood up and screamed at the children in an angry tone.

"What's he saying, Sanjay?" I said to one of the lascars.

"Off his head, miss," Sanjay returned. "Mahmood says the white people are getting more water than the brown-skinned."

"But he must see the same measure is used for each of us?"

"As I say, miss," Sanjay repeated, tapping his forehead with his index finger. Sanjay addressed Mahmood in their common language, then translated for me. "I told him to sit down and be quiet. He is scaring the children."

He's scaring me too, I thought.

Mahmood sat, but he was not quiet. He called out again and waved his arms.

"He says Mister Brown lied to him . . . lied to all of us," was the translation. Sanjay shrugged. "I don't know what he's talking about."

Mahmood bounced upright again, this time balancing one foot on the gunnels and rocking the boat.

"Sit down," Harold Browne ordered. "Immediately. Sanjay, tell that man to sit down."

Mahmood bared his teeth like an animal and howled something.

"He's been sneaking seawater," Sanjay reported. "It has addled his brain."

Then Mahmood leapt overboard and began swimming away from the boat.

"Out oars," Browne commanded. "After him."

The movement to lower the sail and ready the oars was very slow. Mahmood laughed to himself, a foolish giggle both shocking and unsettling.

"I'll fetch him, sir," Wilson offered and jumped back into the sea. With his powerful stroke he soon overtook the other man.

"Row, can't you?" Browne said. "You don't expect Wilson to tow him, do you?"

By this time Wilson had caught up with Mahmood. The two struggled in the water. Wilson pushed the lascar's head under and held it there. When he allowed Mahmood to surface again, the crewman was no longer struggling. Wilson held Mahmood firmly around the neck, keeping the man floating on his back, while the Cockney was treading water.

Number 7 pulled alongside. "Well done, Wilson," Browne praised.

"Good show, that," Barrett agreed.

"Should have let him go," Podlaski suggested, sounding as much like a vulture as he already looked with his stooped shoulders and bulging eyes.

Browne, Barrett, and John combined their strength to drag Mahmood back aboard. He lay in the bottom of the boat, looking dazed.

Leaving him there, Barrett and John turned their attention to assisting Wilson.

That's when Mahmood bounded upright and pushed both playwright and chorister over the edge, on top of Wilson, then plunged into the ocean again.

When the trio of men got untangled in the water, all three of them started out in pursuit of the lascar.

Connor was first to spot the fin. "Shark!" he cried. "Shark!"

A steel-gray blade sliced through the water. No more than twenty yards away, it looked as if it would pass between Mahmood and his pursuers.

Suddenly everyone was screaming at once. "Shark! Come back!"

James called out in fear to his brother. "John! John!"

"Row!" Browne shouted. "Pull hard!"

A tail shaped like a scythe slashed the surface well back from the fin.

It was a big shark.

The three Englishmen turned back toward the boat, while Mahmood continued swimming away.

"Big shark! Big, big shark," Mariah cried. "Lord, help them!"

Fin and tail disappeared. Where had he gone? Which way had he turned? Had all the yelling and the noise of the oars scared the animal off?

Mahmood jetted upright as if launched from beneath. As he fell over sideways, I screamed . . . because the lower half of his body was gripped in the jaws of the beast.

Blood spurted into the sea.

"Don't stop rowing!" Browne urged. "Get them in. Quickly, now. Hurry!"

Barrett was lifted into the boat first, followed by Wilson and then John.

Mahmood was nowhere to be seen, but a pool of crimson rose and fell on the swell.

Angelique fell into Raquel's arms. The girl was sobbing. "Tell him, no more swimming," she said. "No more!"

Fear and stunned disbelief were not the only emotions on Number 7.

One of Mahmood's friends said openly, "He should not have died. Fresh water would have saved him."

"Why should children get as much as we who must row?" another lascar griped.

"Belay that!" Wilson croaked. "He drank seawater, went crazy, and there's an end of it, got it?"

The hostile muttering was squelched . . . but not silenced.

21

We had given up keeping a lookout. After so many days at sea we no longer expected to be rescued. I prayed God would help us reach Ireland.

Ireland captured our imagination in the way I had sometimes thought about heaven before being on the *Newcastle.* Ireland came to represent peace and safety, with plenty to eat and drink. There would be no one trying to kill us there. A roof overhead. No more wind and cold. A warm fire to sit beside. A cup of tea.

A hot bath.

How I dreamt about a tub full of warm water. Once in such bliss I would not emerge for a whole day. Warm, fresh water was what I craved instead of cold, salty fluid that pickled my skin and turned my hands to sandpaper-coated claws. Even my teeth felt gritty with salt. My hair was plastered with salt into phantasmagorical shapes that no amount of patting and pushing could smooth.

Two of the lascars were in terrible shape. I don't know if they had also sampled the seawater like Mahmood, but they were barely alive. Their companions had to spoon their liquid ration into their mouths. They could not eat.

None of us had much appetite. The hard tack was like eating a brick. The canned fruits were too sticky sweet; the canned meats too salty. There was never enough water to wash it down properly.

But I knew I must eat, so I forced myself to swallow a morsel. My throat was so sore and constricted that it might be five minutes before I could attempt another bite.

Third Officer Browne's cheeks were blotchy with sores. His lips were swollen and crusted.

Raquel and Mariah, who had been dividing their rations with the children, were shrunken. Mariah looked especially gaunt, with her eyes sunken in her head.

The children were listless but remained healthier than the adults. Only one of us seemed as hale as ever: Matt Wilson. Though he no longer attempted his daily swim, he still engaged the children in games.

"What's good about being out here on this lifeboat? C'mon, think. Must be some good things, eh?"

Connor lifted his head wearily. "It's an . . . adventure."

"There you go! Right as ever, Connor, my lad. What else?"

"No schoolwork," John contributed.

"No piano lessons," Tomas said.

"No sirens," Simcha offered. "No bombs."

"That's it, in'it?" Wilson agreed. "Had our dose of war, but now seems like we're through with it. Rock along here, being floated to Ireland."

Podlaski shook his head, too exhausted and spent to produce a negative thought.

"Just you remember," Wilson added. "We might see Ireland today or tomorrow, but soon anyways. Soon. Don't forget that."

"What does Ireland look like?" Yael asked.

Raquel petted the girl's hair. "You already know the answer to that, darling. Auntie Mariah told us. Ireland is wet and green and smells of peat smoke and baking soda bread."

"Oh," the child responded. "Then that can't be Ireland, can it?"

No one moved for a time. I worried Yael might be delusional. I knew there was nothing to be seen on the whole expanse of ocean except more and more water.

Cedric Barrett raised bloodshot eyes. "There is something . . . there. I think. Coming out of that fog bank."

Wilson swept Yael up in his arms and stood towering in the boat like a slightly misplaced figurehead. "Starboard bow, Cap'n," he said to Browne. "Give us 30 degrees to starboard."

It was a ship, and from its shape it was heading directly for us.

From almost complete lethargy Number 7 changed in an instant to a hive of activity. "Wilson," Browne ordered, "get the flare pistol and ready a smoke canister. The rest of you: get ready to signal with whatever you can."

"Couldn't be a German again, could it?" Tomas worried.

"Never you mind that," Wilson corrected. "We're too close in to the Western Approaches now. Airplanes'd spot 'em and plaster 'em good. No, this can't be no Heinie this time."

The shape of our deliverer grew larger and noticeably nearer as it emerged from the wall of mist. "I think they've seen us," Barrett said with excitement. "I'm sure of it."

"Are we rescued, Aunt Elisa?" Robert said.

"What are you waiting for, Browne?" Podlaski demanded. "Shoot the flare! Shoot it now!"

The oncoming ship began a slow turn to its left, presenting its flank to us.

"Slowing to rig out boats to come for us," John said to Angelique. "It won't be long now."

The freighter rolled there on the swell, regarding us from a distance. Then there was an eruption of white water at its stern as the propellers revolved forcefully. The stack belched gray smoke, the ship lunged into motion . . . and turned away from us.

"No!" James shouted. "Come back! Don't leave!"

"Don't worry," Wilson comforted. "Just their normal zig-zag course, like. You'll see. That's the zig. Next time, when they zag, they'll be headed right for us."

But he was wrong.

When the ship made its next maneuver, it turned still farther away and began to diminish in size.

"Don't wait, man," Podlaski scolded. "Fire the flare!"

There was a loud pop that made Yael and Simcha cover their ears, and a rocket streaked upward. It burst high overhead and hung there, a bright orange ball of fire drifting slowly back downward.

"Pop the smoke too," Browne ordered Wilson.

Wilson pulled the ring and tossed the device overboard. The canister floated on the gentle swell, puffing out a cloud of vapor that drifted away from us toward the departing ship. "They can see it. They must be able to see it," I said.

Then the freighter was gone, and they weren't returning.

"It's your fault," Podlaski said, accusing Browne. "You waited too long." He buried his face in his hands.

There was the low hum of angry muttering among the lascars.

"What do you say, Wilson?" Browne asked. "I think they saw us. I think they deliberately turned away. But why?"

"It's like this, see, sir. Me brother's in the merchant marine. He says them Nazis, well, sometimes they put out a lifeboat as a decoy. Then the U-boat hangs around, waitin' to pounce on whoever motors up all unsuspecting."

Browne scrubbed the stubble of his beard with ragged fingernails. "That must be it. What else could it mean?"

"But that's still all right, in'it?" Wilson consoled. "They'll still call in this position, so's somebody will check us out. An airplane, most like. Why, we could have a plane here quick as bob's your uncle, eh?"

Then the breeze shifted, bringing the fog bank over us, swallowing us up as thoroughly as if we were buried alive. We never did hear a plane pass by overhead, but it would not have mattered. They could never have seen us anyway.

That night Matt Wilson came forward again, picking his way over grousing sailors and groaning boys. He arrived just as Robert sobbed with hunger and aches in his legs.

"What's this?" Wilson demanded. "Sniffling? Don't you know real heroes never snivel?" Then gathering all the children with his words, he elaborated. "Don't you know you're all the heroes of a real-life adventure? So what if that ship turned away today? Don't you realize what it means? We're in the shipping lanes now. Tomorrow we'll be found or we'll run across another ship or we'll reach Ireland and save ourselves. But turn it any way you like, there's no cause for sniveling, is there? Buck up, mates. We're writing a grand tale here. Don't muck it up here at the end."

The sky darkened and the breeze increased. It blew out of the east, so once again was no assistance in our voyage. We could not sail against the wind. The waves mounted one upon another, as if an unseen hand heaped them together and dashed them against us.

The sea had been so calm, the motion so steady, that we had forgotten what it was to be seasick. The hideous, corkscrew motion of the boat removed the delusion that we could not get sick. It was worse with nothing in our stomachs. Poor Robert retched until he almost choked and gasped for air. I patted his back and tried to console him, but he turned yellow and then green. His head lolled on his shoulders as if it might fall off at the next thundering roller.

Mariah crossed herself and called to me: "Pray! Pray to the Lord who calmed the sea!"

My prayer was only a single word: "Jesus! Jesus!"

We were soaked through, and the boat required constant bailing.

"Row!" Browne commanded. "Keep her head into the waves or we'll capsize. And the rest of you: bail! Use your hands, your shoes!"

With almost no reserve of energy, pulling an oar to keep Number 7 from turning broadside to the waves or lifting a pail to dump over the gunnels seemed nearly impossible. Despite the urging of Officer Browne and the encouragement of Matt Wilson, I had no strength to do either.

Then it began to blow still harder—a gale-force wind.

I think I almost gave up at that moment. A complete sense of the utter futility of fighting wind and wave and hunger and thirst and exhaustion overwhelmed me as never before. If I could just go to sleep—permanently, I thought— then all those pains and aches and fears would be eliminated.

Wilson's voice roused me from my despair. "What's the matter with all of you? Don't you realize it's about to rain? Fresh water, free for the taking, lads. Loosen the sail, John. That's it. You and James hold up the sides. Form it into a channel. Peter, Tomas, get all the empty milk tins, peach cans . . . whatever you can find. Hold them beneath the spout. Don't waste a drop."

Our faces turned upward in expectation. We were starving baby birds in this nest of a lifeboat, waiting for the moisture that would sustain our lives. Mariah raised her eyes heavenward. I saw her lips form the words, "Thank you."

The rain came, slashing violently into mouths and filling the gully in the sail.

I swallowed convulsively, gulping the bounty from the storm, helping Robert do the same, and Connor. Robert lapped from my cupped palm, greedily.

Around Raquel her girls wiped their cheeks, caught drops in their mouths, and laughed.

Just as abruptly as it began, the squall passed.

"There now," Wilson said. "How many tins did we fill?"

"A dozen," John reported. "An extra ration all around."

"That's the way, boy! That's the proper spirit. Hand me one. I was too busy bailing to drink, but I'll take my share now."

Weary half smiles watched the progress of a can of miraculously delivered water as it passed from Peter's hand to his brother's to Wilson's. Expectant eyes were fastened to the sailor's face as he tipped it up.

What happened next caused a convulsive shudder to pass through all of us that had nothing to do with the movement of the sea.

He spat it out and scrubbed his mouth with the back of his hand. "Brine," he said flatly. "Salt trapped in the sail from the spray. Don't drink it," he warned Mariah, who had a pineapple tin halfway to her lips.

The disappointment was crushing.

For once it took Wilson a long time to find the silver lining. At last he said slowly, "Next time it'll be better. Washed the salt loose so with the next squall we can drink all we can catch. Wait and see."

But there was no further rain that evening. Squalls of rain pattered to left and right and behind us, but no more fell on Number 7. We had no strength available to paddle into one of the cloudbursts.

The wind died and the sea calmed. There was even a small breeze out of the west behind the storm. And everything aboard Number 7 went back to what it had been before . . . dismal and nearly hopeless.

Robert's eyes were only half open and the portion that showed was glazed. He stared into the distance at something only he could see. He could not chew even the softest food and had stopped eating altogether. I forced him to swallow a tablespoon of canned milk and drink his water ration, but that was all I could get down him.

As the afternoon wore on, he began to rave. "Mama, I promise I'll be good. Don't punish me anymore, Mama. Whatever I did, I won't do it again, I promise. Please, Mama, please. Can't I have something to drink? Please?"

It broke my heart to hear him. I hugged him and rocked him. Connor, so weak himself he could no longer stand, tried to help. He sang to Robert until he was hoarse and he couldn't be heard above the flapping of the sail.

The sun cast lengthening shadows from the rigging. Black tangles formed by the cables' shades lay across Robert as if tying him down.

He plucked feebly at the dark lines. "Why am I tied up? Why are you making me stay here? What are these bars for? What did I do?"

Matt Wilson came in response to the whimpering. Though he still looked muscled and hardy, the grizzled sailor staggered as he stepped across the thwarts. He put out a hand and caught the mast to keep from falling. It worried me to see him affected in any way. He was the rock of encouragement for all of us. How could we go on if he failed?

"What's this, then? Why are you moanin' and carryin' on?" Somehow Wilson's voice broke through the boy's stupor.

"My throat hurts and my feet hurt and I want to go home."

"And so we will! But real heroes don't whine, do they?"

"I don't want to be a hero," Robert protested. "Please, I want some water."

"Couple hours yet," Wilson returned, squinting at the sun's height.

Robert blubbered silently into my chest. He had no moisture left to make tears, and his mouth left streaks of salt on my blouse.

"Please," Connor pleaded, "can't he have his water early, just this once? I'm . . . I'm afraid."

I shook myself and raised my head. "Connor is right. Robert needs water, and he needs it now. If we wait, he may be . . . it may do him no good."

Wilson fixed his gaze on mine and studied me, then nodded curtly. He went back to the stern and had a whispered conference with Browne.

I saw Podlaski interrupt. I saw Barrett threaten the diplomat with a clenched fist.

Browne shook his head. Wilson persisted.

Eventually Browne relented. "Listen, everyone," the officer said. Exhaustion was evident in the way he spoke. Every few words he needed to marshal his strength before uttering the next phrase. "I am ordering . . . one extra measure . . . of water . . . for the boy. Not trying to . . . hide it. No one else . . . so don't ask."

The angry buzz of protests started at once among the native sailors.

"What about Farouk?"

"Farouk? What about me?"

"English officer for English boy . . . not for lascar."

"Wasted. Boy will die soon any—"

"Belay that talk," Wilson warned. "Clap a stopper over it before I do it for you, see?"

Wilson returned to where we sat with the water—four ounces of precious, life-giving fluid.

Robert sucked it down, then held the measuring

tube upright over his mouth to catch one more clinging drip. "Thank . . . you," he said. "I'll do my best not to whine."

"I know you will, son," Wilson agreed. "Maybe Missus Murphy there will rub your feet and legs for you. Would you like that?"

"Oh, yes, please."

I put out my hand and touched Wilson's arm. "Thank you. I mean it . . . thank you."

"Never mind," he replied. "What it's all about, in'it?"

22

We rocked along on the bosom of the ocean. It was hours since the last water ration and hours still to the next. Two of the lascars were near death. Robert, despite the extra share, lay limp beside me.

A morbid image came into my head, and I could not dispel it. What if we all died? Would Number 7 sail along, a floating hearse, until it eventually bumped into land or a ship? When our desiccated bodies were discovered, would anyone say, "We should have looked harder. We should not have given up so soon."

Or would our fate be ascribed to the tragedies of war: *Dear Sir, we regret to inform you . . . ?*

I had left the *Newcastle* with nothing but what I was wearing. My mind reviewed how many times in my life I had been reduced to starting over. Leaving Germany, leaving Austria, bombed out of London, and now sunk. *Oh, Murphy,* I thought. *I was such a bad investment for you, wasn't I?*

Was there some reason I was reviewing this Shakespearian tragedy of endless woe? What had I been trying to determine?

Finally it came back to me. Was there anything aboard on which I could write a few words so Murphy and my children would know I had been thinking of them? I wondered if Officer Browne would let me scribble a note inside the *Book of Common Prayer. Poetic touch, that,* I thought. *Like something you would read in a novel. It would never happen in real life.*

I resolved to ask him . . . later. The very idea of transforming thoughts into words on paper was just too much effort for now. No one seemed to have any energy left at all. The lascars lay on their oars. The rigging clanged idly against the mast. No one wanted to sing or tell stories or compare likes and dislikes. Each of us retreated further into private shells of misery.

The exceptions were Simcha and Yael. The two young gypsy girls talked softly together in the bow of the boat. They lay in the creases between the canvas awning and the gunnels, one on one side of the prow and one on the other.

"Should we say anything?" I overheard Yael ask her sister.

"I don't think so. Remember how unhappy it made everyone when you saw that ship and then it didn't stop for us? Remember? Let's watch awhile longer and then maybe . . . maybe we'll tell Raquel."

"All right," Yael returned glumly. "I don't want to get in trouble. But won't getting to Ireland be a good thing? They have water there, don't they?"

Dreaming or hallucinating, I wondered. The longer we were adrift, the thinner the line between imagination and madness.

Leaning my head back I stared up into fleecy clouds in an azure sky. When the weather was foul, we feared Number 7 would swamp or overturn or be blown so far from land we'd never get home again.

On days like today, when scarcely a breath of wind rippled the dark green sea it was fair weather that was our foe. We had no strength to row. If God did not send a breeze or a boat, we would languish here forever . . . and never get home again.

It seemed a dilemma without a solution, or perhaps my brain was too fuzzy to put coherent thoughts together.

A dark shadow swooped over my vision, then another. Was I going blind or was I hallucinating? Which was preferable? Crazy people don't know they're crazy, do they?

Another blurry something swept overhead. This time it added a pair of screeches.

Seagulls. So as yet I was neither blind nor delusional. That was comforting.

"Gulls," Barrett remarked. "Seagulls. Isn't it true . . . don't people say . . . I've heard . . ."

What was the poor man trying to convey? I wished he'd hurry and finish the sentence.

Matt Wilson took over for him. "Gulls never go far out from land. If they found us, then we must be closer to land than we think."

"That's what Yael and I wanted to tell you," Simcha said, rising up from her perch. "Is that maybe Ireland over there?"

All who could be roused peered up at the birds still soaring above our mast and then into the distance.

"Fog bank," Podlaski said, folding his arms across his chest and sitting back down with a thump.

Barrett ignored him. "What do you say, Browne? Wilson? Could it be land?"

"Watch," Browne replied.

Ahead of us, almost at the limit of our vision, lay a gray wall. A shaft of sun jetted down from behind a cloud, highlighting steel-colored cliffs and the darker outline of a canyon.

"Connemara?" Mariah wondered. "Donegal? Sure, I can't tell. Me eyes are so fuzzy, so they are."

"Maybe," James offered. "Maybe it's . . . Scotland? Maybe we sailed past the northern end of Ireland. That would explain why it's taken so long."

Wilson stared ahead. "What do you think, Connor, lad? And you, John? You've got good glims. What do you see?"

"I think," Connor said, "I think I see smoke.

324

Could it be from houses or a factory . . . or maybe ships in the bay?"

Excitement increasing, John said, "That looks like the entrance to a bay, right enough! And beyond it. See that lighter line just where the land and sea meet? Couldn't that be a beach?"

"I think I see houses?" James added. "Two-story houses painted white."

"If it's a bay then . . . there'll be ships . . . coming and going," Browne said. "Look sharp. When we see one we'll . . . pop another flare . . . to get his attention."

The current carried us past the mouth of the bay. The headlands rose steep on either side. Any moment now the view into the depth of the harbor would open. Then certainly we'd see ships and houses and rescue.

It was taking a long time to sail across the entrance. I saw what Connor noticed: spirals of vapor rising above the hills.

Then another helpful beam of sunlight darted ahead of us. It glinted against the canyon walls with painful brilliance and shone into the recesses of the harbor to reveal . . . nothing.

The fog bank rose from the horizon as if it had merely been resting there. In the space of a minute harbor, town, homes, factories, ships, food, a cool, refreshing drink, rescue . . . all disappeared. The curtain rolled back to reveal a perfectly flat, unblemished ocean . . . and nothing else.

• • •

I was awakened by someone plucking at my elbow. In my stupor I thought I was back at the Savoy. "Murphy," I murmured drowsily.

When the touch persisted I tried to brush it away.

Fingers gripped my arm and squeezed. A voice hissed in my ear: "Listen! You must wake up."

It was the lascar sailor, Sanjay.

"What? What is it?"

He clamped his palm across my mouth and shushed me, holding my neck so I could neither twist away nor cry out. "I must tell you," he said urgently. "The others. Haji. They plan—"

He never completed the warning. There was a cry of rage behind Sanjay and a whistling sound. Something hit Sanjay in the back of the head and he fell across me, pinning Robert and me against Number 7's rail.

From the other end of the boat came a despairing groan of pain and then a thrashing splash as someone was launched overboard.

"Strike, my brothers," the lascar known as Haji shouted. "Strike now! All the food and water for us. No one will ever know."

The attack was timed to fall just before dawn, when the men standing watch were at their lowest ebb.

By the faint light of predawn I saw three natives wrestling in the stern with Officer Browne. One of them swung a hand axe at Browne's face. It was the cramped space that saved him, because two of the attackers were in the way of the blows aimed by the third.

Two more of the lascar sailors were slumped on their bench, taking no part in the struggle.

Then my attention forcibly returned to my own peril. Haji raised an oar to club at my head. "Kill and throw the Christians out!" he yelled.

Unable to move, I watched in horror as the paddle began its descent.

"No!" Peter cried, popping up alongside me. He lifted both arms to ward off the blow. Haji shrieked with rage. The blade of the oar glanced off Peter's outstretched hands. Though he managed to deflect it from me, the heavy wooden club hit Peter in the forehead, and he dropped across Mariah.

Drawing back the paddle for another blow, Haji jabbed it at me like a lance. As I hunched my shoulders and tried to roll aside to shelter Robert, Haji thrust the oar into my ribs.

I cried out with pain as something cracked. My vision swam, and I struggled to remain conscious.

James from one side and John from the other flung themselves on Haji. As James wrestled with the lascar for possession of the oar, his brother slammed a fist into Haji's face. The native staggered backward, losing his grip on the weapon.

Suddenly I could again see the battle going on at the stern. While Podlaski shrank away in terror, Barrett grappled with one of the attackers while Browne faced off against two more.

Where was Matt Wilson? Why wasn't the sailor, the strongest, fittest man aboard, helping us?

The native wielding the hatchet raised it to strike. Seeing the danger to Browne, Barrett shoved his opponent into the others. The blow of the axe landed, but it fell on the neck of a lascar and not on Browne. The wounded man screeched and threw himself out of the boat.

John had the oar now. Sweeping it around him with a flat swing, he struck Haji in the side. The native retreated, stumbling over his unconscious comrades.

Browne struggled with the pocket of his jacket, while dodging more blows of the axe. Browne and Barrett faced off against two remaining opponents.

Where was Wilson?

Browne had a gun. He produced a small revolver from inside his watch coat and threatened the native assailants with it. "Drop your weapons and sit down!" he ordered.

As John tried again to strike Haji with the paddle, I watched the lascar wave a knife. It flashed menacingly in the pale light. Haji ducked another blow of the oar, then lunged with the blade aimed at John's arm.

The echoing boom of a gunshot shattered the air.

The bullet hit Haji behind the right ear. With his dying leap he fell headfirst into Raquel, who was shielding her girls and Connor.

I could not maintain consciousness any longer.

As blackness swirled in front of my eyes, I heard Browne respond to a question from Barrett. "Sanjay's dead. So are Haji and the one in the water. Missus Murphy and Peter are wounded." As his voice faded away, I heard him add, "Wilson's dead too. They killed him first."

There were more stars shimmering in the sky than I knew existed. I thought how strange it was that on my last night alive heaven seemed closer to me than earth.

I knew the peace of surrender. My spirit was letting go of my body. I was slipping away, and I knew it. I hardly knew if I was still breathing or merely floating above the human misery of Number 7.

Then I moved and gasped. Pain in my rib cage was a reminder that I lived on.

Peter lay exhausted and bruised at my feet. His bandaged brow oozed a dark spot of blood. Did he have a concussion? My ribs screamed agony when I drew a breath. I was certain from the intensity of the pain they had been cracked by the blow of the lascar's oar.

I searched the horizon for the bright constellation of Orion. Peter had once told me that he thought Orion marked the location of heaven. I wondered if we would soon know whether his guess was correct.

Barrett sat at rigid attention between us and the lascars. Barrett's silhouette blocked my view of the surly band of mutineers. I wondered, without compassion, if the men who tried to murder us were also suffering from their wounds. Would they survive long enough to be tried and hanged for what they had done? I hoped Browne would give their share of the water to the children come morning.

As if Barrett heard my thoughts, he turned and looked at me. "Are you all right, Elisa?"

Even speaking caused a dagger of white-hot pain to surge through my left lung. "Okay," I gasped.

The playwright said, "You need a doctor."

I was unable to reply that all I really needed was a cool drink of water and a solid place to lie down.

Mariah answered bitterly, "Too right we need a doctor. The wog broke her ribs with that oar."

I tried to reply but my breath caught. "Oh!"

Barrett's face was close to mine. For the first time I could see his left eye was swollen shut. Blood matted his hair. "You'll live, Elisa Murphy. If any of us in this boat manages to survive, you will be among them."

I did not know why Barrett singled me out for such a prophecy. I only shook my head and fixed my gaze upon Orion.

Raquel sighed. "We have all lived through too much to die."

Barrett cleared his throat. "Yes. Tough. You ladies are tougher than I. That's certain. Elisa? You, Raquel. Your kids. You must live. I pray you will live. However, I don't think that I . . . will. Live, I mean."

I thought of Murphy and wondered if, after two long weeks, he had given me up for dead. If he was awake, did he look at the same stars and wonder how I liked heaven? Would he ever know what had happened to those of us in Lifeboat Number 7? Would he sense the moment I breathed my last?

Barrett reached into his inside coat pocket and pulled out an oilskin-wrapped package. "Here, Elisa. You keep it. That poor little girl. Lindy. You must live, Elisa. You were last to see Lindy alive. Here is her journal. She had a premonition, you see. She wrote a last letter to her mother. You must survive to carry the message home. In person. You must place Lindy's account—all that remains of the dear girl's life—into the hands of her grieving mum." He pressed Lindy's journal into my hands. "That is why you must live, Elisa."

My fingers clamped around the dead girl's last

testament. I resented the responsibility Barrett had given me. Another reason to try, to go on.

I nodded and managed to whisper thanks to Barrett. I would do my best to survive, I promised. I would do my best to be the angel messenger returning Lindy's last words home to her grieving mother.

The boat rocked. I could see around Barrett for a moment. Our enemies were heaped upon one another in exhaustion as Browne, wide awake, sat erect in the stern with the revolver in his hand. His was the first watch, guarding the mutineers.

I wondered if it mattered now. Perhaps by this time tomorrow many more of us would be dead.

From the shadows little Connor said quietly, "One more day. If we can hold on, one more day."

Mariah whispered agreement, "Maybe tomorrow. The gulls. We saw the gulls."

I prayed silently, *One more day, God. Help us hold on. Only one more, and then? What will You do? God, what will You do for us . . . tomorrow?*

The sail hung limply from the rigging. A cross sea slapped the boat's hull, reprising the twelve-count *petenera*, but giving our journey neither impetus nor direction.

How many days had we been adrift in Lifeboat Number 7?

I could no longer remember, nor did it seem important.

Despite our reduced numbers—only seventeen people remained alive—last night we had run out of water. For two days prior we had eked out a barely continued existence on four ounces of water supplemented by any drinkable fluid. Now the canned milk was gone. Likewise exhausted was all the syrup from the juice cans.

Scraping the bottom of the water tank with the dipper produced flakes of damp rust.

Cedric Barrett tried to swallow the oil in which the sardines were packed. It made him violently ill and left him thirstier than before.

No one else made the attempt.

There were only two surviving lascars. They had both been mutineers, so were supposed to be under arrest and guarded day and night by Barrett or Browne.

Even that no longer seemed to matter. Number 7 was full of bodies either sprawling like cast-aside rag dolls or curled into tight balls of misery.

The overcast day admitted very little light and no hope.

Idly, I thought of my desire to write of my love and prayers for Murphy and my children. It might have been possible two days earlier. Now it was not. Even if I could muster the will to make the attempt, I doubted if my fingers would hold the pencil.

I hoped my precious children would have someone to love them and cherish them and tell them stories about me from happier times. My mother would do that for me, I knew.

A vision of Lindy's mother came to me. I saw her sitting at a table, staring out a window across the rolling East Sussex hills. How long would it take before she no longer jumped up at every knock on the door? How many tears would flow before she stopped punishing herself for having put Lindy on the transport ship?

I had doubly failed Lindy's mother: I had not protected her child, and I had not survived to carry Lindy's love home. At least I would die and be released from my guilt.

I would see Lindy soon enough; of that I was certain, and I knew she would forgive me.

When I put on my hundred-year glasses I knew Lindy's mother would also forgive me. So would Murphy and Katie and Louis and Charles. When we met in heaven, they would all forgive me for not coming home as I had promised.

There was a roaring in my ears when there was no wind. Was it the sign of my approaching death? Whether my last breath came during this gray, fog-shrouded half light or during the blackness of night, that did not seem to matter either.

"A plane," Connor's tiny voice croaked. He sounded like the bleating of a newborn lamb.

The roaring increased.

John roused himself from where he lay against

his brother's shoulder. Through swollen, cracked lips he slurred, "He might be right."

James waved feebly at the veil of vapor overhead. "Never see us . . . anyway."

This final taunting angered me. Ships had turned away, whales had offered pretend rescue, fog banks had mimicked safety . . . now this?

"Jesus," I said. "Help."

Engine sounds roared past overhead. The airplane sounded close enough to touch, certainly close enough for us to be seen.

Another craft motored past us. We might as well have already been in a watery grave instead of buoyed upon it.

Tomas sponged his brother's forehead with a brine-dampened rag. "Whole flight . . . of them. Wish we could . . . shout."

Connor stood on unsteady, quaking legs. "I'm going . . . I'm going to climb the mast."

Hallucinating for certain. The child had no strength with which to climb. Even if he did, what good would it do?

Or what harm? Anyway, I had no energy with which to stop him.

Hand over hand, Connor managed it. Halfway up the mast he missed a grip and almost fell. His tin whistle dropped from his pocket, bounced on the railing, and splashed into the sea.

I watched him climb, certain his body would likewise plunge into the ocean.

While I lay there, looking up, something astonishing happened. It was as if the edge of an unseen hand sliced downward through the clouds and swept a portion of them aside. As cleanly as the bow of my violin sawed across the strings, that precise a gap appeared in the fog.

I stared into clear blue sky . . . in time to witness a floatplane with British markings fly past and leave us behind.

"Flare," Browne said, lunging to his feet and falling over Podlaski. "Flare!"

Connor reached the top of the mast. "Another one's . . . coming."

Barrett fumbled with a smoke canister. The igniting ring broke off in his hand.

Browne snapped open the breach of the flare gun but could not locate the shells.

The drone of the flight of planes was diminishing. A last lone member of the group appeared behind the others. In seconds it too would be gone.

Reaching inside his jacket Connor drew out the pocket handkerchief he had offered his mother at the train station. Clinging to the swaying mast with one hand, Connor waved the small scrap of white. "Down here. Look here. We're here."

The plane was already beyond us. I groaned as I realized the pilot could no longer see us. The twelve-count rhythm of the waves was fully victorious at last.

Connor continued to signal valiantly. I did not have the heart to tell him he was wasting what little strength he still possessed.

And then the note sung by the floatplane's engines changed.

"Sunderland flying boat," James offered to no one in particular.

The machine, which had dwindled to a black speck, began to grow larger again. "Seen us!" Connor said triumphantly.

He was right.

Within minutes a rubber life raft was dumped from the plane. It plunged into the sea near us and when it bobbed up again, Browne, Barrett, and John paddled Number 7 toward it.

Lashed to the raft was a supply of food, which we could not use, and five one-gallon jugs of water.

There was also a handwritten note: *Have called for help. Will circle until they arrive to direct them to you. Don't worry. If fog closes in, I will land near you. Thank whoever signaled us. Navigator spotted it at the last second.*

Within an hour a sardine fishing boat out of Galway steamed alongside us. It took another hour for the crewmen to carefully hoist us aboard and lay us amid their nets.

Only Connor was able to climb from Number 7 into the trawler under his own power.

Three hours later we sailed past the Aran Islands and into Galway Bay.

We had been twenty miles from Ireland when we were rescued.

Connor—and his mother's pocket handkerchief—had saved us.

23

Some days after our rescue I awakened in the bedroom of a white-plastered, two-room, thatched-roof cottage overlooking Galway Bay. The local doctor, Ignatius O'Toole, stood over me with a look of satisfaction on his ruddy face.

"Well done. Ye'll live," he pronounced.

Murphy was at my side. He had hitched a ride from England on a military cargo plane when news of our rescue came over the wire at the TENS office.

He received instructions for my care from the physician, who was grateful to hand me off to another and hurry to deliver a baby. Murphy and I were alone. I spoke for the first time in days as tears brimmed in his eyes. "The children?" I managed.

Murphy took my hand. He replied, knowing completely which children I meant. "You did good, my darling. Except for Patsy's two little ones lost in the beginning, all the kids on Number 7 are alive and well."

"Where?"

"Staying with local families."

"Will they go home again? to England?" I

thought of those who would never return to their waiting loved ones. Lindy's notebook was on the lamp table beside my bed.

"We're arranging transport for the kids. Back to their families in England. Elisa . . ." He kissed my fingertips. "It may be awhile before we're able to get back to the U.S."

"They've shut down the evacuation?"

"Several merchant ships have been sunk this week. Too dangerous for kids to cross to America. And Elisa, too dangerous for you to try again."

I closed my eyes as warm tears spilled out. I silently prayed for strength. I thanked God our own babies had made it across the Atlantic before the deadly German U-boat attacks had been ramped up. "Okay, Murphy. Your mother and father . . . I can't think of a better place for our children. Stiff upper lip?"

"There's my girl. We'll do what we can over here."

"The others?"

"Mariah has taken Raquel and her girls home to her father's farm."

"Poor man. Mariah was so worried about him. Losing Patsy and the little ones. I never saw such a courageous woman as Mariah."

"Officer Browne told me. He says a woman is like the makings of a cuppa tea. You never know how strong she'll be 'til she's in hot water. Seems he's developed a liking for Irish tea. He tells me he has fallen in love with Mariah."

I smiled faintly. "And she with him. A good man. We wouldn't have made it without him."

"There'll be an Irish wedding to celebrate, come St. Bride's Day, I think."

The healing of my broken ribs was slow. The recurring nightmares of our ordeal receded day by day as Murphy held me in the night and kept me on a steady emotional keel. Weeks passed too quickly. Autumn turned to winter. I had come to love the peace of Ireland. For the first time in years, I forgot about the war.

News about England's fate and the Blitz and the widely expected Nazi invasion trickled in days after the events. The protective flock of RAF pilots finally pushed back the assault of the German Luftwaffe, ending the Blitz for the time being. Churchill declared to the world on the wireless, "Never have so many owed so much to so few."

In distant lands far to the south, the British army carried on the battle alone against the Nazis. Three times a week, Murphy traipsed the mile into the village for news and mail. He always returned with the question of the Irish on his lips, "When will the Yanks come into this thing? I wonder."

The U.S. remained neutral. Convoys bearing

food and supplies from America braved the dangers of the Atlantic. Many merchant ships were sunk in the crossing. Such information brought the fresh terror of nightmares to me, so Murphy stopped telling me what he heard in the village. We concentrated on being together in a way we had never experienced in our marriage before. It was almost a honeymoon. Hours were filled with long walks, good books, and making love without fear of being interrupted by an air raid siren or bomb exploding.

The cold rains of early December sluiced off the roof as Murphy and I warmed ourselves beside the peat fire. The doctor arrived for my final checkup, carrying a London newspaper. The front page displayed photos of the reunions of the children of Lifeboat Number 7 with their families in England.

I sat silently gazing at the images for a time, loving the small heroes who waved and smiled at the crowds who gathered to welcome them home. No one would ever really know what these young champions had endured. I also knew well that many mothers and fathers who had lost their children on the *Newcastle* looked at those same photos with wistful longing.

I thumbed through Lindy's notebook and realized the time to return to England and to the war had come. When I raised my eyes, Murphy was studying me tenderly.

"Those kids," he said slowly. "Little Connor. The rest. They are some strong tea, huh?"

"It was some hot water."

"Ready to go back to the kettle?"

I squared my shoulders and nodded. "Yes. Ready."

May the LORD give strength to His people!
May the Lord bless His people with peace!
PSALM 29:11 ESV

VIENNA, AUSTRIA
MARCH 14, 1938

Austria is no more. The German army is at the border and will march into this beautiful little nation to devour it. Murphy has come back here to my flat for me. I scribble this final note in haste. When Leah comes we must leave Vienna quickly.

Murphy says my name is on a list with the Gestapo, and they will come knocking on my door. No matter that I am married to an American. They know I have been aiding Jewish children to escape from Germany. Murphy says he will not leave me. He is my safety and protector.

I play the Guarnarius one last time for Austria, for my lost father, and for Murphy.

I ask him, "It's all over, isn't it? Like the night we left Berlin?"

Murphy answers with a nod. I see his compassion for me reflected in his eyes. "I'm so sorry, Elisa."

"I have been running my whole life. When will it end?"

"When the Jews have their own homeland. When Jerusalem is the capital of reborn Israel. Isn't that what your friends are working for?"

"Leah? Yes. And why Rudy was murdered. Oh, Murphy! I pray that day will come."

I am happy now that I wear Murphy's lapis wedding band on my finger. I grieve for all those of Jewish heritage who have no plan, no place to run.

The wind is howling outside, like the night my father left the Reich in a plane. Murphy tells me again the story of my father's escape from Berlin. How Papa bravely climbed into the tiny biplane and, against all odds, flew against the wind into the night. The storm raged around him, and he vanished.

I pray now for Papa. And for Mama. How she must long for him.

I am weary. Murphy's arm is around me, and I lean against him. I know that if I am arrested and these are the last words I write, he will carry my story out to the West.

I hear footsteps now. Heavy on the stairs. Too heavy for Leah. Have the Nazis come for me?

I hear a man cough in the corridor. Murphy stands suddenly. His fists are clenched.

I hear my name! "Elisa?" Is that my father's voice calling to me?

Murphy goes to the door and peers through

the peephole into the hallway. He gasps and throws the door wide. "Theo! Theo! It's you!"

My father asks, "Where is Elisa? Where? I've come so far. Escaped. Where is my daughter? They are coming now! The Nazis will swallow Austria whole by tomorrow! Is Elisa here? We must hurry!"

ON THE TRAIN TO KITZBÜHEL
LATE NIGHT

Leah and Shimon rang as we were leaving for the terminal. She says they have tickets and will cross into Switzerland and meet me in Innsbruck within the week.

Papa is asleep on the bed in our compartment. I watch him and wonder if he will be strong enough for the journey over the mountains. Murphy sits like a sentinel in front of the door.

The chance of escape is past, I think. The Western nations have allowed evil to gain a foothold. England is silent tonight as Austria crumbles. Murphy says there will be a war. The only real refuge will be America, so we must set our hopes on that distant shore. "You're a strong woman, Elisa," Murphy says. "Like strong tea, huh? You never know how strong until you're in hot water."

I tell him this is a compliment I hope to live up

to. Only I am ready to climb out of the hot water.

He laughs and I laugh with him. Strange to be able to laugh at such a moment.

Tonight I know there is no time to think of what might have been. Though I see now that Murphy looks at me with longing, how can I speak of my love to him? I know what I feel is far more than gratitude. I love him, but outside the window the world descends into deep and terrible darkness. Will there come a time for love again? I pray it will come again.

The water grows hotter and, as with tea, I feel myself grow stronger.

EPILOGUE

SOUTHERN ENGLAND
DECEMBER 1940

It was almost Christmas when Murphy and I boarded a plane for the quick flight from western Ireland to Heston Aerodrome near London. It was at this same airfield that, after handing Czechoslovakia to Hitler in 1938, the British Prime Minister Chamberlain had returned to declare, "I believe it is peace for our time." I thought of the mounting cost of Chamberlain's appeasement policy as we circled low over the bomb-blasted landscape. Barrage balloons swam through the air beneath us like giant silver fish in the sea.

"Welcome to the war," remarked a fellow passenger to no one in particular.

I knew there was only one real reason for me to return. Lindy's notebook was safely wrapped in my rucksack. The lock of her hair was tucked into the volume of the *Book of Common Prayer.* I would at least bring that small fragment of Lindy back home to her mother. Lindy's death was the direct result of a weak, deluded British politician who had feared to stand up to the Nazis.

I cried a little when I set foot on British soil.

When I had left England three months earlier, none of us were certain how long the little island nation would survive. I remembered my girls on the *Newcastle*. Lindy's bright smile as she joined in the singing, "There'll Always Be an England."

In my heart, I answered the chorus with a prayer: *So far, so good, Lord. England is still here. Thanks for watching over her.*

Murphy and I spent the night at the Heston Aerodrome Hotel, which Murphy told me looked a lot like the American White House.

I replied that I hoped one day to see the American president's home with my own eyes. We both knew it could not happen for a long time.

The next morning Murphy kissed me good-bye and headed into London while I caught the slow Southern Railway train to Lindy's little village home of Lewes.

The jingle of bells sounded outside the Lewes railroad station as I stepped to the curb and hailed a taxi.

A 1920s-era cab rattled toward me. "Where headed, miss?"

"It's missus. Missus Murphy." I passed the address of Lindy's mother to the driver. "This address in the village, please."

He studied the handwriting briefly as I climbed into the carriage. Glancing at my Irish tweed traveling clothes in the rearview mirror he asked, "Not from round here, are you, Missus Murphy? A Yank, are you?"

I felt encouraged that my Teutonic accent was fading. "Yes. Yank. American. Nearly."

"Well, may I ask y' then? When are you Yanks going to come along and do your bit in this war? Things are pretty rough over here, you know."

I did not answer but remembered the great hulk of the *Newcastle* as it slipped under the water. I could hear the cries of the dying rise up like the roar of a crowd in a sports stadium. I stared silently out the window at the frosty countryside as the little vehicle wound through the streets of Lewes, which must have been so familiar to beautiful Lindy. I pretended to see her memories. I imagined what Lindy's future would have been if only Chamberlain had stood up to Hitler and refused to collapse at the tyrant's threats.

But it was not to be. I organized my thoughts as we headed toward my rendezvous with heartache. What would I say to the woman to whom I had given my pledge of protection for her only daughter? I had failed. Should I ask for forgiveness that I had lived while this extraordinary child had perished?

I hugged my rucksack close to me. *What shall I say, God?*

The taxi turned a corner onto a street of small row houses. The lane was decorated for Christmas—as though there was no war, as if Lindy had not perished on the sea. Imagine! Holly and wreaths on every door!

"Here we are, missus." The house where Lindy lived was a tall, narrow structure with square-paned windows and a green enameled door. A bicycle leaned against the wall.

I paid the cabbie a few pence, then stood outside the picket fence to simply drink in Lindy's street. It sloped steeply downward, and in the distance I could see Brighton, and beyond that, an angry gray sea. Would I ever lose my fear of the ocean?

I held the rucksack in my arms like a baby and wondered if I should have Lindy's notebook out and ready to hand over when the door opened. It had only been a few months since the *Newcastle* sank. Would Lindy's mother still be in mourning? Would she welcome me? Would she want to hear the details of her daughter's death? Would she forgive me for my failure—or blame me that I had not stayed for Lindy to die in my arms?

Was it enough for me to tell her that Lindy's last thoughts had been for her mother and home? This home?

The hinges of the gate groaned as I swung open the gate. An aged border collie barked from the porch and raised himself from the ground one leg at a time until he tottered fiercely, blocking my way.

I heard a woman's voice scold the canine from inside as the green door opened. "Darby! What are you about then?"

Still hugging the rucksack, I managed a smile but remained rooted on the walk. "He won't let me by," I explained.

"He has no teeth." The woman laughed. She was young, in her midthirties, with a mop of pale curly hair closely matching the lock I carried with me.

"He has a wicked bark," I replied, unmoving.

Grasping his collar, she stroked his head. "Bark is worse than his bite . . . obviously. My protector. Nothing like a faithful dog. Man is gone with a wind, but a dog? Now he'll stay with a soul through a howling gale."

Protector. The description stung me. Yes. A dog was more faithful and true than I.

I blurted, "I was on board the *Newcastle.* With your daughter. With Lindy."

She released the dog, who resumed his place at her feet. Lindy's mother straightened slowly. Her eyes considered me first with awe, followed by curiosity.

"I am . . . my name is Elisa Lindheim . . . Murphy."

The woman's expression filled with compassion.

"Elisa. Yes. I would know you anywhere. You were . . . there."

"Yes." I patted my rucksack. "I have something that belonged to your daughter. Her diary. I've brought it. For you."

Her eyes brimmed as she held out a hand to welcome me. "All this way you've come. I read in the newspaper you were rescued off the coast of Ireland. Please, please. Do come in. I'll make a cuppa tea. My name is Dora. You must call me Dora."

My chin quivered as I tucked my head and followed her into the small cluttered foyer. A garland of scented evergreen wound around the banister of a flight of stairs that rose abruptly from the tiled floor. A coal fire flickered in the sitting room to the left. A corridor led away to a kitchen in the back of the house. A pair of muddy shoes was beside the entry. A girl's coat hung on the rack. I knew these were Lindy's things, still in the place where she had last worn them.

I could hardly breathe. On the radio I heard the music of "Silent Night" playing softly.

Dora linked her arm in mine. "Elisa! You must have a lot to tell. So many days adrift. A miracle, they say. A miracle you survived. We read all about it in the papers. Please come along. I'm so glad to see you. I never expected—"

I breathed deeply at her welcome and inhaled the aroma of baking cinnamon apples. More relieved than I had been at any time since the sinking, I followed Dora into the kitchen and sat in the plain wooden chair at the table. I began to rummage in my rucksack, removing Lindy's paper-wrapped journal and the *Book of Common Prayer* containing her golden curl.

My eyes upon the lock of hair, I relived in a moment the officer who had ordered me to run to the lifeboats while he stayed below with the dying child. I stammered, "I don't know how much you would like me to tell you about what happened. She loved you so much." The kettle whistled.

"Tell me everything. You must. I've heard only bits and pieces. 'Twas an angel carried my daughter though the waters, I'm sure of it . . . lifting Lindy up and up. The thought of it gives me such peace. Most who survived were rescued the first night, but you were lost, overlooked somehow." She brewed the tea. "I like strong tea. You?"

I nodded my agreement. "Strong tea. Yes. Someone once told me . . . women are like tea. You never know how strong they are—"

Behind me a girl's sweet voice finished the proverb, "Never know how strong until they're in hot water."

"And here's my girl! Where've you been, darlin'?" Dora smiled over my shoulder.

I turned to follow her gaze and gasped.

"Hello, Elisa!" The beautiful child greeted me with her arms opened to enfold me.

Her mother exclaimed, "Look, Lindy! Look who's come a-visitin'. It's Elisa Murphy, darlin'. She's come all this way to Lewes, just to return your diary!"

TAKING IT DEEPER . . .
Questions for individuals and groups

1. If you were going to write your "Last Will and Testament," who would you address it to? What possessions would you list? What instructions would you give? What would you want to make sure that those left behind knew?

2 Elisa says, "I see one child who is a hero in this story" (p. 13). For her, it's Connor Turner. Why is Connor so special to Elisa? In what way(s) does Elisa identify with Connor's mother's story? What person in your life do you see as a hero or a heroine? Why? Tell the story.

3. Psalm 91:11 says, "He shall give His angels charge over thee, to keep thee in all thy ways" (KJV). Do you believe God's angels have charge over you? Why or why not? Give an example from your own experience.

4. Elisa received a very special Christmas present from her mother in 1936—a red leather-bound diary stamped with roses. Of all the gifts you've received, what one

special gift do you remember most? Why was that gift so significant?

5. In 1936 Elisa feels that "the whole world is crumbling around us. Do we still imagine that everything will return to normal somehow?" (p. 18). How does that statement apply to our world today? Do you have hope that "everything will return to normal somehow"? Why or why not?

6. If you were a parent living in London in summer 1940, would you:

   • risk sending your child on a ship to America, hoping for safety along the way?
   • keep your child with you in London?

Explain your answer.

7. Rudy Dorbransky, and later Elisa, take tremendous risks hiding visas for Jews in the case of the precious Guarnerius. If you had the opportunity to save lives by doing so today, would you take the risk—of what it might mean to you and to your family if you were discovered? Why or why not?

8. Elisa says, "My friendship with Irish actress Mariah Fitzgerald and the Spanish flamenco

dancer Raquel Esperanza was first forged in flames of the Blitz and later sealed on the high seas of the North Atlantic" (p. 47). How does living through crises knit people's hearts together? When have you developed an unlikely friendship as a result of going through a difficult time? What has each of you gained from the experience? Tell the story.

9. Elisa says, "I remember Christmas past in our beautiful home in Berlin. Music and laughter. Snow falling on the ground. A whispered secret and knowing glances. The scents of pastries and the Christmas goose filling our house. The midnight chiming of the tall old clock in our foyer" (p. 55). What special memories do you have of Christmas, or other holidays in your home growing up? What childhood traditions do you still carry on, and why are those traditions, in particular, important to you?

10. "I wonder sometimes if God is asleep. Why has He been silent? Why do my prayers go unanswered?" Elisa asks when her Papa disappears, and there is no word of his fate for a long time (p. 85). Have you ever wondered the same thing—if God is asleep or silent? Why He doesn't answer your prayers? If so, in what situation(s)? What

have you learned about yourself, God, and faith as you've waited for answers?

11. Why do you think Miss Pike is so disapproving of Elisa and the way she handles the girls onboard ship? Have you faced a personality like Miss Pike's in your own life? If so, how have you handled that disapproval? How might looking at that person with a long-range perspective—and a sense of humor—help you from becoming discouraged?

12. What about Lindy's character and personality makes her so special to Elisa and to others? How might you develop the sensitivity to see others in a different way? to feel what others feel? Give an example of one way you could exhibit Lindy character and personality traits this week . . . and then follow through on that action.

13. Lindy asks Elisa to write a postscript on her letter to her mum—a promise that Elisa will look after Lindy. Elisa is heartbroken when she can't keep her promise. Have you ever failed to keep a promise? How did that make you feel?

14. "I thought of Otto Wattenbarger and his brother, Franz—how what had come upon us

was tearing families, cities, the whole world apart. I remembered the place where Franz had shown me that two snowflakes, identical in every way, could fall mere inches apart. Yet one would melt to flow south into light and warmth while the other would join the black uniforms, the marching rivers of the north.

"The division of families and hearts is that clear . . . and that permanent" (p. 159).

Have you and a loved one ever been divided in heart over an issue? What was the issue, and what sides did each of you take? Have you ever reconciled over that issue? Why or why not?

15. "You know," Lindy says, "maybe Mister Barrett will write about us when he gets to Hollywood. Heroic British youth escape from bombing to adventure on the high seas. What do you think?"

"I think Mister Barrett doesn't think much of the high seas," Nan observed.

"He'll be better soon," I offered. "But if our adventure is merely about how well they feed us, there may not be much to write about" (p. 163).

How does Elisa and the girls' journey end up quite different from the one they've imagined it would be? If you were one of the girls, writing about what you learned on your lifeboat, after the sinking of the *Newcastle*, what would you say? When has a journey of yours ended up differently than you expected? Tell the story. What elements of your surprising journey are ones that you can pass on as significant lessons for the next generation?

ABOUT THE AUTHORS

BODIE and **BROCK THOENE** (pronounced *Tay-nee*) have written over sixty works of historical fiction. That these best sellers have sold more than twenty million copies and won eight ECPA Gold Medallion Awards affirms what millions of readers have already discovered—that the Thoenes are not only master stylists but experts at capturing readers' minds and hearts.

In their timeless classic series about Israel (The Zion Chronicles, The Zion Covenant, The Zion Legacy), the Thoenes' love for both story and research shines. With The Shiloh Legacy and *Shiloh Autumn* (poignant portrayals of the American Depression), The Galway Chronicles (dramatic stories of the 1840s famine in Ireland), and the Legends of the West (gripping tales of adventure and danger in a land without law), the Thoenes have made their mark in modern history. In the A.D. Chronicles they step seamlessly into the world of Jerusalem and Rome, in the days when Yeshua walked the earth. Now the Zion Diaries cover the time period between their best-selling Zion Covenant series (1936–1940) and Zion Chronicles series (1947–1948). "These timeless tales are the missing pieces of the lives of some of the most beloved characters from our Zion Chronicles and Zion Covenant series," the

Thoenes say. "Their compelling stories of courage and love chronicle the darkest of times, when good seemed lost, but God's Truth stood firm and shone as a beacon in the midst of Hitler's evil. Based on decades of interviews and divine encounters, the Zion Diaries are our most up-close and personal books ever."

Bodie, who has degrees in journalism and communications, began her writing career as a teen journalist for her local newspaper. Eventually her byline appeared in prestigious periodicals such as *U.S. News and World Report*, *The American West*, and *The Saturday Evening Post*. She also worked for John Wayne's Batjac Productions and ABC Circle Films as a writer and researcher. John Wayne described her as "a writer with talent that captures the people and the times!"

Long intrigued by the personal accounts of history, and the romantic and often mysterious stories based in Hawaii, Bodie has also authored *Love Finds You in Lahaina, Hawaii*. "There, the past and the present overlap through the lives of elders sharing their memories," Bodie says. "When I met an old Hawaiian woman who was making *leis* in the shade of Lahaina's banyan tree, I was entranced by her photos—and her personal remembrances of Princess Kaiulani. The rumors she shared shed new light on the old story, as if Romeo and Juliet had a happy ending. As she told me the legends and the romance, I knew I must write it one day."

Brock has often been described by Bodie as "an essential half of this writing team." With degrees in both history and education, Brock has, in his role of researcher and story-line consultant, added the vital dimension of historical accuracy. Due to such careful research, the Zion Covenant and Zion Chronicles series are recognized by the American Library Association, as well as Zionist libraries around the world, as classic historical novels and are used to teach history in college classrooms.

Bodie and her husband, Brock, have four grown children—Rachel, Jake, Luke, and Ellie—and seven grandchildren. Their children are carrying on the Thoene family talent as the next generation of writers, and Luke produces the Thoene audio books. Bodie and Brock divide their time between Hawaii, London, and Nevada.

www.thoenebooks.com

Center Point Publishing
600 Brooks Road ● PO Box 1
Thorndike ME 04986-0001 USA

(207) 568-3717

US & Canada:
1 800 929-9108
www.centerpointlargeprint.com